DEDICATION

For all my family & friends.
Especially Erica and Owen for their endless support and encouragement!

ACKNOWLEDGMENTS

Thanks to Fairlee Anderson for the cover design.
Thanks to Corey Cain Photography for the postcard photo.

Although the characters, dialogue, and scenes are loosely based on the author's experiences, make no doubt about it — this book is a work of fiction!

I'm sure there were many times I probably took my summers at York Beach for granted, but looking back on it now, I am so very fortunate to have grown up in such a beautiful place!

For Tony, Jason, Tim, Ian, and all the *summer friends (and friends in general)* who have come in & out of my life over the years. No matter how long or short the friendships — you've all left a handprint on my life!

1

"WHEN I GROW UP" – Garbage

For *The Empty Beach* novel, I took you back to the summer of 1995. For *Between Hello and Goodbye*, I fast-forwarded four years to 1999. And now, for the final installment of my Soundtrack to My Life trilogy, I decided to center it around two different summers – 2003 and 2004.

I'd like to say a lot has happened between 1999 and 2003, but sadly, not so much. Well, nothing monumental like marriage or kids or anything. I don't even think anyone I dated over that stretch had serious marriage potential. You might think that weighed on me more than a little bit, but not really. Ever since Anna, I'd become pretty good at going with the flow. I didn't get too caught up worrying about if the girl I was dating was "the one." I just tried my best to enjoy their company for however long it lasted. And yes, a few of them only lasted twenty-four hours. It is what it is.

It did take quite a few months after Anna for me to be anywhere near ready to start dating again. Over that stretch, I must have reread her letter and looked through her pictures a hundred times. I think what really helped me was my writing. I apparently caught the writing bug, because not only did I finish *Between Hello and Goodbye*, but I started and finished a handful of other screenplays in that time period as well. One of them was *The Empty Beach*, which focused on 1995 (otherwise known as "the summer of Elise"). The other screenplays were fiction—strictly from my imagination.

Although I had made a few small-time Hollywood connections over the years, I was still nowhere near getting my screenplays made into movies, especially getting them made here in Maine. Throughout all my discouraging dead-end roads, I somehow kept my head up and just kept on writing. My friends and family were supportive of my writing, but I could tell that deep down they thought I was crazy for thinking I could ever get my silly stories out to the masses. I was determined to prove everyone wrong.

In 2003, probably the most stable thing in my life was my job. In early 2000, I finally succumbed to Doug's offer, and I became his partner at Here Hey Hoohahs. With each passing year, the business grew exponentially. We killed it in the summers and had a big enough local following to stay open all winter. In my heart, I knew I was destined to do something else, but until I knew exactly what that was, I was more than content being a co-owner at Hoohahs.

Surprisingly, working that closely with Doug every day, we rarely had disagreements. We actually saw eye-to-eye on most things, which was a huge relief to me. The last thing I wanted was for our partnership to come between our friendship. What was even more surprising in my 3½ years as partner, was the fact that Doug was pretty good at keeping business and pleasure separate. I mean, there was that one time he had sex with an employee in the bathroom, but he was quick to point out that she had already given her two-week notice. I chose my battles wisely, so I didn't really bother arguing with his logic.

Besides the bathroom quickie, Doug kept his flirting and sexual advances professional-like. In other words, his flirting was relegated to customers. I suppose I can't bust on him too much, seeing as I may or may not have also flirted with some of our female customers. And yes, some of the flirting might have led to other stuff.

Speaking of Doug, not a lot has changed with him. He had a few short-term relationships, but other than that, he was still fully enjoying the single life. Pete on the other hand, was eyeball deep in marriage, kids, and his career. His girls were now four and seven, and by all accounts, were a handful. Of course, Doug didn't help matters as he continually warned Pete that this was nothing compared to when the girls become teenagers.

I think Doug's exact words were, "If I were you, I'd get their vaginas sewn shut before they hit sixteen, that way you don't have to worry about all those teenage dicks going in there."

Like I said, nothing much had changed with Doug, including his unfiltered comments. Anyway, I think Pete's girls were the least of his stress. As you'll see later in the book, Pete's job was slowly sucking the life out of him. He desperately wanted (needed) a change, but seeing as he was the bread winner of the house, he was kind of stuck.

For years, Michelle relished being a stay-at-home mom, but by 2003, she also desperately wanted (needed) a change. She originally was going to wait until both girls were in school full time before going back to work, but she got so stir crazy that she started the process earlier than planned. Although she graduated with a business degree, I don't think she ever had a specific career in mind. And seeing as she was married with a kid by age twenty-six, she never got to use her degree.

Now, seven years later, she decided to switch directions and go back to school to be a paralegal. I'm not really sure where that came from, but who am I to judge, I'm trying to be a frickin' screenwriter! Anyway, between going back to school and raising two little kids, she too was stressing out, but like I said, more on Pete and Michelle later.

2

"BETTER MAN" – Pearl Jam

One of the perks about working at, or owning a bar, is you get to sleep-in the next day. While Doug usually took full advantage of this, I had regimented myself to wake up early to get some quality writing done. Well, it wasn't always quality, and my time wasn't always spent on just writing either. There was usually coffee drinking involved and the occasional banter with the local baristas. And by local, I mean Portsmouth. Even though I lived in York, there were really no coffeeshops there that were conducive to writing. That's not a shot at any of the York shops, but they were more the in-and-out type places. You know, grab a coffee, grab a bagel, and then get to work. I needed a place a bit bigger, a place I could lounge for hours at a time if needed. Also, in case I had writer's block, I needed a place that provided plenty of people watching. My ideal coffeeshop would be one with a cozy, creative atmosphere with comfortable chairs and great tunes.

My usual place of choice was Breaking New Grounds. It was located in Market Square, which is the heart in downtown Portsmouth. It didn't provide everything I just listed, but it provided enough of them for me to bang out five screenplays over the past four years.

Also, it definitely provided the best people-watching in the area. So much so, sometimes it was difficult to remain focused on the task at hand, and on that particular day, my task at hand was my newest script called *Livin' on a Prayer – The Untold Tommy and Gina Story*. Yes, it's my little play on the Tommy and Gina characters from the classic Bon Jovi song.

The story itself had nothing to do with actual song—*my* Tommy didn't work on a dock, and *my* Gina didn't work the diner all day. My script was a straight-up comedy with a creative twist. It started off in the 80s and slowly moved to present day. I loved that I was able to throw in plenty of 80's pop culture and musical references from my most favorite time period.

Now, with regards to my *bantering* with the baristas, you might assume what I really meant to say was *flirting*. You would be assuming wrong. Not 100% wrong, but mostly wrong. Working the last few years behind the bar, especially with Doug, one couldn't help but develop a flirtatious nature. Personally, I think I'm flirtatious for the sake of it rather than looking for something from it. I'm not sure if that makes sense or not, but in my head it does.

So, when I wasn't behind the bar, it was nice to just banter with the baristas. One of the baristas that I particularly dug was Joanna. She recently turned thirty and was going through the whole *what am I doing with my life* phase. I think you all know, I have been there and done that! Besides our musical tastes, we had other things in common. Joanna was also a writer, and even though she concentrated more on poems and short stories, it was still enough in common to give us plenty to talk about. She was my main go-to person for feedback on my screenplays. I used to go to Doug for his thoughts, but all he ever said was I needed more F-bombs, and that I needed to add more gratuitous sex scenes. As you can fuckin' see, I've obliged him on the F-bombs, but I've never really written any sex scenes—gratuitous or otherwise.

Anyway, I met Joanna about a year earlier when I first started going to Breaking New Grounds on a regular basis. Another thing we had in common was our search for Mr./Mrs. Right. More times than not, all we ever found was Mr. & Mrs. Wrong!

In 2003, the whole internet thing was becoming more and more prevalent, as too was this thing called online dating. I wasn't very computer savvy yet, so my methods of meeting women remained old school. It was either through friends, or friends of friends, or at the bar, or just by starting up a random conversation with someone. Joanna, on the other hand, had just started to dip her toe into the online dating pool. It was a pool my toe wanted nothing to do with.

That particular morning, before I even got to the counter, she had my order waiting for me. A blueberry muffin and a coffee (house blend). After we exchanged pleasantries, I stood there, giving her a look of anticipation.

"What?" she asked.

"Sooo… did you read those scenes I gave you yesterday? As always, be honest. I can handle it."

"I sent you my thoughts," she said. "Didn't you get my

email?"

"You know I don't check that. I'm not even sure I remember my password."

"You really need to get with the times, Josh. The computer is your friend," she smiled.

"Oh really? So how is your *friend* working for you with the online dating thing?"

Her smile quickly disappeared.

"Ugh. Don't even go there. Last night's date turned out to be forty-seven years old—NOT like his profile suggested. He played dumb and claimed it was a typo. Trust me, the whole night felt like a typo. Do you realize I've yet to go on a second date with any of them?"

"They've all been that bad, huh?"

"Well, no. I would have gone a second date with a couple of them, but… they never called me again. Seriously, Josh, what's wrong with me?"

"There's nothing wrong with you, Joanna. Personally, I just don't think you can find true love over a computer screen. I think it needs to be more organic."

Joanna shrugged then changed the subject.

"Where's your backpack? Aren't you gonna do some writing today?"

"Not today. I'm actually meeting Dalelyn here in a little bit."

"Which one is Dalelyn again?"

"You know, the one who works at the Gaslight."

"Oh yeah," she nodded. "Doesn't she have a boyfriend?"

"For now," I smiled.

"Ahh, ever the romantic optimist. I wish I could be like that. I think I'm becoming more and more jaded with each passing day."

Hearing this, I couldn't help but sympathetically laugh. This was totally me a handful of years ago.

"One day it'll all fall into place, Joanna. On the bright side, it's good fodder for your poetry."

With that comment, I smiled at Joanna and took my coffee and muffin over to an available table. Within minutes of me sitting down, Dalelyn showed up.

Dalelyn Hayward—Age 27—Originally from Berwick, Maine—Now resides in Portsmouth, NH.

She's been dating the same guy for a year and a half (four different breakups in between). Like Joanna, Dalelyn was a great girl, and also like Joanna, Dalelyn and I had a lot in common. She wasn't a writer, but she was a very heavy reader, and yes, she had read a couple of my screenplays.

While Joanna always offered honest, straightforward critiques, Dalelyn was way too kind and sweet for that. She always had the highest praises for my writing. My ego needed and appreciated both girls.

So, the big question you might be thinking is: why would I waste my time pursuing a chick with a boyfriend—a year and a half boyfriend? I guess Joanna had it right, I had reverted back to my younger self, and I was indeed a romantic optimist (AKA – a naive idiot).

I met Daleyn four months earlier at the Gaslight. We were all there celebrating Pete's big promotion (more on that later). Physically and personality-wise, I was immediately attracted to Dalelyn. Also immediately, she and I totally hit it off. She was smart, full of life, and although five years younger than me, she totally got 97% of my pop culture references.

When we originally met at the Gaslight, I wanted to invite her to come have a drink at our bar sometime, but I felt a little pretentious telling her I co-owned a bar. That's why I had Doug do it for me. Yup, we were 33 years old and still playing the wingman roles for one another.

Dalelyn's face beamed with excitement as she accepted Doug's offer to come by our bar sometime. Doug's face beamed knowing he had just flown another successful wingman mission. My face beamed for all of the reasons above. Of course, 5.7 seconds later, the beaming dimmed considerably. Technically, the beaming turned into a blackout.

"I would love to check out your bar sometime!" she excitedly said in my direction. "I've been meaning to hit York Beach for a while now. I'm sure my boyfriend would love it too."

Although my face remained stoic, my gut felt like I had taken a punch from Mike Tyson. My wingman quickly turned into my cornerman as he tried giving me smelling salts to bring me back from the near knockout.

About a week later, true to her word, Dalelyn showed up at Hoohahs, but instead of her boyfriend, she just brought a friend. A female friend named Kacie. In retrospect, it probably would have been better if she showed up with her boyfriend. It might have hammered the point home to me more. It might have prevented me from pursuing a "taken woman." Eh, let's be honest, probably not—but it might have.

When Dalelyn and Kacie showed up at Hoohahs, she explained to me that her boyfriend didn't "do" York Beach. Supposedly, he was strictly a Hampton Beach dude. That pretty much told me everything I needed to know about him. Of course, that didn't actually stop her from telling me all about him herself. As a matter of fact, from that night on, every time Dalelyn and I would talk or hang out, 72% of the conversation would be about him. And 97% of the 72% was all negative stuff.

Yup, her boyfriend was a giant douchebag. And that, my friends, was probably why I continued my pursuit of a taken woman. I would have never pursued her if her boyfriend was a nice guy—a cool guy—a guys' guy. Because then, even though he wasn't a close friend, he still would have been covered by the guy code. You know, the code that states it's not cool to flirt or bang another guy's girl. That same guy code also states that it's NOT okay to hit on, flirt, or bang the ex-girlfriend of one of your friends. It's even frowned upon to do those things to a girl that one of your friends is simply interested in. Yes, even if she isn't interested back.

So why did I not feel guilty about flirting and pursuing a taken woman? It was all in the fine print of the guy code. All of the rules (guidelines) I just mentioned only went into effect with one's "close circle of friends." Think of it as a pyramid with close friends being at the top. This would then be followed by friends, acquaintances, and at the bottom, just below acquaintances, would be people labeled – "I have no fuckin' idea who you are."

Personally, my inner circle only included Pete and Doug, and even though I hadn't seen him in years, Scott as well. Other than those three, the rest of my friends were a judgement call. So, long story short, seeing as Dalelyn's boyfriend fell into the "I have no fuckin' idea who you are" category, and more importantly, seeing as he appeared to be a giant douchebag, all bets were off concerning the guy code!

That being said, my four-month friendship with Dalelyn never got physical—not even a kiss. At times, there was definitely sexual tension. She knew I was interested in her, and she made it clear that if she was single, she too would pursue something more. In the four months that we knew each other, there were two occasions that she was on the brink of dumping his ass. And yes, on both occasions I highly encouraged the ass-dumping. To be fair, I would have done the same even if I wasn't interested in her. Like most of her friends, I hated seeing him treat her like that, and I thought she deserved better.

Both occasions involved her crying her eyes out on my shoulder, claiming that she wanted out. Unfortunately, on both occasions, she called me the next day and told me how she might have "over-reacted," and that "he didn't actually hit me, he just grabbed me," and "I kind of deserved it. I threw his video game controller across the room," AND the ever-popular, "Anyway, he apologized and said it would never happen again." Seriously, what is it with nice girls falling for bad boys? You also might be thinking, what is it with nice guys trying to save nice girls from the bad boys? Touché.

Seeing as Dalelyn and her D-bag boyfriend didn't live together, we ended up talking on the phone at least four times a week, and we would hang out a few times in person. Most of the time, we'd just grab a coffee and talk. Sometimes we'd go out and do things—things her boyfriend refused to do with her.

Anyway, back to Breaking New Grounds and my coffee with Dalelyn. After coffee, we walked down to Prescott Park. The park was located in downtown Portsmouth directly on the Piscataqua River. It was well-landscaped and full of scenic gardens, and it also contained a large stage, which they used for summer concerts and plays.

As usual, the conversation revolved around Dalelyn

complaining about her boyfriend.

"Ugh, I'm sorry to be talking about this to you again. You've gotta be sick to death of me bitchin' about him to you."

"You're the one who should be sick of it," I said. "I hate seeing you get treated like this. Over and over again he treats you like shit. The way he talks to you, the way he orders you around… you deserve better, Dalelyn. I mean, from what I can see, you're like the perfect girlfriend."

"Ha ha. Yea, right."

"I'm serious. How about his birthday last month? You made him his favorite dinner—a candlelight dinner, I might add, and not to mention a homemade cake. And did he show up to enjoy it? Nope. He was out drinking with his friends."

Dalelyn sipped her coffee and looked out at the tug boats on the river.

"I know this isn't an excuse, but in his defense, he was under a lot of pressure at work that week. It just slipped his mind."

Yea, because there's a ton of pressure working 23 hours a week at a Sears!

I wanted to say that, but I didn't. I knew the moment didn't call for honest sarcasm. So instead, I put my arm around her and said, "You need someone who will treat you the way you deserve to be… like gold."

"Aww, Josh. Why do you always say the sweetest things to me?"

"Because you deserve it, even if you don't think you do."

She smiled at me then returned her gaze out towards the river. As the tug boats guided the large freight ship under the raised bridge, she turned to me and said the classic line, "He's really not as bad as I portray him to be."

My only response was an *are you fuckin' kidding me* look.

"I know, I know, what am I gonna do?" she said, hanging her head in shame.

You're gonna dump the sorry son of a bitch and start dating me! That's what you're gonna do!

Yea, you're right, I didn't say that either.

3

"THE GHOST IN YOU" – Psychedelic Furs

If you remember from *Between Hello and Goodbye*, our head bartender at Hoohahs was Taylor. She was sexy, sarcastic, and pretty much Doug's perfect match. Although they had hooked up in the past, and although Doug once had legitimate interest in her, ultimately nothing came of it.

Taylor ended up getting her teaching degree and had since moved a few towns over and now teaches high school. She usually stopped in a few times a year to visit us—and to get free drinks—and to bust Doug's balls. We had quite a few workers over the years, but there was definitely no replacing Taylor.

Hoohahs had its share of regulars, but as of late, our number one regular was Pete. Seeing as he was one of our best friends, this might not seem very strange, but until recently, he rarely stopped in for a drink. Lately however, he's been coming four or five times a week. As I mentioned earlier, I met Dalelyn at the Gaslight while we were all celebrating Pete's big promotion.

With a big promotion usually comes longer work hours, and longer hours usually means more stress, and more stress almost always requires a drink or two to relax and unwind. Pete absolutely adored his two little girls, and he loved Michelle more than anything, but seeing as he was the only committed one of us three, I think he liked living vicariously through our wild tales. (Truth be told, Doug's tales were usually wilder than mine.)

It was 9 PM on a Sunday—the cash registers were ringing up a storm, Pete sat up at the bar with a Sam Adam's in hand, and Doug had his eye on two cute chicks. All was right in the world.

"Are you gonna make your move or what?" Pete asked, motioning to the girls.

"My move?" said Doug. "Pfft, I already tapped the blonde one the other night."

"Yea, right," laughed Pete.

Doug looked over at me for confirmation. I nodded and indeed confirmed his tapping-of-the-blonde proclamation. Not that I had first-hand knowledge he actually did the deed, but after hearing Doug fill me in on the sordid details of their wild sex-filled night together, I assumed not even Doug could make that shit up.

I listened as Doug retold the story to Pete, and even though he spoke in hushed tones, it was loud enough to cause the older couple sitting close to Pete to huff off in disgust. They paid their tab and hastily started to leave. Well, the older gentleman was really the one doing all the huffing. His wife turned a bright red, and I swear, on her way out, she winked at Doug.

Doug's sexual exploits with the blonde were so wild, that at one point, he had to draw us a diagram on a cocktail napkin. After Pete stared in awe at the napkin, he said to Doug, "So why the hell ain't you tapping that again?"

Doug shrugged and matter-of-factly said, "Eh, she's a snapper."

"She's a what?"

"You know, she snaps her gum when she chews. Loudly. Very loudly. I fuckin' hate that."

Doug was known for having silly (stupid) reasons why he didn't go out with girls a second time. One girl, he claimed was just too tall, "Way too fuckin' tall," were his exact words. FYI, she was an inch taller, maybe.

There was another girl, who he really liked, but refused to go out with her again because she had a "rogue hair sticking out of her left nipple." He kept mumbling to us —"It's just not right… it's just not right… just take a pair of tweezers to that thing!"

I could literally do a whole chapter on Doug's stupid pet-peeves, but I'll spare you.

As the blonde and her friend slowly stood from their chairs, all three us couldn't help but stare. The blonde had on an extra short mini skirt. Doug took one look at her long, tanned legs then said, "Well, I suppose I could put ear plugs in and let her ride the Doug Express one more time."

"You're such a womanizer," Pete said, shaking his head.

"Whoa, whoa, whoa! I think you need to check your definition of a womanizer because I'm definitely not one of them!"

Without hesitation, I said, "Womanizer—a noun meaning a man who likes many women and has short sexual relationships with them."

Doug pondered a second then shrugged and conceded Pete's point. By now, the blonde and her friend made their way over to the two vacant seats left by the older couple.

"Hey Doug, how's it going?" she asked.

"Heyyyy… you," he returned.

Pete and I smirked, knowing full-well he had forgotten her name.

"This is my cousin, Julie," said the blonde.

"Nice to meet you, Julie," said Doug. "This guy right here is one of my best friends, Pete. He's married with two kids," Doug pointed out. "And this is my other best friend and business partner, Josh. He's totally single. Like completely and utterly single."

Both Pete and I politely smiled, but make no doubt about it, we were shooting daggers at Doug. Out of the corner of my eye, I noticed the cocktail napkin still sitting on the bar. The same napkin Doug had drawn his re-creation of his night with blondie. I was tempted to show her Doug's X-rated artwork, but I decided to spare him. I discretely reached over and swiped the napkin from view and threw it away. In retrospect, considering the next thirty minutes were spent on him making me look like a fool (a hopelessly romantic fool), I should have embarrassed the fuck out of Doug!

Pete got the whole ball rolling by asking me if I got any writing done that morning. I responded by saying, "No, not really. I hung out with Dalelyn most of the morning."

That was all it took. The flood gates were now officially open.

"She still got a boyfriend?" asked Pete.

"Yea," I shrugged. "For now."

"I hate to say it, my friend, but she's never gonna leave him," said Pete.

First of all, it pisses me off when people start a sentence with, *I hate to say it.* If you hate to say it, don't fuckin' say it then!!! That being said, Pete was right, she was probably never going to leave him. I think Pete knew he hit a nerve, so he decided not to harp on it any further. Doug, on the other hand, was just getting started harping.

In front of both girls, Doug said, "I hate to say it, Josh, but I'm afraid you're just the DISCO."

My curiosity for what the fuck the DISCO was, outweighed my urge to yell at him about the *I hate to say it* phrase.

"I'm just the what?" I snapped.

"You're the *DISCO*. Without the *I,* though."

Both Pete and I were still completely confused.

Finally, Doug explained. "You're just the Designated Shoulder to Cry On. The DSCO!!"

At this, Pete nodded in agreement with Doug's asinine acronym.

"You guys have no idea what you're talking about. I am so not the DSCO (I was totally the fuckin' DSCO)! I'm telling ya, one day she's gonna see what a jackass he really is, and—"

"And then she'll come running to her knight in shining armor. Sir Josh-A-Lot! The most powerful knight of hopeless romantics everywhere," laughed Doug.

I knew there was no sense in defending myself, so I simply walked away and waited on the next customer at the other side of the bar. Doug knew there was no point in embarrassing me any further, yet he did it anyway. He turned to blondie and her cousin and gave them a brief synopsis of me.

"See that guy right over there?" Doug loudly said, pointing over in my direction. "That's Josh Wentworth. Not only is he one of my best friends, but he's one of the nicest guys you'll ever meet. Unfortunately, that's one of his downfalls."

Don't you love it when your friends give you backhanded compliments?

"Awww, being a nice guy isn't a downfall," said Julie.

Before I could thank her, Doug continued.

"I'm telling ya, his nice guy persona has caused him to have the worst luck with women. Well, it's not so much bad luck, he just chooses the wrong women, that's all."

The only thing that would have made his statement worse, was if he started it with, *I hate to say it.*

"Oh Doug, I'm sure you're exaggerating," said blondie.

"Umm, nope, I don't think I am," he replied. "Take for instance, his newest project, Dalelyn."

Yup, Doug went there. Over the next fifteen minutes, Doug (and Pete) filled the girls in on everything Josh & Daleyn. They filled them in on us going to the movies, on our coffee get-togethers, and yes, on our frequent late night phone calls. You're probably thinking this all could have been avoided if I never told my friends my personal life to begin with. You wouldn't be wrong.

Doug and Pete then filled them in on the douche bag known as Dalelyn's boyfriend. I was actually a little impressed with just how many details they remembered about him. I guess it shows my friends really do listen to me when I talk.

"That's horrible," said Julie. "We have more than a few friends who have assholes for boyfriends, and no matter what we say, or how much sense we make, they never break up with them."

"Yup, that's why good ol' Josh here is the poster child for hopeless romantics everywhere. Always thinking chicks will fall for nice and sweet. Too bad that nice and sweet don't cut it in the real world."

Before I could even shoot Doug a hot glare, Julie gave me a sweet smile and said, "I think more guys should be the nice and sweet type."

As I returned her smile, Doug just rolled his eyes and walked off. Pete and I bantered with the girls for a while until Pete decided he needed to go home. As the night went on, Doug and blondie seemed to be talking and laughing a lot, and it quickly became obvious that he was indeed going to tap that again. It didn't hurt that she had run out of gum hours earlier. When we started to close up the bar, Doug informed me that we were all going to go out afterwards.

"We are?" I said.

"Well yea. Her cousin is totally into you. I figure we can all take a walk on the beach, and then I can do the old shoestring trick."

Oh man, where do I start? First of all, Julie seemed like a nice enough girl, but the more we talked that night, the more I knew she just wasn't my type. If I would have gone along with Doug's scheme, it would have been purely a one-night thing. A hit it and quit it, if you will. And why would I want to do that, especially knowing I was solely interested in Daleyn?

Doug reminded me how wild blondie was (Yup, I never found out her name either), and he claimed he knew her cousin would be the same way. To his dismay, I politely passed on his double-date proposal. He was gonna have to go this one on his own.

4

"BROKEN HEARTED SAVIOR" – Big Head Todd & the Monsters

The next morning, I met Pete for breakfast around 10 AM. My go-to spot for coffee, writing, and chit chat was Breaking New Grounds. Pete's spot, however, was the Friendly Toast, which was also located in downtown Portsmouth. His new office was just a couple of buildings down.

The Friendly Toast was an extremely popular local restaurant. I would describe the atmosphere as eclectic, quirky, and overall, quite funky. Not only are you greeted by a hostess, but a strangely dressed mannequin as well. The place is filled with vintage signs, classic old board games, and a real-working stop light. Most of the memorabilia throughout the place is definitely on the kitschy side.

Mostly, however, the walls are adorned with many, many old and unique framed paintings. And by unique, I mean strange, disturbing, and just plain fucked up. Case in point: the weird painting of a long-eared rabbit wearing a turtleneck shirt underneath a suit jacket. And don't forget the painting of a boobless woman posing with a white bunny. I don't know what their infatuation is with rabbits, but it kind of freaks the shit outta me! They're the type of paintings that are disturbing to look at, yet you can't look away.

Seeing as Joanna had the day off at Breaking New Grounds, I decided to do my writing at the Friendly Toast while I waited for Pete to arrive. By the time he showed up, I had banged out four or five pages of amazing dialogue. Like most of the waitstaff there, our waitress was heavily pierced and tattooed.

She greeted Pete with a wide smile and said, "The usual?"

He nodded and winked, and then proceeded to sit across from me.

"Hey Cat, this is Josh. Josh, Cat,"

"Nice to meet you," I said.

"So, you're the writer friend, huh?" she smiled.

"Ha ha," I laughed. "Is that what I'm known as?"

"Actually, you're known as the hopelessly romantic best friend who's trying to play the broken hearted savior to that Dalelyn chick. Her name is Dalelyn, right?" she asked in Pete's direction.

While he smirked and nodded, I just sat there dumbfounded. I was, however, slightly impressed with her use of the phrase broken hearted savior. It was a song title by the band Big Head Todd & the Monsters.

"I think I prefer being known as the writer friend," I pointed out.

They both smiled at each other as she headed off into the kitchen.

"Since when do you talk about my personal life with strangers?" I asked.

"Oh relax. Cat's not a stranger. I've known her for like three weeks now."

"Oh, well that makes me feel a whole lot better," I said, shaking my head.

"She's cool. We talk about everything."

Before I could delve into the whole broken hearted savior comment, Doug entered and sat next to me.

"S'up, my brothers?" he said with a little too much enthusiasm.

Pete saw the glint in his eye and laughed. "Let me guess, you had round two with blondie last night?"

"That I did," Doug smiled, giving Pete a fist bump.

"What happened to all your pet peeves about her?"

"Eh, it's not like I'm planning on dating or marrying her. Besides, she's heading back to New York tomorrow. I figured I'd give her a little going away present, if ya know what I mean?"

Cat returned and asked Doug, "Coffee?"

"Absolutely!" he said.

Pete then started to introduce them.

"Cat, this is—"

"The infamous Doug, I presume? Otherwise known as the lifelong bachelor and the last of the famous international playboys."

After she walked off, Doug turned to me and smiled, "The last of the international playboys! That's a Morrissey song, ya know?"

"Yea, Doug, I know. I'm the one who introduced you to that song."

"Geesh, relax, dude," Doug said, and then looked over at Pete.

"Josh is just mad because she compared him to a Big Head Todd song."

"Broken Hearted Savior?" asked Doug, smiling. "That totally fits!"

I sat there and watched as they fist bumped at my expense.

"What's her name again?" asked Doug.

"Cat," replied Pete.

"She's a cool chick."

I wasn't happy being called a broken hearted savior, but anyone who could work a Big Head Todd AND a Morrissey reference into a conversation was indeed pretty frickin' cool.

"She also just started her own graphic design business. She actually designed all of her tats."

"That's pretty bad ass," said Doug. "I'm thinking about getting some ink done."

"Dude, you've been saying that for fifteen years," I snapped.

"Just waiting on the perfect idea, that's all," he said. "And why are you snapping at me? You should be thanking me! More importantly, your dick should be thanking me. That Julie chick was hot, huh? Soooo? Was she as wild as her cousin or what?"

"You hooked up with that Julie girl?" Pete asked me with a smile.

Before I could respond (confirm), Doug interrupted.

"After work we all went for a walk on the beach and I pulled the old shoestring trick."

"Nice!" said Pete as he and Doug, yet again, did a fist bump. Pete offered me a bump, to which I hesitantly reciprocated.

Okay, my readers, let's get this out of the way. You're probably calling bullshit on me for *maybe* leading you to believe that I had passed on hooking up with Julie the previous night. Technically, I didn't really lie to you because I honestly had no intentions on hanging out with her after work or having a one-night stand with her. Honestly, I didn't!

Was I telling the truth when I said she wasn't really my type? Yes, yes I was… kinda. She wasn't *girl I want to date* material, she wasn't. But… she was kind of, definitely the *girl I wanted to bang* material. Sorry, I don't mean to sound so crass or so Doug-like, but I'm just keeping it real.

So, in regards to the one-night stand with Julie—in my defense, she seduced me. We were walking on the beach together and out of the blue she said, "Whatever happens tonight is completely no strings attached. Let's not feel obligated to exchange numbers or say all the proper PC things. We're both adults, so let's just have a fun, uninhibited night."

What can I say, she had me at *no strings attached*, not to mention, the word *uninhibited* definitely sealed the deal. And what an uninhibited night it was!! Don't get me wrong, it wasn't sketch-a-diagram on a napkin uninhibited, but it was pretty frickin' hot.

You also might be wondering if I felt guilty about having a wild night of meaningless sex, knowing my heart and hopes lay with Dalelyn. The answer is nope, I didn't feel guilty at all. Why should I? Although I really liked Dalelyn, the fact of the matter was she had a boyfriend and that would probably never change. Nope, zero guilt here.

Fuck!! I just lied to you guys again. I guess I did feel a little guilty. I know that makes no sense, especially considering I was single and that Dalelyn had a boyfriend. But yes, I admit it, I did feel a twinge of guilt. I promise though, from here on out, no more lying to you guys. Promise.

Okay, back to the Friendly Toast and our breakfast. Oh wait, you're probably still wondering about the shoestring trick. It really wasn't a trick, but rather it was more of a method—a method to get each couple alone. All four of us started off walking, talking, and laughing on the beach. A few minutes in, Doug stopped, and he bent down and began the long, slow process of tying his shoe—his shoe which was conveniently untied. Blondie paused to wait for him, but I kept walking. Naturally, Julie kept walking with me. By the time Doug finished tying his shoe, Julie and I were far ahead and on our own.

Fun Fact: The shoestring method was first used in 1989 by Scott. We had just left the Aqua Lounge with two chicks, and we all walked down to Long Sands. Shortly after we passed the Cutty Sark Hotel, Scott paused to tie his shoe. Stupidly, I paused as well. It wasn't until he shot me a *get the fuck going* look that I knew what he was up to. I kept walking and my chick followed, and before long, we had the whole beach separating both couples. I think you know where this is going. Anyway, that was the birth of the shoestring method. Since then, it's been used many times by all of us, with a 99% success rate.

Okay, back to our breakfast. After Cat brought us our food, we continued to fill Pete in on our fun-filled night with the McPherson cousins. Poor Pete. You could tell by his expressions and his many questions that he wasn't getting any from Michelle. It was obvious that he was living vicariously through Doug and I.

I have to admit, it was kind of cool to have someone deem my sex life worthy of living vicariously. That being said, Doug's description of his night far outweighed mine. And yes, at one point, Doug flipped his paper placemat over and sketched the crazy positions they had done.

After we finished our breakfast, the conversation took a dramatic turn from sexual to serious.

"I'm thinking about quitting my job," announced Pete out of the blue.

"What? Are you serious?" I asked.

"Completely serious."

"But you're doing so well, not to mention you've been doing it forever," said Doug.

"When I first started back in '95, it was new and exciting, but slowly over the years, it's just become something I completely dread. The fun and excitement has long since been sucked out of it."

"You do work a shit-ton of hours," said Doug. "And personally, I never saw the draw in working all those hours behind a computer screen. Well, not unless computer porn was involved."

"Ha ha," laughed Pete. "Let's just say, more times than not lately, computer porn has indeed been involved."

"What does Michelle think about this?" I asked. "Not about the porn surfing, but the fact you want to quit your job?"

"I haven't really told her yet. Now that she's back in school, she stressing out. I really don't wanna add to that. Besides, there's no way we could afford for me to quit my job, and I'm sure it'll be years before she's actually making the kind of money where I can even think about changing careers."

"You've been with that company since before you were married. What kind of job would you do if you quit?" I asked.

Pete shrugged then said, "I don't know. I've kind of been

toying around with some different graphic design programs. It might be cool to get into something like that."

I'd say you've been doing more than just toying around," Cat said from behind us. "Have you guys seen some of his sketches and designs?"

Pete blushed at her comment.

"Sketches and designs? What, are you holding out on us?" Doug asked.

"Ya, no shit," I added. "Let's see what you got."

It took a little coaxing, but eventually Pete opened up his laptop and showed us some of his stuff.

"Holy shit, dude. You really did all this?" questioned Doug. "It's really good."

"Yea, it really is," I agreed. "You do all this on the computer?"

"I usually sketch most of it on paper first," he said, handing us a sketchbook out of his bag."

Doug and I were more than impressed as we flipped through his drawings.

"Jesus Christ!" exclaimed Doug. "How have we been friends all these years and yet this is the first time we're finding out about this side of you?"

"Pretty cool shit, huh?" Cat said, walking by again. "Maybe you should have Pete do your little sex-sketches," she laughed, looking down at Doug's placemat."

Instead of blushing, Doug beamed with excitement and was quick to respond with, "That's a great idea! Could you do this on the computer? Like with more details and in color? Or maybe in 3D?"

"Relax, dude. I'm not that good yet."

"What does Michelle think about your sketches and

designs?" I asked.

This caused Pete to laugh. "Seriously, guys, it's not a big deal. It's just a silly hobby, that's all."

It was clear he hadn't mentioned any of this to Michelle, so I decided not to push the issue. I did come up with a great idea, however.

"You should design us a new sign for the outside of the bar," I said.

"Yes!" shouted Doug. "We've been talking about getting a new sign. And you should come up with a cool new logo for us too."

I smiled and nodded in agreement. "We'll even pay you for it."

"Whoa, settle down. Let's not get carried away," joked Doug. "Just kidding. Of course we'll pay you… as long as the logo doesn't suck."

Pete didn't say much after that, but I could tell by his big smile that his wheels were already turning regarding our new sign and logo. Doug was right, it was crazy that we had known Pete all these years and never knew about his hidden talent, or as he put it, his "silly hobby." Either way, we were glad we could offer him a project that utilized his talent. I think Doug and I were both hopeful this would help take his mind off his real job.

5

"THAT'S WHAT I GET" – Nine Inch Nails

Later that week, on one of my nights off, I swung by Hoohahs and had a couple of drinks with Pete. My first beer was spent listening to him excitedly talk about some of his ideas for our new sign and logo. He only verbalized his ideas to me and never actually showed me any drawings. He said he wanted it to be a surprise.

Unfortunately, the entirety of my second and third beers were spent listening to him bitch and moan about his real job. So much for our project taking his mind off of it. The more he complained, the more I realized just how much he really, really hated doing what he was doing.

Although he's explained it to us dozens of times, embarrassingly, I still can't tell you exactly what he does for work. I know that probably makes me a shitty friend, but I prefer to think of it as me just being computer illiterate. I do know, when he first started out, they only had a couple dozen employees, and now they have close to three hundred. I also know the company has switched hands a few times, and I'm sure that has added to his unhappiness.

Hating your *job* is one thing (we've all been there, felt that), but when you hate your chosen *career*, that must be extremely stressful on a person. I didn't have a wife. I didn't have kids. I didn't have anywhere near the financial pressures as Pete. I did my best to listen and offer my thoughts, but I'm sure it just came across as your typical cliché-filled shit.

Stupid shit like, "Maybe you just need a vacation." Or "You're probably just in a funk. I'm sure it'll pass." Eventually I decided to keep my mouth shut and just listen to him vent.

When I got home from Hoohahs, I turned on the Sox game, and before I knew it, my eyes slowly closed and I was out for the night. Well, I was out until just after 2 AM. That's when my phone started ringing. My first thought was it must be Doug wanting to go for a late-night walkabout. Either that, or it was Doug wanting to know who sang a certain song. Seriously, he did that a lot.

Doug, like me, was still anti-computer, so he wasn't able to simply google his silly questions. Just three nights earlier, he called me at 3:30 AM just to ask me who sang the 1991 hip hop song, "Mistadabolina." He said he couldn't sleep until he found out (btw, it was Del the Funky Homosapian). My life would have been so much easier if Doug had a computer so he could google that shit.

My eyes were half-closed as I reached for the phone. They became fully-opened when I saw the caller ID. It wasn't Doug.

"Hello? Dalelyn?"

Yup, I had just received a 2 AM call from Dalelyn Haywood, and at the time, it was one of the best 2 AM calls I had ever received! Through her tears, she told me about her night. Apparently, her parents were in town for a couple of days, and all four of them were supposed to go out to dinner. Of course, her D-bag boyfriend never showed up, which forced her to do what she did best—make excuses for him.

"I called Randy like every five minutes but just kept getting his stupid voicemail."

By the way, Randy is the name of her D-bag boyfriend. If it's all the same, I'll still refer to him as D-bag.

"After dinner, I even had my parents drive me by his place. And whose car do I see there? His ex-girlfriend's!"

"Did you confront him," I hesitantly asked.

"Nope. They drove me home, and I spent the rest of the night crying and getting lectured by them. You were right, Josh. You were right all along. I don't deserve to be treated like this. I'm tired of it. It's over! It's totally over!"

Although I was smiling like a mofo on my end of the phone, I really did feel horribly for her. No, really, I did.

"I'm so sorry, Dalelyn," was all I could muster through my smiling face.

"No, I'm the one who should be sorry. You have listened to me bitch and moan for months, and now you're listening to me ball my eyes out at 2 AM."

"You don't need to apologize, Dalelyn. I told you, I'm always here for you."

"Why can't more guys be like you, Josh?"

I assumed it was rhetorical so I didn't answer.

"My parents are driving up to Bar Harbor tomorrow for a few days, and I'm thinking of going with them. I just need to clear my head."

"I think that's a great idea," I said.

"Maybe when I get back, we can go out to dinner or something? It'll be nice to be on a date with someone who treats me so well."

That's right, my friends, did you hear that?? She said a date with someone who treats her so well. And that someone was me! I had been waiting and preparing for this moment for months. I immediately initiated the proper protocol.

"How about next Saturday night? I can pick you up at six."

She emitted a chuckle then said, "Saturday night at six sounds perfect."

We talked for a little while longer, but to be honest, I wasn't really listening. My mind was already planning the perfect date. After we hung up, I was tempted to call Doug and wake his ass up and tell him my persistence had finally paid off, but I didn't. I knew he probably wouldn't hear the phone ringing over his own snoring. Instead, I simply sat on my couch and reveled in my victory. There is nothing better than when a scenario plays out exactly the way you dreamt it up! Pffft, broken hearted savior my ass!!

***

The rest of the week was spent in pre-date preparation. I had learned my lesson years ago with the Elise debacle that there was no point planning out a huge elaborate date. I decided to keep it simple, with maybe a couple of small, sweet presents thrown in. Dalelyn had always mentioned how she was dying to go eat dinner down at the North End in Boston, but her D-bag boyfriend always refused.

My first pre-date preparation was to make reservations at a small, authentic Italian restaurant in the North End. I made sure they gave me their most romantic table. I could already see us sitting there, and as we were drinking our wine, she would say, *A toast—to Josh, the sweetest and nicest guy I know. The kind of guy I want to be with*!

Yup, this date was going to be epic.

The rest of my pre-date rituals took place on the day of the actual date.

Shopping for a new shirt.

Shopping for a new cologne (CK-1).

Shopping for some hair gel. (Dep-Level 6)

Car wash and vacuum.

My final stop before I picked her up was a quaint little flower shop in downtown Portsmouth. It was owned by this older couple, Mr. and Mrs. Miller. Seeing as I had maybe been there only once or twice in my life, I was sure they wouldn't remember me. As I entered, the bell on the door jingled, causing them both to enter from the back room.

"Hey, it's Joshua!" said Mr. Miller.

"We've been worried about you," said Mrs. Miller. "We haven't seen you in here since last fall."

Mr. Miller pondered then said, "No, he was here around Christmas time."

"Oh, that's right," Mrs. Miller exclaimed.

"Oh, and Valentine's Day too," pointed out Mr. Miller.

Mrs. Miller smiled and said, "That's right. I made you that wonderful arrangement. How could I forget that? I guess I'm getting old, huh?"

I politely smiled. And yes, I might have downplayed how many times I had been in here over the years. I didn't lie to you guys, per say, I just—misremembered? Anyway, back to the Millers.

"So, what's the occasion this time?" asked Mrs. Miller.

"A first date with a special lady," I answered.

"Red roses?" asked Mr. Miller.

Before I could say a word, Mrs. Miller said, "No, dear, don't you remember, red roses say too much. Not to mention, they're also the kiss of death!"

"Ah yes, I remember now," he said, running his fingers through his grey beard.

"I do want roses though," I said. "They're her favorite."

"White?" asked Mr. Miller.

Both Mrs. Miller and I shook our heads and said, "Nah. Says too little."

Again, he ran his boney fingers through his beard and pondered. Finally, a light bulb went off and a twinkle appeared in his eyes. He snapped his fingers and said, "Just this morning we got in some beautiful peach colored roses."

I looked over at Mrs. Miller and we both smiled.

"Perfect!" I said. "How about two? I don't wanna over do it."

He gave me a wink then hurried into the back room. Well, he didn't really hurry, bad hip and all. But I suppose compared to most 68-year-old dudes with bad hips, he was moving as fast as the Flash!

"Sooo, what's her name?" Mrs. Miller curiously smiled.

"Dalelyn."

"Ohhh, that's quite unique… and pretty."

Before I could get into the story of how we met, my eyes were drawn to a little candy display in the far corner.

"Oh yes! This will be perfect," I said, grasping a netted bag of chocolate gold coins.

"Ahh, she has a sweet tooth, huh?"

"Actually, it's more of a symbolic gift than anything. I just want her to know she deserves to be treated like gold. Hence, gold coins!"

"Aww, Joshua, why can't more men be as romantic as you?"

"I heard that!" grumbled Mr. Miller from the back.

"That's why I said it loud enough," she giggled.

A second later, he appeared carrying a couple of beautiful peach roses.

"You said two, right?" he asked.

"Yup, two dozen would be perfect, thanks."

The Millers exchanged a look, then Mr. Miller and his bad hip reentered the back room.

"Would you like to pick out a card?" she asked, pointing to a small rack.

"No thanks. I already bought one and wrote in it."

By the time I left the Miller's shop, it was fast approaching game time. I gave my arm pits another quick swipe of deodorant, fixed my hair in the rearview mirror, and topped it off with a spritz of CK 1.

As I pulled into her driveway, I proudly gazed over at the passenger seat, which was adorned with roses, gold coins, and a special little gift. No, not a mixtape… or a mix CD. I was serious when I said I was retired from making them for girls. That being said, I did have a mix playing in my car that was filled with songs I knew she liked. Hey, cut me some slack! I've made great strides in the mixtape/mix CD making biz!

I exited my car, took a deep breath, then made my way up the walkway to her front door. Do you remember when I said that there was nothing better than when a scenario plays out exactly the way you dreamt it? Well, on the flipside, there is nothing worse than when a scenario takes a drastic turn—one that you totally didn't see coming.

I knocked three times, and when she finally opened the door, she had a weird look on her face. I should have known right then and there that something was up, but my (hopelessly) romantic optimism took hold and I said, "Are you ready for the best date of your life?"

"Umm, didn't you get my message?" she hesitantly asked.

"No," I said as I started to feel that pit-of-your-stomach sickness thing. "When did you leave it? I just checked my machine a couple of hours ago."

"Yesterday," she quietly said. "I left it on your cell phone."

"My cell phone? You know I never use that."

It's true, I had only just gotten a cell a few months earlier, but I very rarely used it. I happened to be with Pete when he was picking out a new one, and he pretty much peer-pressured me into getting one. I caved and got the cheapest flip phone they had. He tried to pressure Doug into one too, but Doug simply said, "Um, no! What the fuck do I need a cell phone for?"

In retrospect, I should have said the same thing. The phone was pretty much useless. Whenever I would call someone, I would just get their voicemail, and ten seconds later, they would shoot me a text asking what was up. Like you couldn't just answer the phone to say that?? All anyone wanted to do was have text conversations. Do you know how long it takes to text a sentence on a keypadless flip phone? By the time I typed and answered their first question, they had already sent me seven more texts. Soon after I got the phone, I decided to just stick to old school phone calls on my cordless phone—

calls that involve actual talking, not texting.

Every time Dalelyn and I talked on the phone, it was almost always my home phone to her cell phone. I wondered why in the fuck would she call my flip phone, but the look on her face said all I needed to know.

"No. Please don't tell me you took him back?"

Her head lowered, and she avoided eye contact.

"Seriously? What happened to 'You were right, Josh. You were right all along.' Or 'I don't deserve to be treated like this.' Huh???"

She shrugged and quietly said, "I think I might have overreacted last week. The reason Randy never called me back that night, was his answering machine was turned off. And he also said that he had been working so much that week that he totally forgot about dinner with my parents."

Just like you guys, I wasn't buying his bullshit excuses either. I was having a hard time believing that she bought them as well. There was no way I was letting her off the hook.

"And what about his ex's car at his house?"

Ha! Let's see her defend this one!

"Oh, that. Randy said she just showed up out of the blue. He said she had been drinking, and she kept telling him how much she wanted him back. He said she started crying, and at one point, she tried to kiss him. He said he pushed her away and told her that he was happy with me."

Dalelyn had more to say, but I won't torture you guys with it. Honestly, I don't want to torture myself by writing it. It was at that point, I finally realized, that no matter what that little prick did, she would always take him back. I swear, she could have walked in on him having sex, and he would eventually convince her that he simply tripped, and his dick accidently fell into her.

"I can't believe you bought that story, Dalelyn."

"I know it sounds crazy, but trust me, his ex-girlfriend is a nut job. I can totally see her doing something like that. Anyway, we had a long talk the other night on the phone, and he promised that things would be better between us. And look, he even bought me flowers and a new book!"

She motioned to a small table, which had a cheap prepackaged mini-bouquet of red roses. The kind of flowers you'd find on the counter of a convenience store.

"Are you fuckin' kidding me?" I said, moving closer to the table. "Are these flowers even real?"

I shit you not, on the cellophane was a Cumberland Farms sticker that read: $4.99 Special. Before I could offer a sarcastic word, I gazed at the book he bought her. It was one of those stupid romance novels. You know, the kind with a shirtless hunk on the cover wearing a cowboy hat, or a construction worker with just a toolbelt on, or a half-naked cop with handcuffs dangling off his… It was like the fuckin' Village People went into the erotic book business.

"You hate these kind of cheesy romance novels."

"I know, but I had mentioned a while ago that I was eagerly awaiting the newest Jody Clark book (see what I did there?)"

"Umm, that's *not* the new Jody Clark book. It's not even an old Jody Clark book."

"Yea, I know. He couldn't remember the name of the book… or the author, so he thought I might like this one instead."

"Well, yea," I sarcastically said, pointing to the half-naked cop on the cover. "Who wouldn't love a book called, *Hard Justice*, I laughed."

She gave me a smile and had the nerve to say, "Oh well, at least he tried. It's the thought that counts, right?"

I could have spent the next hour explaining to her how stupid and naïve she was, but I just didn't see the point.

"I gotta go," was all I could say.

"Aw, Josh, don't be like this. You should be happy that I'm happy."

There was no way I was going to respond to that.

She then had the nerve to ask, "Do you wanna meet up for coffee tomorrow morning?"

"I don't think so. I care about you too much to watch you get hurt again."

"I told you, this time will be different."

With a slight chuckle, all I could say was, "Goodbye, Dalelyn," and then I left.

I left without a hug, a kiss, a handshake, or any other form of physical contact. I was officially done being her DSCO!

I climbed into my car and immediately ejected the CD and tossed it on the floor. That's right, I was that mad! I replaced it with another mix, and as Nine Inch Nails came on, I cranked it up and headed home.

At one point, I pulled along the side of the beach at Long Sands. I looked over to my passenger seat and saw the roses, the gold coins, and yes, the brand-new Jody Clark book adorned with a bow. Yup, that was the special gift I had bought for her.

It was high tide, and I was tempted to pull a Doug and toss the flowers into the crashing waves, but I didn't. Nor did I barricade myself in a darkened house with candles lit, all the while The Cure blared out. Nope, I had indeed come a long way from that guy.

Did I still make the occasional Depression Session mix? Yes, yes I did, but not nearly at the fervent pace as I did years earlier. Don't get me wrong, I was hurt, and depressed, and most definitely angry over the whole Dalelyn disaster, but I had other methods now to deal with this. Methods other than long, drawn-out sessions of depression. You think I'm joking, but I'm not! My bounce-back-ability over girls had dramatically improved over the years.

With that in mind, I left the beach and drove straight home. I got out of my car and walked around to the passenger door and opened it up. After I grabbed the flowers, the book, and even the chocolate coins, I casually headed to my small backyard. I stopped in front of a bare (burnt) spot of grass, and I released the presents onto it.

Next, I entered my garage for a brief moment, and when I exited, I was carrying matches and a bottle of lighter fluid. I squirted a plentiful amount (half bottle) onto the flowers and gifts, and then I lit the whole fuckin' thing on fire. It was glorious, yet depressing. Gloriously depressing, if you will. Most of all, it was cathartic. I watched it for a few minutes, squirted a little more (rest of bottle), then turned and went inside for a cold beer.

No sooner did I crack one open, I heard a car door shut—two doors actually. I peered out the window and saw Pete and Doug walking up the driveway. Doug pointed to the fire in the backyard then held out his hand. Pete shook his head then slapped what appeared to be a twenty-dollar bill into Doug's hand. Those fuckers were taking bets on me. I wanted to be pissed, but I suppose it served me right. I earned this one.

By the time they entered my house, I had two opened beers waiting for them. I think they were a little taken aback by my lack of sadness. There were no candles burning, no incense, and no Depression Sessions playing. As a matter of fact, I had just turned the TV on and was watching *Jeopardy*.

To their credit, they held off on their *I told you so's* and their sarcastic jokes. They asked how I was doing and curiously asked what exactly went down with Dalelyn. I filled them in on every miserable detail. Usually, it would take me three to seven days to reveal details of my latest female catastrophe, but like I said, I had made huge strides over the years.

"Well, on the bright side," said Pete, "you have a clean, fresh-smelling car."

What can I say, I'm surprised they held off their sarcasm this long.

"What's the scent this time?" asked Doug. "Strawberry?"

"Shut up, dude!" I said then mumbled, "Vanilla."

"Ha!" yelled Pete, holding out his hand.

Doug begrudgingly gave him back his twenty bucks.

"Seriously? You guys are taking bets on me?"

They both nodded and laughed.

"Do you know what you need?" asked Doug.

I knew exactly where he was going with this.

"No, Doug, I don't need to go to a strip club."

"Dude, it's like visual medicine for a broken heart. And if you go the right club, it can be physical medicine as well."

"Thanks, but I'm all set. I don't need any medicine—visual or physical."

To our surprise, Pete announced, "Well, I do!"

We were surprised because Pete never advocated for strip clubs. It wasn't that he didn't like them (I mean, who doesn't like strip clubs?), it's just that out of us three, he was always the reluctant one. Usually, the pecking order was this: Doug would (excitedly) suggest going to a strip club, and if I declined, then Pete would follow suit and decline as well. If I agreed to go, then nine out of ten times, Pete would also agree—reluctantly, but he would go. But never had he agreed to go before me!

The poor guy must have been more stressed than I thought. Although, I suppose it didn't surprise me; married seven years, together twelve, two kids, and a job he hates. I was afraid to ask him what his masturbation-to-sex ratio was these days. It was probably 12 to 1. Hell, maybe even 15 to 1!

So yes, I agreed to go to a strip club, but I didn't do it for me, I did it for Pete. I was being a good friend, that's all. Needless to say, Doug was beside himself with excitement. Not only was he going to one of his favorite places, but he didn't even have to spend the energy convincing us to go.

"Ten's Club here we come," announced Pete.

"No, no, no," said Doug. "The Ten's Club is too… um, too…"

"Too classy?" I said.

"Yes! Way too classy. We're going to Kitten's! Where a lap dance actually means they're *on* your lap."

"They don't do that at the Ten's?" asked Pete.

"Fuck no!" snapped Doug. "They charge more money for their private dances, and it only consists of them *hovering* on your lap, not grinding."

"Really?" said Pete. "It's been a couple of years since I've been there, but I could have sworn they did more than just hover."

"Nope!" insisted Doug. "Besides, how would you know? You're usually too cheap to ever pay for a lap dance."

Doug was not wrong. Pete was known to be very cheap, especially at strip clubs. As a matter of fact, the first time we all went to a strip club (Fun Fact: it was the Fuzzy Grape in Webster, Ma), Pete pulled a major strip club no-no. It was me, Pete, Scott, and Doug, and we all were sitting front and center along the main stage. The dancer known as Cinnamon sexily made her way down our line of crisply folded one-dollar bills. It was our first time, so each of us were widely smiling (& slightly blushing) as we deposited our dollars into her garter. All of us except Pete.

When Cinnamon got to him, she gave him the sexy-as-fuck stripper eye contact and then turned and did the ass shake. She finished it off with a slap to her right cheek. Instead of sliding a creased George Washington into her garter, Pete motioned her closer and I shit you not, he asked if she could break a five. The only thing that would have been worse was if he placed quarters in front of her. I think she would have rather had him touch her (#1 strip club no-no) then to pull that cheap shit.

Anyway, the three of us went to Kitten's that night, and a good time was had by all. Don't get me wrong, I was still upset about Dalelyn, but Doug was right, Kitten's provided a well-needed distraction for all of us. And I'll be damned, Doug was also right about their lap dances. There was no hovering, just some old-fashioned grindage.

6

"CREEP" – Radiohead

A few days after our guys' night out, Dalelyn called me (on my landline) and left a message on my machine. I was actually home when she called, but when I saw the caller ID, I chose not to answer it. The old Josh would have answered it before the second ring, but like I said, I was more mature and less pathetic than my younger years (minus the sacrificial fire and lighter fluid thing).

Dalelyn's message basically said that she was sorry about how things went down the other night, and that she hoped it wouldn't affect our friendship. Unfortunately, our friendship was never the same again. It wasn't that I was mad or hated her, not at all. She was an amazing girl, and I loved being around her, but I hated seeing her energy being drained by Mr. D-bag himself. I just hoped that one day she would finally realize that she deserved better. But until then, I had no intentions on being the DSCO.

Doug used to say, the best way to get over someone is to find a new someone. I would like to think this wasn't totally true and that I could get over a girl on my own terms without the help of finding someone new. And less than two weeks after the Dalelyn fiasco, I was doing just that! I had not only attended a strip club with the guys, but I wasn't moping around, I wasn't a sad fuck at work, and I didn't listen to depressing music in the dark (no more than normal, that is).

That being said, on the ten-day mark, I did start making a song list for what might be considered a Depression Session mix. You'll be happy to know that the mix never actually saw the light of day. Creating and writing down the song list was as far as I got before I stopped. I have to admit, my self-control was impressive. See, Doug was wrong, I didn't need to find someone new to get over someone old.

Aw shit! I just remembered I promised I wouldn't lie or stretch the truth to you guys anymore. Okay, okay, full disclosure: my stoppage of the mixtape(CD) had less to do with my self-control and more to do with receiving a phone call from… well, from *someone new*. Technically, she was someone old, but she was about to provide me with a huge distraction from Dalelyn. Actually, way more than a distraction.

The phone call got me so pumped up that I decided to head down to Hoohahs on my night off for a drink, but when I saw that Pete was having another shit day, I decided to put my good news on hold. Instead, I just sat there drinking my beer and listening to Pete vent.

"I really think you should tell Michelle how much you hate

your job and how you need a change," I said.

"Trust me, it wouldn't go over well. Right now, she's laser-focused on her classes and on getting her own career going. Besides, when am I supposed to tell her? Between my work schedule, chasing the kids around, and house chores, Michelle and I barely have time together. And don't even get me started about sex."

"I'm sure by you hanging out here every night, it isn't helping add to your together time," I half-joked.

"Hey! I deserve a little me time! Right now we're in between daycares, so during the days I watch the girls and attempt to work from home. Then, when Michelle gets home from class, I head into the office to get some real work done. So, yea, I think I deserve a beer or two!"

I had known Pete since grade school, and he has pretty much always been the poster boy for long-term relationships. In high school, he had two separate serious relationships. After that, he had a brief four-year window where he was single and had his fun, but then he met Michelle, and the rest was history.

Can you imagine not having to deal with the whole dating scene? Or never having to try and get a girl's digits? Or never having to wonder if the girl likes you? Or having to come up with ways to impress her? Shit, for nearly twelve years now, Pete has never once had to worry about going to bed alone. Yup, the guy had it made and he didn't even realize it. I tried to remind him just how lucky he was, but it didn't go over so well.

"Oh, I have it made, do I?" he scoffed. Do you wanna hear how my night went yesterday? If you remember correctly, I was only here for fifteen minutes tops. Just long enough for a quick beer. I went home, gave the girls a bath, read them a story, put them to bed, then attempted to have a little alone time with my wife. I came up from behind her in the living room and kissed her neck and said, 'the girls are in bed, and I will be too in a few minutes… hint, hint.' She just turned around and glared at me, literally glared."

"Why?" I asked.

In his best Michelle voice, Pete said, "These clothes aren't gonna fold themselves, and in case you didn't notice, there's also a sink full of dishes."

I took a long sip of beer as Pete continued his story.

"I tried to kiss her neck again and told her that we'd get dishes and clothes tomorrow. She wasn't thrilled with my response. 'What's with the we?' she said. 'I have class all morning tomorrow, and then I need to study for a big test.' I tried one last time to kiss her and I said, 'Whatever, I'll do them tomorrow then.' Apparently, that was the wrong response as well. She just laughed and said, 'Like the way you did the dishes and clothes the other day?'

Pete finished his beer and angrily said to me, "Do you wanna know why I didn't get the dishes and clothes done the other day?"

It didn't matter how I responded, I knew Pete was going to tell me anyway.

"I spent the morning on a mandatory conference call with our London office, all the while the girls were running around the other room screaming like banshees. And of course, one thing leads to another and Kayla accidently knocked over Lindsay. At that point, their screams were replaced with crying. Loud, loud crying. Needless to say, I was forced to end the call and tend to Lindsay. She spent the next hour on my lap with an ice pack on her forehead. When she finally got off my lap,

Kayla announced that it was her turn, so she climbed up and we all watched cartoons."

Doug slide us another round and Pete continued his story.

"Don't get me wrong, I love spending time with my girls, and who doesn't like watching cartoons… but because of that, none of my work or my house chores got done that day. As soon as Michelle got home, I headed to my office to get caught up."

Pete stood up, and before he headed towards the bathroom, he looked at me and said, "So you might wanna keep all of that in mind the next time you get jealous of my life."

After Pete walked off, I beat Doug to the punch and said, "Wow, someone needs to get laid."

"Ya think?" Doug said, laughing.

By the time Pete returned from the bathroom, he had calmed down a bit.

"Sorry, I didn't mean to lay all that on you guys like that."

"It's no biggie," I said. "I'm sure once Michelle gets settled into her school routine things will get better. And when you guys finally get a new daycare, everything will get back to normal. And I'm sure things will work out with your job too. Life just has a way of challenging us sometimes, that's all."

With that positive affirmation, I happily took a long swig of beer. When I finished, I felt both of them staring at me.

"What?" I said. "Can't someone be positive and upbeat?"

"Someone can, but not Josh Wentworth. Besides, didn't you just get your heart stomped on a week ago?" asked Pete.

"Ten days ago, to be exact," I smiled. "And I don't know about stomped on, just a little setback, that's all."

Pete looked at me and laughed. "I tell you what, Josh, your bounce-back-ability from heartbreaks is getting shorter and shorter."

Doug suspiciously looked at me and said, "You've got another chick lined up, don't you?"

"Is it that brunette from a couple weeks ago?" asked Pete.

I shook my head no.

"Sooo, who is it?" they both said.

"Jane," I said with a smile.

"Jane who?" they both said worriedly.

When my smile grew bigger, they both knew exactly Jane who.

Just to recap: I met Jane Wheeler back in the summer of 1990, and we have since experienced multi-occasions of "great time but bad timing." For a short while in '97 our timing was perfect! She even moved in with me for a bit. Then, what always happens, happened. She got antsy, she got an amazing job offer, and she eventually moved out and moved on—without me. I always knew she was never one to let the grass grow under her feet for too long, but being the hopeless romantic sucker that I am, I always held out hope that our paths would one day cross for good.

Although we had stayed in close contact over the years, she hadn't actually been back to York since 1999. I think I covered that meetup in *Between Hello and Goodbye*. We had met for breakfast at Rick's restaurant and reminisced. Later that night, we had a few drinks at Hoohahs, and then, like always, she spread her wings and flew away; figuratively and literally. Her destination was Chicago, and she loved it so much that she made it her new home. She immediately landed a job as the lead photographer for a popular Chicago magazine.

I actually flew out to see her a couple of years later in 2001. It was my first time there, and the city was amazing. Jane was the perfect tour guide, showing me all of the classic sights. I have to admit, I was very tempted to rent a car and drive over to Iowa to see the famous Field of Dreams, but I didn't. I figured it would be more meaningful if I waited until I had a son to take there with me. Yes, I did realize I could be an old man before that happened, and by then, Shoeless Joe Jackson might be toothless Joe Jackson. Either way, I decided to hold off on my Field of Dreams pilgrimage.

While I was in Chicago, our friendship picked right up where we left off. We had tons of fun, tons of laughs, and yes, tons of adult beverages. And in case you're wondering, no, we did not hookup. There was no sex or kissing involved at all. We did however, sleep in the same bed together, but that was it. All in all, it was a pretty fuckin' great time. Since then, we talked plenty on the phone, but that weekend back in 2001 was the last time I had physically seen Jane. I didn't allow myself to have any sort of romantic aspirations, but still, I was very excited to see her again. Doug didn't really share my excitement.

"Are you fuckin' kidding me?" said Doug.

"Apparently, she just quit her job and wants to take some time off to think about her future."

"Good for her," mumbled Pete, completely relating to her job situation.

"So how does this involve you?" asked Doug.

"Because she wants to come to York for the summer and relax," I said.

"Didn't her parents sell their summer house a while ago?" asked Pete.

I nodded.

"Where's she staying then?" Doug hesitantly asked.

My smile clearly gave it away.

Both of them shook their heads at me. Just then, Doug cracked open two Coronas, shoved a couple of limes in them, and handed them to two regulars, Gwen and Christina. They had approached the bar as I was informing the guys about Jane. Doug continued shaking his head at me as he addressed the girls.

"This is bad news. Very bad news," he said.

"What's bad news," asked Gwen.

"Jane coming to stay with Josh for the summer."

"Who's Jane," Christina asked.

Do you guys see a pattern here? Doug constantly finds the need to tell complete strangers at the bar about my personal life.

Doug took their money then said, "Who's Jane? Let's just say, there have been a lot of girls in the past 15 years that Josh has either dated or has been infatuated with, but none of them could hold a candle to Jane."

"Aww, that's sweet," said Gwen. "And she's coming to stay with you for a while?"

I smiled and nodded.

"Trust me," began Doug, "the last thing Josh needs is for Jane to reappear in his life… especially for the summer."

"Why?" asked Christina. "Is she a bad person?"

"No, not at all," said Doug.

"We love Jane," Pete chimed in.

"Yea, we love Jane. She's a cool chick, but—"

"But what?" asked both girls.

"It's just that Jane has always been Josh's Achilles elbow."

"Achilles heel," corrected Pete.

Doug shrugged off Pete's correction, and before I could

defend myself, Pete said, "Jane is the first girl that Josh really, really, really fell for. And we're not talking, *Hey, here's a mixtape I made you* type of fallen for. This was the first girl I ever remembered him using the 'L' word with."

"Pfft, even worse," added Doug, "he used the 'S' word on her."

Both girls (and Pete) looked over at me puzzled. I had no idea what he was babbling about, so I just shrugged. Besides, even if I did know what the 'S' word was, it was obvious that I was just a bystander in this conversation about me.

When all of our eyes looked curiously over at Doug, he matter-of-factly said, "You know, the 'S' word—soulmate. Whatever the fuck that means."

I'd love to say the conversation was nearing the end, but it was just getting started. Two other people up at the bar overheard Doug's soulmate statement and decided to add their thoughts on the word. The next thing you know, there was a large Hoohahs-debate over the actual definition of soulmate. A large debate which didn't include any input from me. I thought about using that moment to quietly slip away and go home. Trust me, they wouldn't even had noticed I left, but instead, I just sat there and drank my beer. And for the record, I NEVER called Jane my soulmate!

Okay, I'm going to pause here for a moment. Long story short, after the soulmate debate, Pete and Doug continued filling the crowd in on the history of Josh and Jane. Luckily for me, I was getting pretty good at tuning out my friends. I know they were only looking out for me, but I was still very excited about Jane coming to stay with me for the summer. And no, I didn't have any expectations of us getting back together. No, seriously, I didn't! I was just looking forward to us hanging out again. The one thing you could always count on with us, is no matter how long it's been since we'd seen each other, we could easily and immediately fall back into a familiar place.

Even when we had our breakup and didn't see each other for nearly two years, our friendship didn't miss a beat once we were face to face. I knew Jane's visit would be fun, and I knew we'd get along perfectly, but what I didn't expect, was just how fun and just how perfect it would be.

7

"MOTORCYCLE DRIVE-BY" – Third Eye Blind

On that following Saturday, when I returned home from some errands, I saw the best sight ever. It was a white Volvo with Illinois plates. Okay, maybe the car was the second-best sight ever, for sitting on my porch reading a book was Jane Wheeler. She placed her book beside her, widely smiled, then stood up and gave me a long, overdue hug. When we finally separated, I gave her a once-over.

"Wow, you look great, Jane. Not that you don't normally look great, it's just now you look really, really great."

"Aww, I'm here seven seconds and you're already making me blush."

"Yea, yea, yea, I'm sure you hear that all day long."

"Ha! I wish," she shrugged.

"How was your trip?"

"It was good. I've been in Massachusetts at my parents' house the last three days, which was about two days too long. It took less than a day for my mom to start harping on me."

"Let me guess—when are you gonna settle down and get married?"

"That, and when is she gonna get a grandchild. She also doesn't get why I'd rather stay here at the beach for the summer instead of with her and dad in Massachusetts."

"What did you tell her?"

"I told her my goal this summer was to just relax, and that would not be possible if I stayed with them. I then told her, if I play my cards right, maybe by the end of the summer I could be not only married, but knocked up as well. Needless to say, she wasn't very amused by my sarcasm."

"I'm sure not," I laughed.

Oh, and in case you guys are wondering, I totally knew Jane was being silly. I didn't think for a second that she was referring to me as the guy who would knock her up and marry her. I meant it when I said I had zero expectations of her coming here. I was just looking forward to having some fun with an old friend. That's all!

I gave Jane a quick walkthrough of my place. I lived in a small two-bedroom cottage a few side-streets away the beach. No, I didn't own it. It was just a year-round rental. You rarely find year-round rentals this close to the beach, so I was actually quite lucky finding it. There was a sweet older couple who used to come in the bar all the time, but they had since retired to Florida. They didn't really want to deal with the hassle of renting their place out on a weekly basis, and they also didn't want to deal with hiring a company to take care of it for them.

One night, I sarcastically joked that I would gladly rent it all year round from them. The next thing I knew, they placed the keys in my hand. There were only a couple other cottages on my road that were winterized, so it was very quiet in the off-season, but I kind of liked that.

Anyway, after I gave Jane the quick house tour and got her stuff settled in, we decided to take a ride around town. Jane was always amazed at how much had changed since the last time she was here. I suppose by me living here, I didn't really notice the changes as much. We drove around the beaches and even drove by her parents' old summer home.

"Aww, so many great memories," she sadly said as we parked out in front.

"I can't believe they sold it," I said.

"Yea, they used the money to buy a winter home in Old Folk's Alley in Florida," she joked.

"Ah yes, Bingo and early bird specials."

"You have no idea," she laughed.

After she reminisced a bit about her old summer house, we continued our drive down memory lane. Jane filled me in more about why she quit her job. Apparently, the magazine was becoming more and more focused on local hotspots—as in, restaurants, bars, nightclubs. Jane was getting bored with that type of photography, and finally, she just up and quit and decided to leave Chicago all together.

I cannot stress this enough—I had ZERO hopes that York Beach would be Jane's permanent landing spot. I knew she was just here to relax and recharge her batteries.

Eventually, we drove away from the beach and out towards the mountain. Of course, Jane made me stop at Flo's for lunch.

"It's good to see not everything has changed around here," she said, stuffing her face with a Flo dog.

When we had our fill of Flo dogs, we continued our drive. Our drive took us up Pete's road, and I noticed both cars were in the driveway.

"Looks like they're both home. Do you wanna stop in?"

"Sure. I haven't seen them in forever."

"Well, if you came back home once in a while…"

"I know, I know. It really sucks that my parents sold their beach house," she said as we headed up the walkway.

"Wait until you see the girls," I said.

"How old are they again?"

"Umm, seven and four I think."

We knocked on the door, and after a few seconds, it slowly opened. On the other side was Cinderella. Well, Kayla dressed like Cinderella. From the other room, Michelle yelled to Kayla.

"Kayla! I told you never to open the door to strangers."

Kayla giggled and yelled back, "It's not a stranger, it's Uncle Josh and some woman."

Jane looked over at me and said, "Wow, I guess it's been longer than I thought since I've been back here. Cinderella doesn't even remember me."

Just then, Michelle entered the foyer. She excitedly smiled when she saw Jane.

"Kayla, that's not some woman, this is Jane. Don't you remember her?"

"I actually babysat you once," Jane smiled. "But you were teeny tiny. Remember, we made puppets and did a very cool puppet show?"

Slowly, Kayla's eyes lit up. "Ohhhh yea! I remember! We made a puppet of Uncle Doug, and he kept saying silly things and falling down."

"So this was a realistic puppet show?" laughed Michelle as

she gave Jane a hug. "I didn't know you were coming to town."

"I told Pete," I said.

"Pfft, like he tells me anything," Michelle said, rolling her eyes.

"Like you listen when I do," exclaimed Pete, entering from the other room.

Pete and Michelle were the masters of playful sarcasm. It was always one of those qualities I admired about them. In this case, however, it seemed it was less of the playfulness and more of the sarcasm. Pete also approached Jane and gave her a hug. Just then, Kayla gave Jane's shirt a tug.

"Me and my little sister are playing princesses, do you wanna play?"

"Oh, honey, let Jane visit for a little bit, okay?"

"I tell you what," said Jane, "I'm not sure I'd fit into any of your princess dresses, but I brought my camera, and maybe we can do a princess photo shoot later with you and your sister."

"Really?" Kayla said with a big smile. "That would be the bomb!"

Our questioning gaze went directly to Pete and Michelle.

Michelle shook her head and said, "Looks like someone has been hanging out with Uncle Doug way, way too much."

Pete nodded and said, "He could have taught her worse phrases."

This caused all of us to nod in agreement. Our laughter was interrupted by the royal entrance of Princess Lindsay.

"Oh my God," exclaimed Jane. "She's so big. The last time I was home, you were pregnant with her."

"Hey, Lindsay, Auntie Jane is gonna do a photo shoot with us later! We should go get ready!"

With that, Kayla grabbed Lindsay's hand and they both

scampered off.

"Wow," laughed Jane. "I went from some woman to Auntie Jane in less than five minutes."

As we entered the living room, Michelle apologized for all of the toys and clothes strewn about.

"Sorry for the mess. *Somebody's* slacking on their chores," she said, looking over at Pete.

"I've been outside fixing the damn lawn mower. If you wanna trade places, be my guest."

Their exchange was even less playful than the previous one. Pete grabbed a couple of beers, and I followed him out back to the lawn mower.

"Sorry for showing up out of the blue," I said. "I hope we didn't interrupt anything."

"Nah, don't mind Michelle. She's just stressing about her classes. She has a huge work load this summer, and we're scrambling to find daycare for the girls."

"I thought *you* were watching them during the day?"

"Michelle might have a huge school load this summer, but it pales in comparison to my work load. Ever since our company switched hands, it's been nothing but chaos. There's just no way I can work from home while watching the girls."

"What about your parents?"

"Too unreliable. Now that they're retired, they like to just take off and travel on a whim."

"Sounds like a good gig," I smiled.

"Yea, no shit. I can't wait for that to be us."

I stood back and watched Pete clutch various tools and tinker with the mower. To be honest, I wasn't sure he knew what the hell he was doing, but seeing as neither did I, I kept my mouth shut.

"When did Jane get into town?" he asked, searching for the right-sized socket wrench.

"Today. We've just been driving around looking at the old haunts."

"Ahh," he said, still not finding the proper tool. "She looks good."

"Yea, I guess," I shrugged. "I didn't really notice."

"Uh huh," he said sarcastically.

***

After we left their house, Jane and I drove back to my place to get her settled in.

"Is it me, or are they both completely stressing out?"

"Yea, bigtime. Pete's job is really getting to him. I think he's ready to quit and try something new. Unfortunately, he needs to wait until Michelle finishes school and gets established with her own career."

"And she's totally stressing out over that, by the way," said Jane. "I think she's overwhelmed and feels she waited too long to go back to school. I have to admit, that's the most tension I've seen between them ever."

I nodded in agreement.

"At one point today, I was looking at the girls, and I made a comment how I felt so old and single. Michelle told me I should enjoy every minute of it. I mean, she was quick to point out how much she loved her family, but she told me I'd be amazed at how boring and routine things get."

I laughed and replied, "I hear that from Pete all the time. He compares his life to the movie *Groundhog Day*. Same shit, different day."

"It's kind of depressing," she frowned.

"Eh, it's just a phase, that's all. I'm sure they'll be back to their old cheery selves soon enough," I reassured.

"Well, I did volunteer to watch the girls a few days a week. Hopefully that'll relieve some of their stress."

"I thought you came here this summer for a little R&R?" I smiled.

"Trust me, hanging out with kids will be way more relaxing than dealing with some of the morons at my job."

"Speaking of morons at work, I gotta head out in a few to Hoohahs. You just gonna chill here?"

"Yup," she happily smiled. "I'm gonna do a little unpacking and then maybe plant my ass out on the back deck with a good book."

"Sounds good. Enjoy."

"Oh, and by the way, when I'm finished with the book I'm reading, I wanna dig into some of these screenplays you've been working on the last few years."

"We'll see," I smiled.

"Am I in any of them?" she curiously smirked.

I gave her a playful shrug then waved goodbye as I headed off to work.

***

It wouldn't be long before I'd see Jane again. She ended up showing her face down at Hoohahs later that night.

"Well, look what the wind blew in," yelled Doug across the bar. "Jane fuckin' Wheeler… in the flesh."

"Aww, you even got my middle name right," she shot back. She then leaned across the bar giving Doug a hug. "Still in business, I see."

"Hell yea!" he exclaimed. "Doing better than ever, actually."

She looked around at the full bar and said, "It looks like it. Good for you," she said sincerely. "You guys deserve it."

Over the next hour or so, Doug caught her up on everything in his life, which basically meant he informed her on his last few sex-capades. Thankfully, he didn't do any napkin sketches for her. Also thankfully, he didn't fill her in on my latest crash and burn with Dalelyn. Jane hadn't even been here a day yet, so I was hoping to hold off for at least a little while on my embarrassing heartbreak stories.

Like clockwork, right around nine, Pete showed up for his nightly beer or two. He took a seat next to Jane and proceeded to thank her for volunteering to watch the kids a few days a week.

"No problem at all. It'll be fun."

"It'll really be a huge help for us," he said. "I love being around my girls, but it is nearly impossible to get any work done at home."

"You just getting done work now?" she asked.

Pete looked over at Doug and I then said, "Yea, kinda. I sorta told Michelle I'd be at the office until ten-thirtyish, so I'd appreciate you not telling her you saw me here."

"Yea, sure," she hesitantly said.

As soon as Pete got up to go to the bathroom, I clued Jane in further on Pete's nightly habits.

"So Michelle thinks he's working late most nights, but he's really here drinking?" asked Jane.

"Well it's not like he's drinking here all night," I said. "He usually just has a couple. I told you, his job has really been stressing him out bigtime lately. He just comes here to unwind a bit."

I didn't give Jane the full lowdown about how Pete doesn't go home too early so that he can avoid, as he put it, "mundane conversations and arguments." I certainly didn't agree with Pete's avoidance of his home life, but who was I to cast judgement on the life of a married couple.

When Pete returned, the conversation switched to our lack of help at the bar. Doug informed me that one of our part-time bartenders, Lisa, had just given her notice.

"Don't worry," I reassured, "I'm sure we'll find someone. We've never had a problem before finding help. Besides, she only worked a few shifts a week anyway."

"I'll fill in until you find someone new," Jane said out of the blue.

"Really?" Doug said, slightly shocked.

"Sure. As long as it doesn't interfere with the days I watch Pete's kids."

"So much for a relaxing summer, huh?" I laughed, shaking my head.

"Are you kidding me?" she smiled. "Working at the most popular bar at the beach… it'll be a blast."

"Just remember," Doug pointed out, "if you work here, we'd be your boss. So you'd need to treat us accordingly."

"Yea, treat us accordingly," I jokingly reiterated.

Jane sat up straight and gave us both a salute.

So, just like that, Jane was not only living with me but was working a couple shifts with me as well.

8

"JANE, I STILL FEEL THE SAME" – Matthew Ryan

It was a little strange having Jane stay with me, especially considering the last time she stayed with me was six years ago when we were dating (& having sex). It was strange, but it was a good strange. We were having so much fun with each other that before I knew it, it was almost August. It didn't really surprise me that we were getting along so well, but what did surprise me, was the fact that Jane had been here all summer and I never once got the impression that she was getting restless. She didn't seem like she missed Chicago or her job, for that matter. Dare I say, she seemed quite content.

I do have to admit, even though I didn't have any expectations, there were definitely more than a few times I wanted her to crawl into my bed at night. And no, not just for sex. Although, yes, that also crossed my mind. Bottom line, I just really missed my arm wrapped around her, not to mention, her smell. It's funny how people have a distinct smell that can immediately transport you back in time. It's not unlike hearing a certain song. As a matter of fact, there are times I hear a song on the radio, and not only does it remind me of a specific time, place, and girl, but I swear, I can also smell those memories. I know that sounds completely whacked, but it's true.

Anyway, despite my innate desire to have Jane sleep in my bed, I kept everything perfectly platonic. We were getting along so well and having so much fun, I didn't see any reason to push the limits and go down that road again. So, that being said, for the record, it was Jane (not me) who decided to take a stroll down that road again—kinda.

***

Sometime around early August, I organized a friends' night out. Doug and I got coverage at Hoohahs, and we all met up over at the Portsmouth Brewery. In addition to drinking with friends, I figured with all the stress and tension Pete and Michelle were feeling, this would be a good release for them. I was hoping it would allow them to have some old-fashioned laughs together.

I also invited Joanna and her newest online date. I even prearranged a designated driver for all of us, so we could all drink to our hearts' content. Michelle and Jane took full advantage of this, and they started their night off with shots of tequila.

After sucking her lime, Jane looked at Michelle and said, "Remember drinking that whole bottle of tequila out on the rocks by the Nubble?"

Michelle cringed and said, "I remember throwing up that whole bottle of tequila on the rocks by the Nubble."

Their laughter was followed by another shot. Oh, did I mention one of the bartenders was none other than Doug's former employee/former sex/former crush, Taylor?

"What the hell are you doing working here?" Doug asked as we approached the bar. "I thought you were doing the school-teacher thing?"

"I am," she smiled. "But unfortunately, I still have to work part time in the summers to make ends meet."

"Ahh, I see," Doug said suspiciously. "And you chose this place over Hoohahs?"

"Ha, you guys couldn't afford me," she laughed. "Just kidding, Doug."

Taylor went on to explain that she had run into the owner of the Brewery, and he asked her if she wanted to work for him in the summer. She agreed, but seeing as she was living up in the Portland area, she only wanted a few shifts a week. Luckily for her, he gave her the most profitable shifts.

Just like old times, we stood by and witnessed Doug and Taylor playfully exchanging verbal jabs.

"So, Taylor, how's the love life going?" asked Doug.

"Eh, it is what it is," she said, less than enthusiastic.

"Well at least you're keeping the battery business going strong." Doug laughed at his own joke.

Without missing a beat, Taylor said, "Just as I'm sure you're keeping the tissue and lotion businesses going."

"You know it!" he laughed, raising his drink to her.

Yup, it was just like old times. We all drank, laughed, and reminisced. Pete and Michelle seemed to be enjoying themselves, and more importantly, they were enjoying each other. This night out was exactly what we all needed.

Doug and I also made a toast to Pete. A few days earlier, the new logo and sign that he'd been working on was finally unveiled, and we loved it. He had Cat help with the actual production of the sign, but his design and creativity literally blew us away.

It wasn't until around 10 PM that Joanna showed up. I introduced her to Michelle, and before I could say another word, Joanna said, "And you must be the one and only Jane?"

Jane laughed and said, "I'm not sure about the one and only."

"According to Josh you are," she smiled.

"Awww," emitted from Pete and Doug.

Before it got too awkward, I quickly turned the tables on Joanna.

"Hey, didn't you have one of those computer blind dates tonight?"

Slightly embarrassed, she corrected me by saying, "It's not a blind date, but yes, it was from an online dating site."

"Which one are you using?" asked Jane.

"I started with Friendster, but now I'm trying Match.com."

"Ah yes," grinned Jane, "I've tried them both. Hopefully you'll have better luck than I did."

I couldn't believe what I was hearing. It was shocking enough that someone as cool and cute as Joanna was forced to resort to a dating site, but Jane?? Unbelievable! Was it really that hard to organically find a decent guy to date? Or to find a decent guy period? Either way, I was still shocked that both Joanna and Jane were forced to resort to this online dating thing. Was this where my own dating life was heading?

Before I could worry too much about what my future dating

profile would look like, I heard Doug insensitively ask Joanna, "I'm assuming tonight's date was a giant crash and burn, huh?"

"Actually, our date just got started about an hour ago. He was in Boston for a meeting and got caught in traffic. We grabbed a late dinner at Rosa's and then decided to join you guys for drinks."

"Where is he now?"

"He's outside. He had an important phone call to take."

She motioned to the front window, and there, standing on the sidewalk was a well-dressed man talking on his phone.

"Mr. Suit & Tie is your date?" laughed Doug.

"Yea, why?"

"He looks old enough to be your dad."

"Doug!" chastised Michelle.

"What? I'm just saying the dude looks old. And who wears a suit and tie on a date?"

"Someone with some class, that's who," said Jane.

"First of all," started Joanna, "he's only eight years older, and like I said, he just came from a meeting, so that's why he's dressed like that."

"Joanna, you don't need to defend yourself to us," said Michelle. "Especially to *him*," she said, pointing at Doug.

"And there's nothing wrong with a well-dressed older man," said Jane.

"Pfft, he looks boring and stiff to me," said Doug. "And by stiff, I don't mean the good kind. If ya know what I mean?" he winked.

"Really? You're into stiff men?" said Taylor over our shoulder.

We all laughed as Doug flipped her off.

Our laughter didn't deter his comments.

"What does he do for a living? A maître d'? A funeral director?"

"No," laughed Joanna. "He's a trader."

"Like Benedict Arnold?" asked Doug, stupidly.

After we all stared blankly at him for a few seconds, Pete said, "That would be a *traitor*. Her date is a *trader*."

"Like stocks and bonds and Wallstreet type of shit?" asked Doug.

Just at that moment, Taylor again walked by our table and said, "No, like pelts and spices type of a trader."

The louder we laughed, the higher Doug raised his middle finger at all of us, especially Taylor. Just then, Joanna's date entered the bar and made his way over to us.

"Good evening all. Sorry about the phone call," he said. "Business knows no hour."

"Everybody, this is Bradley. Bradley, this is everybody."

Sometimes a person's name fits them perfectly. This was one of those times.

"So, what are you drinking, Brad?" asked Doug, motioning to our waitress.

"Scotch on the rocks for me, please and thank you. Oh, and by the way, I prefer Bradley over Brad."

I think everyone at the table fought the urge to burst out laughing. Doug just gave him a vacant stare, and before he could say something sarcastic, Jane stepped in and initiated conversation.

"So, Bradley, Joanna tells us you're a trader of the stocks. That sounds very interesting."

I nearly spit my beer out. A trader of the stocks? Jane gave me a slight, embarrassed shrug as Bradley answered her ridiculously worded question.

"There's quite a bit more to it than that," he said. "There's constant research on market trends and…"

I'll be honest, after the words "market trends," all I heard was Charlie Brown's teacher saying "Wah, wah, woh, wah, wah."

"Bradley went to Yale," boasted Joanna.

Well, it was less boasting and more to just save us from him boring us to tears. For the next fifteen minutes or so, Jane carried the conversation with tales of her many travels. Usually, I would feel a little uneasy listening to her talk about this. Not because I wasn't happy that she had all these amazing experiences, but because I knew if it wasn't for those experiences, she would have stuck around here, and we would probably still be together. Still, that being said, I loved seeing that twinkle in her eye as she talked about her travels.

To my surprise, she ended her story with, "Yea, I definitely had a lot of fun traveling over the years, but I'm very much looking forward to settling down back here at home."

As you guys can see, at age 33, I had made great strides in many things; I'd cut way back on my Depression Session mixes, my bounce-back-time from a broken heart was practically overnight (practically), and I had seriously cut back on the over-analyzing thing. That being said, did you guys hear the words that came out of Jane's mouth?? She was "*very much looking forward to settling down back here at home!*"

Was that her way of saying she was here for good? And when she said "home," was she referring to Maine in general or to my house? It was at that very moment, I relapsed and began over-analyzing like an insane person. My thought process was interrupted when Taylor came over to our table with a tray full of shots (paid by Doug). After we did our shots,

I introduced Joanna and Bradley to Taylor.

"Taylor is one of the best bartenders around," I said. "And rumor has it, now she's one of the best school teachers around as well."

"What grade to you teach?" asked Joanna.

"High school," replied Taylor.

"Is it me," asked Doug, "or do high school chicks nowadays look like they're in college?"

Taylor (and the rest of us), stared blankly at Doug.

"It's a good thing I'm not a teacher," continued Doug. "It'd be hard not succumbing to my students flirting with me."

"Oh God!" exclaimed Taylor. "Get over yourself already. That is one of MANY reasons why you're not a teacher."

"Hey! I could be a teacher. I'd be a great teacher actually," he said.

"And what subject would you teach?" asked Michelle. "How to shotgun a beer?"

"Ha ha," Doug fake-laughed. "I would teach lessons of life. Life lessons, if you will. Shit they can really use one day. For instance, one of my classes would be called Flirting 101. I would touch upon some of the more postmodern pickup lines, and even delve into some pre-Renaissance lines as well."

"You're such an idiot," laughed Taylor.

"I'm amazed there are actually girls who fall for your stupid lines," said Michelle.

"It's more about the delivery than the actual line," said Doug. "Of course, you'd know that if you took my class."

All of us laughed at Doug being Doug. All of us except Bradley. He had no idea what to make of Doug's comments. If he thought that was bad, he probably should have left then because it only got worse.

After Taylor went back behind the bar, Bradley's phone vibrated and he looked down at it then politely said, "I know this is rude of me, but do you guys mind if I return this text?"

We all shook our heads no, and Bradley graciously smiled and then began texting.

It was at that point, Doug slouched down low in his chair and quietly exclaimed, "Oh, shit!"

When we looked curiously at him, he motioned to the front door. Two women entered and sat in the corner.

Still slouched, Doug said, "Shit, I slept with that redhead like a year ago."

"Let me guess," said Michelle, "you promised you'd call her the next day but never did?"

"Nope. Much worse. We both got wicked shit-faced and ended up banging back at my place. After we finished and fell asleep, I kinda, sorta… pissed the bed."

"Ewwwww. Doug!" cringed Michelle.

Pete and I, who had heard this story before, laughed. I had known Doug for many years but was still shocked, and somewhat impressed, how easily he could tell self-effacing stories like this. Let it be noted, if I ever piss the bed (with or without a girl in it), I would certainly never ever tell a soul—including Pete or Doug.

Bradley was still texting on his phone but was also half-listening to Doug's story.

"Do you guys ever have that dream where you have to go to pee really bad? Then you wake up and realize that you really do have to pee, so you get up and go to the bathroom and pee?"

Everyone hesitantly nodded.

"That's the dream I had that night. But in the dream, I just let it flow, and when I woke up, I realized I let it flow for real. All over myself and all over the sheets."

"And all over her?" asked Jane.

"Actually, no. But at one point, she must have rolled over in it."

"I hope she punched you in the face," said Michelle.

"Umm, well, actually, I woke up first, and when I realized what I had done, I quickly changed into dry clothes, so when she finally woke up…"

"She assumed she had pissed the bed?" Joanna said, shocked.

Doug slyly smiled and nodded.

"Total dick move!" said Jane.

"What? I was nice about it. I told her it could have happened to anyone."

"So this whole time, she thinks she was the one who pissed the bed? You really are a pig," said Michelle. "I have a good mind to go over and tell her the truth."

"Oh, no, no, no!" Doug said, straightening up in his chair. "You can't! I told you that as a good friend, and you can't break the *good friend code*!"

"Pfffft, this is about the *girl code*," said Michelle.

"No!" snapped Doug. "The good friend code comes before the girl code. Besides, you girls don't even have a code! You're all too catty and shit."

Knowing he was mostly right, the girls smirked and shrugged in agreement.

"FYI, you're never sleeping over our house again," announced Michelle.

"Not without plastic sheets," I pointed out.

After our laughter subsided, Bradley finished his final text and rejoined our conversation.

He took a sip of his scotch on the rocks, looked over at Doug then said, "Umm, Douglas, did I hear correctly? Did you say you urinated on a girl in bed?"

"No, Bradley. If you were listening more carefully you would have heard that I pissed *next* to her, not *on* her."

Bradley looked at all of us and then back to Doug. "Umm, what's the difference?"

"You're the Yale man, you tell me. And by the way, I prefer Doug, not Douglas."

Needless to say, that was the first and last date Bradley and Joanna had. Also needless to say, I think Joanna was secretly appreciative and relieved of that!

Overall, our night on the town was a huge success, filled with a lot of drinks and a lot more laughs. I was glad to see Pete and Michelle relaxed and getting along like old times. I think they, more than any of us, needed that night out. Unfortunately, it wasn't enough to prevent future tensions from arriving in their marriage. But for that night—all was right with the world.

All was definitely right with Jane and I. Whether it was the reminiscing or all of the alcohol, we ended up sleeping together that night. And by "sleeping together," I don't mean sex or even making out. We merely cuddled and slept in the same bed. It wasn't awkward, or weird, or anything of the sort, it was actually pretty God damn nice. The conversations we had in bed that night were also pretty damn nice, even though they didn't initially start off that way.

"So, what was the deal with that chick we ran into tonight?" Jane asked. "You know, the one out on the sidewalk?"

"Ahhh, Dalelyn," I said.

Oh, did I mention we ran into Dalelyn that night? She was with her D-bag boyfriend. It was on the sidewalk on our way into the Brewery. The exchange was quick and polite—and uncomfortable—with very little eye contact on my part—especially at her D-bag boyfriend.

I ended up telling Jane the whole pathetic story, which in turn, caused Jane to share some pathetic guy stories of her own.

"I'll be honest with ya, Josh, I'm starting to think my Mr. Right might not be out there."

"Ha. I'm thinking the same about my Mrs. Right," I laughed.

"I'm thinking I should probably start learning how to knit," she said.

"Knit?"

"Yea. It'll come in handy when I'm an old maid."

"An old maid, huh?" I laughed. "Are you also gonna be one of those crazy cat ladies? You know, the type who knits hats and mittens for them?"

"Sadly, no. I'm allergic to cats. No mittens for kittens for me," she smirked and sighed.

"I tell ya what," I joked, "if we're both still single at age fifty, we should just do it—get married!"

She pondered a second then smiled and stuck out her hand. "Deal!" she said, shaking my hand. "And just think, if I start practicing now, I'll be able to knit you a wicked cool sweater. Or maybe even an afghan or something."

"Perfect! It'll keep me warm while I'm sitting there watching golf."

"Golf?"

"Yea. Old guys love to watch that shit."

My comment caused us both to crack up laughing. The

entire conversation was us simply being silly and facetious, but I must say, it kind of got me thinking a little bit.

So even though we didn't have sex that night, it was the start of a brand-new chapter for us. It was the catalyst for us to slowly head down the road that would lead us to where we once were—to feelings we both once had. I always, always knew we'd find that road again. This time, I took it slow and enjoyed every step we took together.

Over the next week, more times than not, we found ourselves sleeping together. For the record, there was still no sex. I know exactly what you guys are thinking. You're thinking, the more we just sleep and cuddle without sex, the more this means we're only destined for the friendship zone. On most cases I would agree, but I had the distinct feeling this was different. The closeness and intimacy with us went beyond the friendship zone. I was sure of it.

I was so sure, in fact, that I decided to take the next step. I planned a very romantic mid-August getaway up to the White Mountains of New Hampshire. And in case you're wondering, no, I didn't mention ANY of this to Doug or Pete. I didn't mention the White Mountains or the fact that Jane and I might once again be walking down the relationship road. And I certainly didn't mention the cuddling without sex thing. I didn't need any wise-ass remarks or negative energy bringing me down. I had a romantical weekend to plan!

9

“JUST LIKE HEAVEN” – Katie Melua (The Cure Cover)

The last time Jane and I traveled up to the White Mountains was about ten years ago. Ironically, we weren’t boyfriend and girlfriend that time either. We were just “enjoying each other’s company.” Take that as you will.

The trip ten years ago kind of sucked. It poured the entire weekend, and considering all of our planned activities were outside, we were left hanging out in our hotel the whole time. And by hotel, I mean motel. A very, very run-down motel. I was in my early twenties at the time and apparently on a tight budget. But to be fair to me, the internet was still brand new, and it was way before all of these hotel sites were created. So basically, I booked the place via the phone and sight unseen. The place sounded good—The Mountain View Inn. In reality, it should have been called The Non-Mountain View Inn, or better yet, The Parking Lot View Inn.

I was determined to make this trip a thousand percent better. Being 2003, not only was I able to plan the whole itinerary online, but I was able to get an advance weather report and pick the perfect couple of days. Not to mention, my money situation had improved greatly since the last time, so I planned on moving up from motel status to something a bit nicer.

We got an early start, and it was mid-morning when we arrived up in the Franconia Notch area of the White Mountains. After we grabbed breakfast, we took a hike through the Flume Gorge. The Gorge is an amazingly scenic mile loop featuring waterfalls and covered bridges and is surrounded by towering granite walls. Ironically, it was our first time there.

From there, we set out to see the iconic Old Man of the Mountain. In case you're not from New England, The Old Man of the Mountain was a natural rock formation high up on the cliffs of Cannon Mountain. Nearly 40 feet in length, its jagged rocks naturally formed a profile of an old man.

Technically, we weren't there to see the Old Man, but to pay our respects. A few months earlier, due to years of deterioration, the iconic Old Man came a crumbling down. Surprisingly, it didn't really stop people from flocking there and taking pictures of where he once was.

Before we headed east through the mountains, we stopped at another iconic attraction—Clark's Trading Post. Clark's was famous for their trained black bears and their steam-powered train ride through the woods. While we didn't take the train ride, we did catch the bear show.

As soon as we hit the road again, Jane turned to me and said, "This is way better than the last time we came up here."

"Ya think?" I laughed.

"I'm really glad you planned this," she smiled. "I'm having so much fun."

"You better pace yourself. Our weekend is just getting started."

"Is that so?" she said. "So, what's next on our agenda?"

"I'm thinking we should go pick up some food and drinks and make our way along the Kancamangus and maybe stop for a picnic along the way."

"Perfect," she smiled.

The Kancamangus Highway is a fifty-mile-long scenic byway that cuts directly through the White Mountains. Waterfalls, hiking trails, swimming holes, and breathtaking views for miles; the Kancamangus had it all.

It was nearly 2 PM when we arrived in the popular tourist town of North Conway. Our laughter and great conversations hadn't let up since we left York at 7:07 AM that morning. Jane and I had done a lot of cool things over the years, but for whatever reason, that particular day was fast-becoming my most favorite day ever with her. It wasn't that we were doing anything extraordinary, and by all rights, we weren't even a couple—not yet anyway.

There was most definitely a feeling of possibility in the air. An air of possibility, if you will. There was also the feeling of hope—hope of a brand-new start. Either way, there was just something special about how that day was going, and by the end of that weekend, I would be left with a clear vision of my future.

While we were in North Conway, we sat out on a patio and grabbed a mid-afternoon drink.

"Where to next, Mr. Master-planner?" she asked.

"Umm, I'm thinking we go check into the hotel and just relax for the night."

"Sounds good. Not to be picky, but please tell me you didn't book the same place we stayed at last time?"

"What are you saying, you didn't dig their cozy lobby and their sweet vending machines?"

"Don't forget the perma-rust stain in the toilet, or that funky smell coming from the air-conditioner."

"Ha! Yea, I almost forgot about that," I laughed. "Well, I assure you, you'll be more than pleased with tonight's lodging."

"I'm sure I will," she sweetly smiled.

From North Conway, we traveled north into the Crawford Notch area of the mountains. Don't forget, Jane's true passion was photography, so she came well-prepared. She kept her very expensive camera by her side at all times. I don't think ten minutes went by without her asking me to pull over so she could take a picture. There were times when her picture-taking and her excitement reminded me of the day Anna and I drove up the coast on our lighthouse sightseeing trip. The difference being; Anna had never been to Maine before, so she was taking it all in for the first time. Jane on the other hand, grew up here in New England. She must have visited the White Mountains dozens of times, yet her smile grew bigger with each snap of the camera.

"You would think the last thing you'd want to do in your downtime is take pictures," I said.

"Why, because it's my job?"

"Well, yea. If I built houses for a living, the last thing I'd want to do on vacation would be to build a house."

"Unless it was your own house you were building," she answered. "Photography was my passion long before it was my job. Especially landscape photography. Trust me, I'm in heaven right now," she said, clutching her camera lovingly.

I would like to think "in heaven" was referring to more than just her photography that day, and by the way she was looking at me, I think I was right.

"Speaking of photography," she said, "when we drive past the Mount Washington Hotel, can you pull over so I can get some shots? I love that place. One day I'm totally gonna stay there."

The Mount Washington Hotel was the crown jewel of New Hampshire, maybe even all of New England. It's one of the last-standing grand resort hotels from the early 1900's. It was the quintessential summer resort back in the day. Ever since I was a little kid, I remember saying that one day I'd make enough money to stay there.

Also, ever since I saw *The Shining*, I always associated the Mount Washington Hotel with the hotel from the movie. Yes, I know it was neither filmed or based here, but for whatever reason, I'll forever associate the two.

True to my word, as soon as I spotted the large white hotel off in the distance, I pulled over to let Jane do her magic. Knowing she might be there awhile, I shut off my car and joined her as she attached her telephoto lens. The mid-afternoon sun shone brightly off the hotel's classic red roof. As she carefully took one photo after another, I mentioned how I associated this place with *The Shining.*

"Oh my God, totally!" she agreed. "Here's a little fun fact for you: the hotel that inspired Stephen King to write *The Shining* was actually in Colorado. The Stanley Hotel, to be precise. And while I never stayed there, I did drive by it and take plenty of cool pics."

When Jane finished taking her pictures and reciting her fun facts, we got back into my car.

"Happy?" I asked.

"Very," she answered. "Thanks for stopping for me."

I started the car, and as I pulled back onto the road, I immediately turned right, down the long entrance-way to the Mount Washington.

"You don't have to go up closer to the hotel," she said. "I got enough pictures, thanks."

I smiled and said, "But I thought we were gonna check into our hotel and relax?"

I didn't need to look over at her to know she was wide-eyed and smiling.

"Are you shitting me? We're staying here?"

"Looks like *one day* has finally arrived for both of us," I smiled.

"Aww, Josh, this is so sweet of you, but there's no way I'm letting you pay for this on your own."

"Seriously, Jane, it's my pleasure."

As we walked up the steps of the grand (& expensive) hotel, Jane grabbed my arm and said, "This is going to be amazing!"

And amazing it was. The lobby alone took our breath away. After we checked into our room, we spent the next couple hours exploring the entire hotel inside and out. From the beautiful gardens to scenic walking paths, Jane was in heaven. We both were. Dare I say, it was perfect. The only thing that would have made it better, was if they had that giant hedge-maze from *The Shining.*

Despite that, we both kept pretending we were staying in the infamous Overlook from the movie. I swear, if we had Big Wheels, we would have been riding them up and down the long hallways. I think some of the guests thought we were crazy as we just stood there staring at the elevator, waiting for blood to come rushing out at us. We even searched out room 237, which was the haunted room from the movie. We were like two dorks, taking pictures of ourselves in front of the door, just daring each other to touch the door handle. Jane took countless pictures of me clutching the handle while giving her my most scared expression. Like I said, two dorks. We were so into our little photoshoot that we didn't notice one of the staff members approaching us.

"Ahh, room 237 from *The Shining*, huh?" he said.

Jane literally let out a shriek. Okay, maybe it was me, but either way, the dude scared the bejesus out of us.

"Sorry," he laughed, "I didn't mean to startle you."

"It's okay," Jane said. "We were just being silly. This place always reminded us of the movie, so we've just kinda been pretending."

"Oh, it's quite alright," he smiled. "We get this all the time. A lot of folks think the movie was either filmed here or based on this place."

"So what you're saying is we're not the only idiots?" I said.

"Nah. It's not like you're riding down the hallways in Big Wheels," he laughed. "Or staring at the elevator, waiting for blood to come rushing out."

"Well that would just be plain crazy," Jane said, smirking at me.

The staff member started to continue on his way, but then stopped and asked us, "You guys do know we also have a haunted room here at the hotel?"

"Really?" we both said.

He grinned at our child-like excitement, and then he

proceeded to speak into his walkie-talkie.

"Hey, is anyone staying in room 314 right now?" he asked.

When the reply came back no, he smiled and motioned us to follow him. On the way there, he filled us in on the backstory of the hotel and of room 314. Once we arrived at the room, we again took turns posing in front of the door. When we were done acting like fools, he carefully unlocked the door and let us in.

"Feel free to take pictures if you want," he said to Jane. "Who knows, maybe you'll catch an orb or something."

While we were in the suite, he told us story after story of the sightings and the crazy things that have occurred to guests who stayed in that room. Jane must have taken a hundred pictures, and although no apparitions or orbs showed up in any, it was an experience we'd never forget.

After our super-cool and eerie room 314 experience, we hit the pool and hot tub. It was "the type of day you didn't want to end." Those were Jane's exact words, and I most-definitely agreed. We went back to our room, showered, put on some nice clothes, and headed downstairs for a fancy (& expensive) dinner.

Afterwards, we moved into the bar for a few drinks. It was the perfect way to cap off a perfect day. Well, the real perfect cap to the day would actually come back at our room after drinks. Yup, that's right, we had sex! Lots and lots of sex—hotel sex! Expensive hotel sex!

Even though we had a full day of events planned for Sunday, which included a train ride to the top of Mount Washington, it was the event of Saturday night that changed the course of our relationship. It went well-beyond us just having sex (lots of sex). I even think it went beyond us just *getting back together.*

We've had sex before, but this was different. And we've gotten back together before, but this was also different. As a matter of fact, from the moment Jane arrived back in town that summer, things were different, but different in the best way possible!

By the time we arrived back in York late Sunday night, I knew that particular weekend would be the turning point in our relationship.

10

"DANDELION" – Antje Duvekot

So, what is the first thing one would do after returning from an amazing weekend like that? Have more great sex of course! The next thing one would do is go tell his best friends about his amazing weekend—and the great sex.

My opportunity came the following night on my shift at Hoohahs. Throughout the first part of the night, I played it pretty close to the vest with Doug. I told him I'd fill him in more once Pete arrived for his nightly beer.

It was just after 9 o'clock when Pete showed up. Before his ass hit the stool, I had his beer waiting for him.

"Hey, bro, how's it going?" I said enthusiastically.

Apparently, it was a bit too enthusiastic for him.

"How's it going? It sucks ass, that's how it's going," he answered. "Why I ever chose this profession, I'll never know.

And to think, I actually enjoyed it once upon a time."

"You really need to just fuckin' quit," added Doug.

"Not gonna happen," Pete replied.

"Have you told Michelle how you're feeling yet?"

"As a matter of fact, I have."

"And?"

"She said I need to suck it up until she gets her career going."

"She said that?" I said, questioning his accuracy.

"More or less," he shrugged. "I know she put her career on hold for me and the girls, and I swear I'm not trying to rain on her parade, but I'm just so fuckin' done with my job."

"I'm sure if you really express that to Michelle, you guys can work something out."

"Trust me, Josh, between her classes and the girls, she has no patience dealing with my bitchin' and moanin'. Besides, she's always on edge."

I looked over at Doug and then back to Pete and said, "To be fair, it seems like you're always on edge too."

"No shit," Pete snapped. "Why do you think I work late and then hang out here for drinks? I just want to avoid all the bullshit at home."

I was tempted to remind Pete that this *bullshit at home* he referred to was called marriage, and that he couldn't just avoid it by ignoring it. I decided to keep my thoughts to myself, however. I didn't want to start a big fight between us. I also decided to keep my weekend story to myself. It was obvious that now was not a good time to gush about my happiness.

"I'm sorry," said Pete. "I don't mean to lay all of this on you guys. Besides, I come here to forget my problems, not to bitch about them. Hey, by the way, how was your weekend with Jane?"

Wellllll, seeing as he asked, I suppose it was as good a time as any to gush. And gush I did. I filled them in on every amazing detail of my weekend. Yes, every detail; from our driving, to our hiking, to our ghost-hunting, and yes, to our sex!

Pete focused on the hotel.

"I've always wanted to stay there. Was it as cool as it looks?" he asked.

"Way cooler than it looks," I replied.

Doug focused more on the sex.

"How long has it been since the last time you banged her?"

Pete's attention swayed to Doug's side of the road. "Yea, how long has it been?"

I did a quick calculation in my head then answered, "Nearly six years."

"Holy shit. That's a while ago," said Pete. "Was it the same as you remembered it?"

"It's just like riding a bike," interrupted Doug.

At that point, I probably should have kept my mouth shut, but I decided to go with Doug's analogy.

"It kinda was like riding a bike again, except she definitely learned some new bike tricks," I laughed.

"Really? Do tell," smiled Doug.

I went on to describe some new positions she had us doing. I also mentioned the deadly-sexy new thing she did with her tongue on my… anyway, you get the picture.

When I was finished, Pete gave me a high-five and said, "Good for you, Josh. At least one of us is getting hot sex—or any sex."

"Pfft, speak for yourself," said Doug. "I too had some hot

sex this weekend."

"Of course you did," said Pete. He then looked over at Doug and I and said, "Just make sure you stay single, my friends. Stay single."

"Duh!" exclaimed Doug as he headed over to wait on a someone at the end of bar. When he came back, he turned to me and said, "Did you ever wonder about how Jane learned all her new positions and tongue tricks?"

"What?"

"I'm just saying, there was probably a lot of guys over the last six years that she practiced on. Did you ever think of that?"

"Well not until now!" I said, cringing. "Thanks a-fuckin'-lot, Doug."

"Oh relax, dude. Besides, it's not like there hasn't been plenty of girls that you've honed your sex-skills on over the past six years, right?"

I knew Doug was right, but it still didn't stop my cringing, and it certainly didn't stop me thinking about these unknown dudes who aided Jane in the mastery of sex and the subsequent tongue tricks. Leave it to Doug to put those disturbing thoughts in my head.

"We're just bustin' your balls, bro," Doug laughed.

"Yea, we're glad you guys had a fun weekend," said Pete.

Doug pulled out a paper from under the register, stared at it, then said, "But what we're *not* happy about, is neither of us won the pool."

"The pool?" I hesitantly asked.

"Yea, the *When will Josh and Jane have sex, pool*," Doug matter-of-factly said.

"Are you shitting me?" I said looking at both of my idiot friends.

"I had two weeks ago," Doug said.

"And I had two weeks from now," smiled Pete. "You guys couldn't have held out for me, could ya?" he joked.

"How many people were in this stupid pool?" I asked.

Doug shrugged and said, "Just seven or so."

I was both irritated and annoyed at them for yet again placing wagers on me. Irritated and annoyed, but I was also a little curious.

"Who won?" I quietly asked.

Doug scanned the paper, smiled and said, "Mulder."

"Oh God. Mulder was in this pool?"

The dude's real name was Christopher, but we refer to him as Mulder. You know, like the guy on the X-Files. I'm assuming he had some form of schizophrenia, and no, I'm not making fun or making light of this, but he would come in a few times a month claiming the government was after him because of what he knew.

What exactly did he know? Well, apparently he knew about the aliens, and apparently the government knew he knew about the aliens. Hence, that was why they were after him. For the longest time, he thought Doug was an undercover government agent sent to spy on him. We finally convinced him that it was more likely that Doug was an alien rather than a government spy.

So, yea, the guy who brings a metal detector into our bar looking for hidden listening devices is the same guy who won the stupid sex-pool bet. Normally, I would have reached over and ripped up their silly sex-pool paper, but I was still on a high from my weekend with Jane, so I simply shook my head and laughed along.

"Does this mean you guys are an item again?" asked Pete.

"I think it means we're much more than that," I said, a bit cryptically.

I watched Pete look over at Doug, and I knew at any moment I would be blasted with their negativity. Strangely, they never blasted. As a matter of fact, they did the opposite, and they were, dare I say, supportive.

"Good for you, Josh," said Pete. "I hope everything works out."

Doug nodded in agreement and added, "Yea, congrats. And hopefully the sex continues too. You're way more fun to work with when you get some."

I wasn't sure if they were truly being supportive, or if they were just saying what I wanted to hear to avoid an argument. Either way, I was fine with it, because like I said, I was still riding my high. Pete finished his beer then reluctantly headed home. On his way out, he offered a fist bump followed by some advice.

"Just do us a favor and take it slow, bro… take it slow."

I returned his fist bump, smiled and said, "You know it."

Although Pete's comment was simple and innocent enough, it became stuck in my head the rest of the night. On my drive home, his words echoed in my head - *Take it slow, bro… take it slow.*

No! I'm not going to take it slow! I've been taking it slow with Jane since the first summer we met. I spent that whole summer crushing on her but never revealing it to her. And even on the final night that summer, when we hooked up and had sex, I still hesitated about revealing my feelings to her. My hesitation and taking things slow led to a whole year passing by before telling her how I felt. By then, she had a boyfriend, and I was left thinking what if… what if I hadn't hesitated or taken things slow?

As I pulled into my driveway that night, I knew exactly what I had to do. I needed to do the opposite of taking it slow. I loved that Jane and I had found our way back down the relationship road together, but I wanted more than that. I wanted more than just the familiar relationship road. Actually, the road I was thinking about wasn't really a road at all, but more like… an aisle.

11

"HEY JUPITER" – Tori Amos

As you guys probably guessed, by aisle, I meant wedding aisle. I had never been so sure of anything in my life. So, that next morning, I decided to immediately get the ball rolling and go buy a ring. I was so happy and determined, but I was also smart enough NOT to say anything to Doug or Pete. At least not until after the big proposal. I knew if I told them before, there was no way they could contain their negativity. I also had this disturbing image of Doug snatching the ring from me and playing keep away with Pete.

Smartly, I told no one about my big plan. Well, no one except Joanna. I headed over to Breaking New Grounds that morning and filled her in on everything. I filled her in on our amazing weekend, our amazing sex, and yes, about my impending proposal. I could tell by her expression that she thought I was a little crazy, but to her credit, she was supportive of whatever I had planned. She was also flattered that I asked her to go with me to pick out the ring.

I came back that afternoon and picked her up when her shift was done. From there, we drove straight over to a jewelry store. Joanna's eyes widened as the woman behind the counter showed us one diamond ring after another. My eyes also widened but for different reasons. I was looking at one huge price tag after another. Luckily for me, Jane wasn't really a diamond girl. She really wasn't into much bling at all.

It took us three hours and four stores, but we finally found the perfect ring. I had been pretty good at putting away money for savings over the years, so I was able to pay cash for the ring.

"Thanks again for coming with me today, Joanna. I appreciate it," I said.

"Of course. Thanks for inviting me. So, have you got the proposal all planned out yet? You know, the when, where, and how?"

"I'm thinking maybe this weekend. Not really sure about the where and how yet."

"I'm sure you'll come up with something good," she said. "Are you nervous?"

"No, not really. More anxious than anything."

"And you're not gonna tell Doug or Pete until after?"

I thought for a second then smiled, "Yea, I think that's best."

She returned my smile and said, "You're probably right. Doug's liable to snatch the ring from you."

"I know, right?" I laughed.

After I dropped Joanna off at her car, I headed over to

Hoohahs for my shift. FYI: I'm horrible with secrets. It was all I could do to not reveal my proposal plans to Doug or Pete. Thankfully, the topic of me and Jane never came up, so that made it a little easier on me.

Pete mostly talked about how he was dreading an upcoming business trip. It was a three-day trip to Charlotte. Personally, Doug and I thought it sounded fun, but Pete was quick to point out that he'd be attending with a couple of big wigs from the company. A couple of big wigs who were strictly there for business, NOT fun.

After Pete finished telling us about his upcoming trip, there was a slight lull in the conversation. At that point, I was more than tempted to blurt out my news, but luckily, I was saved by Doug's topic of discussion. Although, I'm not sure I should use the word *luckily*, considering what his "topic" was. It all started when Pete yawned.

"Uh oh," Doug said, watching Pete yawn. "You know what they say about yawning, right?"

"Umm, that it's contagious?" I said.

"No," laughed Doug. "A yawn isn't a disease. How can it be contagious?"

Pete and I looked at each other and just shook our heads. Neither one of us had the energy to explain to Doug what the saying meant. I figured it was best to just play along.

"You're right. A yawn can't be contagious. So tell us, Doug, what do they say about yawning?"

Doug smiled then proudly boasted, "Every time you yawn, a ghost sticks its dick in your mouth."

Pete and I literally spit our beer out.

"What?" Pete said, blankly staring at Doug.

"It's like a famous saying and shit," Doug answered.

"No it's not," I laughed.

"Yea, I'm pretty sure it is," Doug said confidently.

"I'm pretty positive it is not!" laughed Pete. "I think you're confused with that other popular saying. You know, the one that says every time a bell rings, an angel gets its wings."

Doug looked at Pete like he had three heads.

"I've never heard that saying before," laughed Doug. "Like, who the hell believes in angels anyway?" he said, continuing to laugh.

"Let me get this straight," I said. "you don't believe in angels, but you believe in Casper the cock-sucking ghost?"

Pete cracked up, but Doug held to his guns.

"No. If you were listening to me, I didn't say the *ghost* would be sucking your dick, I said that you'd be sucking *his*!"

Fun Fact: After his comment, Doug motioned as if to drop the mic. Although it would take years to catch on, to the best of my knowledge, that was the first time in history that anyone would do the *drop the mic* move.

Disturbing Fun Fact: From that point on, every time I yawned, I found myself having a gag-reflex. Fuckin' Doug! Needless to say, Doug's yawning comment completely curbed my urge to inform them about Jane and me.

On my ride home that night, I started thinking about the question Joanna had asked me earlier. The one about if I was nervous about the proposal. I told her I wasn't, but truthfully, I was a little nervous. Did I read too much into our romantic weekend? Did I read too much into us having sex? Did I read too much into just how amazing our summer was going? Was I rushing into this whole proposal thing?

Before my head hit the pillow that night, I would have the reassurance I needed that this was meant to be. When I got home, she was all cuddled up on the couch watching a movie.

"Hey hun, how was work?" she asked.

"Good, thanks," I answered, catching a peek at what she was watching. "Ahh, a little *When Harry Met Sally* action, huh?"

"Yup! One of my faves," she smiled. "You gonna join me?"

And join her I did. With candles lit and a blanket over us, we watched the movie and spooned. Yup, my questions were answered!

How did I get reassurance from this you might ask?

1. When I walked in, she called me hun. Even when we dated, she never called me hun. Definitely a sign that we were evolving into something deeper.

2. She was watching *When Harry Met Sally*. A movie, I might add, about a man and woman who start out as just friends, but as their lives intersect over a ten-year period, they realize that they are destined to be more than friends. Harry and Sally are us!

3. Halfway through the movie, Jane turned to me and sweetly said, "Thanks again for this weekend. It was one of the best times I've ever had." She then gave me a kiss (like a kiss, kiss). And that was followed by her saying… wait for it… "I'm so glad I came here this summer."

4. The fourth and final thing that reassured me I was not rushing into things, was the end of the movie when Harry said to Sally, "*When you realize you want to spend the rest of your life with somebody, you want the rest of your life to start as soon as possible.*" As soon as he said that, Jane turned to me and said, "Favorite movie line ever!"

And that my friends, is how I knew I was absolutely doing the right thing by proposing to Jane. As a matter of fact, I was so amped that I was tempted to just propose right then and there, but I didn't. I fought the urge and decided to do it the following weekend.

12

"PLEASE, PLEASE, PLEASE LET ME GET WHAT I WANT" – The Smiths

I spent the rest of that week dreaming and scheming of the perfect proposal. Should I book another night up at the Mount Washington Hotel and propose to her in the grand dining room in front of everyone? Or should I do it one night at Hoohahs in front of family and friends? Or maybe, I should wait until she's asleep and stand outside our bedroom window with a boom box in one hand and the ring in the other. Or maybe I should just keep it simple and propose to her up at the Nubble Lighthouse. And maybe, I could take another chunk of my savings out and have a fireworks display going off in the distance.

I had a few more ideas, but they ranged from stupid to really fucking stupid. I mean seriously, did I really think I'd be able to get Billy Crystal and Meg Ryan to be present at the proposal?

Anyway, I finally settled on simple. I would do it Saturday night up at the Nubble. I also decided against the fireworks display. It would have taken weeks and a ton of paperwork to get a permit, and I would also have to hire a barge out in the ocean to set them off from (more paperwork). I decided it just wasn't worth my time and effort. Oh, also, it would have cost me around twenty thousand dollars for the whole thing.

So, seeing as Jane was a low maintenance kinda gal, I decided the simpler the better. My proposal would, however, involve a few creative gifts, including a beautiful flower bouquet from Mr. and Mrs. Miller's shop. To my surprise, they didn't charge me a penny for the bouquet! Mrs. Miller said if I invited them to the wedding, they'd call it even. Mr. Miller mumbled something about me getting them for free because of all the frequent-flower miles I had earned.

I had to work Saturday night, so I asked Jane to meet me at Hoohahs. I told her we were going out after work. I didn't tell her where, just that it was a surprise. Even though I was 100% confident in my proposal, I knew it was going to completely catch Jane off guard. With that in mind, I mentally prepared myself for her to be shocked, hesitant even. It was all going to work out. My life was finally falling into place.

With the flowers and gifts in my trunk, and with the ring in my pocket, we drove from Hoohahs up to the Nubble. My nervous and sweaty hands kept slipping off the steering wheel. I don't believe I said a word on the drive over. I was focusing on the task at hand and rehearsing the perfect words in my head.

As we pulled up the Nubble road, she turned to me and said, "So this is your surprise, huh? It's been awhile since we've done it up here." She then giggled in a naughty and irresistibly sexy way.

Oh shit. Jane thought I brought her here for sex. It was like I was a squirrel caught in the middle of the road. Do I run to the left and have sex with her and then propose? Or do I run right and propose first and then have sex? Either way, I knew I needed to make a quick decision as to not get run over by the car. I decided to dart right.

It was well after midnight, but there were three other cars parked at the lighthouse. It wouldn't have mattered if there were thirty cars up there, I was laser-focused on the task at hand. Laser-focused, but still nervous. After I parked, I suggested we take a walk down on the rocks. It was low tide, so we were able to climb down pretty low. We found a giant flat rock and sat watching the red light of the Nubble.

"Everything alright? Jane asked. "You seem a little fidgety tonight."

"Um, yea, I'm fine. I just kinda have something I want to talk to you about."

"Oh, okay. What's on your mind?" she said, brushing her wind-swept hair out of her eyes.

"Actually, let me go grab a sweatshirt first. Do you need anything in the car?" I asked.

"Nope. I already came prepared," she said, tugging on her own sweatshirt.

"Yea, yea, you always were smarter than me," I joked as I headed back up the rocks.

Once I returned to the car, I popped the trunk. I placed the flowers on her seat, and then I grabbed her gift. Oh, and for good measure, I did actually grab my sweatshirt. I carefully made my way back down the rocks and approached Jane from behind. I reached over her shoulder and handed her my gift.

"What's this?" she curiously asked.

I sat down next to her and motioned for her to open it. As she slowly unwrapped it, I took a deep breath and began my proposal.

"Do you remember when you said you were gonna be an old maid, so you should probably learn how knit now?"

"Umm, yea," she said, giggling as she finished opening it up.

Inside was knitting needles, a ball of yarn, and a *Knitting for Dummies* book.

She continued to giggle as she said, "You are too funny, Josh. This is perfect."

As she started to flip through the book, I took another deep breath and continued.

"And do you remember when we said if we were both still single at fifty then we should just get married?"

Her giggling slowly subsiding when she realized this conversation was going down a more serious road.

"Umm, yea," she hesitantly answered.

"You know I've always cared about you, right?"

She nodded.

"Well, the truth is… in all these years, you've never really left my heart."

It was at that point, I made the mistake of looking up at her face. I say mistake, because for a brief moment, I got lost in her eyes and completely lost my train of thought. I was struggling to remember the perfect speech I had rehearsed all week.

All I could manage was, "I guess what I'm saying is… I don't wanna wait until we're fifty. There's nobody I'd rather walk through this world with."

I reached into my pocket and dug out the ring box. By now, Jane knew exactly where this was going, and as I opened the box in front of her, she covered her mouth in shock.

"Oh my God, Josh, it's beautiful," she said as I handed her the box. "Are you serious?"

"I couldn't be more serious, Jane. I guess it's kind of like, when you realize you wanna spend the rest of your life with someone —"

"You want the rest of your life to start as soon as possible," she finished the quote.

I nodded. She then flashed me her warmest smile and continued to admire the ring.

As a happy tear formed in her eye, she hesitantly said, "I… I don't know what to say. This completely caught me off guard."

"I know. I'm sorry. But I've just been thinking a lot about it this summer… especially this past weekend. Look, I know this is totally out of the blue, and you don't really need to give me an answer right now, but take this ring, and just know this is my ultimate goal with us."

Speechless and still shocked, she looked from me to the ring and then back to me.

"Oh, Josh," she sweetly said as she leaned over for a big kiss and a hug.

For the next five minutes or so, we just sat there in each other's arms, staring at the lighthouse and watching the waves gently lap against the rocks. When we finally made our way back to the car, her face lit up again when she spotted the bouquet of flowers on her seat.

"Awww, they're gorgeous. Thank you," she said, putting them on her lap as she sat down. She continued to admire them as I started the car. "You and your flowers," she smiled then leaned over and gave me a kiss on the cheek.

It didn't matter that we were both too emotionally drained for *after-proposal-sex,* I felt like I was on top of the world. And even though I forgot half of my rehearsed speech, it still turned out pretty damn perfect. I mean, a fireworks display would have been the ultimate topper, but whatever. I was happy. She was happy. That's all that mattered. The only thing left was to finally tell my friends and family the great news.

13

“COMEDOWN” - Bush

A couple of weeks after the big proposal, I was still on cloud nine. My sister invited us out to the Berkshires for a big family Labor Day weekend. Unfortunately, that was the weekend Pete was out of town on his business trip, so Jane was already committed to helping Michelle with the kids. Apparently, Michelle had a huge exam coming up, so Jane volunteered to watch the girls so she could study.

I was disappointed, but I knew how important this final exam was to Michelle, so reluctantly, I went without Jane. My whole family was going be out there, so I used it as my opportunity to update them on my big news regarding Jane and I.

Needless to say, my mother was beside herself with joy. Also needless to say, she had to ruin the moment by asking me if this meant I'd be giving her a grandchild before she died. She was joking—sorta. Overall, it was a nice weekend, but it would have been much better with Jane by my side.

Oh, wait, you're probably wondering what Doug and Pete's reaction was to my big proposal, aren't you? I ended up telling them the morning after the proposal. We all met up for breakfast at the Friendly Toast. Let's just say, they were a little taken aback. Here's a quick summary:

Pete: "Yea right. You're just fuckin' with us."

Doug: "You better be just fuckin' with us or else I'll punch you square in the nuts.

Pete: "Well, if he actually *is* getting married, he's not gonna need his nuts anyway."

Doug: "Did you really propose to Jane? Like with a diamond ring and shit?"

Me: (big smile)

Doug: "Fuckin' numb nuts!"

Pete: "Seriously Josh, this is the *opposite* of taking it slow."

Me: (continues to smile)

The good news is by the time we finished breakfast, they had calmed down a bit and were more supportive… well, semi-supportive. Also good news—Doug never did punch me in the nuts. As a matter of fact, by the time we finished breakfast, they were arguing over who should be the best man.

"Technically, I've known Josh longer than you," said Pete.

"So. Technically, I've been a better friend to him over the years," Doug retorted.

"How do you figure that?" laughed Pete.

Their little pissing contest went on for another ten minutes. I just sat and said nothing. Finally, Doug offered up a compromise of sorts.

"Ya know what, you can be the best man, Pete. I don't really want that kind of responsibility. I'd probably lose the ring anyway."

Both Pete and I laughed and nodded in agreement.

"BUT," Doug loudly declared, "I get to plan the bachelor party! If you plan it, we'd probably end up at Chuck E Cheese or some shit. Also, we *both* get to do a best man's speech."

"You better not turn it into a roast," I said.

"Don't fret, dude. I'm phenomenal at speeches."

So, even though a wedding would be a long ways off, and even though Jane technically didn't even say yes yet, at least I had the best man/bachelor party thing straightened out.

Okay, back to my Berkshires trip. I didn't end up leaving my sister's place until late afternoon on that Labor Day Monday. With all the holiday traffic, I didn't get back to York until around 7 PM. When I came home to an empty driveway, I assumed Jane was over at Pete and Michelle's watching the girls still. I was exhausted from my drive, but I was eager to see Jane again. I decided I was going to take a quick shower then head over to Pete's house. I figured we could maybe go out for a late dinner or something.

With my bags in tow, I entered my house. I dropped my bags by the door and made my way through the living room and towards the bathroom. As my foot hit the hallway, I stopped and hesitantly reversed my steps back into the living room. Something had caught my eye. On the sill of the corner window sat the small ring box.

Why the hell would Jane leave that there? I thought to myself. I made my way towards the window, and on closer inspection, there was also a folded note sitting next to it. My heart dropped like a heavy fuckin' stone. There were a thousand negative thoughts that filled my mind, but there was only one positive one. Maybe it was just a sweet note telling me not to worry about the ring being gone. You know, maybe she actually decided to put it on and wear it—to show it off.

I hesitantly opened the box, and there, glistening in the fading sunlight was the ring. It was official, all I was left with was my thousand negative thoughts. My body fell into the chair next to the window, and my eyes fixated on the note.

I knew it was going to be the worst note I had ever read. Even worse than the note I got from Kimberly Foley in 2nd grade. I left a note on her desk that read: Do you like me? Yes. No. Maybe. I then put three boxes next to them, hoping and praying she would check the Yes box. I would have even settled for the Maybe box.

Kimberly returned my note to me at recess, and as all of my friends gathered around me, I eagerly opened it up. Not only was the Yes and Maybe box *not* checked, but neither was the No box. She had created a new box with a big, fat checkmark which read: No way in hell!!! Yup, three exclamation points.

My heart sank, and my so-called friends all laughed and made fun of me. I was very much tempted to go tell the teacher that Kimberly used the H word, but I didn't. My heart was too broken. It was even too broken to join in the kickball game. I know, right?

Anyway, for the first thirty-three years of my life that was the worst note I'd ever received—until now. I knew once I opened Jane's note, it would put Kimberly's to shame. For sure, this would be a whole new level of heartbreak.

Finally, I couldn't take it anymore, and I reached over and grabbed the note.

Josh,

I know you'll probably never forgive me for leaving like this, and I'll probably never forgive myself for breaking your heart yet again. You need to know, it's NOT because I don't love you, because I do. I really, really do. But just not in that way – the way one needs to feel to get married. I would give anything in the world to feel that way for you, I swear I would. I'm so sorry, Josh, you don't deserve to get your heart broken like this. You deserve to have someone who loves you as much as you love them, and I know that one day you will find her, but I also know that person can't be me. You also don't deserve to come home to this impersonal note, but I just couldn't bring myself to tell you this face to face. I'm sorry. I promise this isn't goodbye forever, and I promise as soon as I'm settled and can muster up the courage to talk to you, I will call. I promise.

Love, Jane

I must have sat in that chair for hours, just staring at the ring on the sill and the note in my hand. Sadness, foolishness, and anger were just a few of the emotions which ran through my body. I wasn't angry at Jane, more so at myself for not only rushing into things, but for causing her to leave town—maybe this time for good.

I had just spent the entire three-day weekend boasting to my family about our big news. How the hell was I going to explain this one to them?

Dealing with my friends would be even more difficult. Joanna and I were supposed to meet for coffee the following morning, and I was scheduled at Hoohahs later that night. On the exterior, I'm sure they would be supportive and say the right things, but on the interior, I'm sure they'd be screaming out, "*We told you so, Josh. We told you so!*"

How the hell could this have happened? A week earlier, I was sitting on cloud nine, reveling in my lighthouse proposal. Two weeks earlier, I was riding high from our amazing weekend in the mountains, and I was on the verge of being the proud owner of a brand-new, shiny diamond ring.

But now, I had nothing. Well, nothing except a stupid, brand-new shiny diamond ring. I was about as far away from cloud nine as I could be. And that wave that I was riding so high on, it came crashing down on me, leaving me gasping for air.

I know this all sounds overly dramatic, but I swear, drowning is exactly how I felt. I truly thought I had hit the lowest point of my life. I also felt the most alone I'd ever been. These were truths, NOT exaggerations.

By the time I finally stood up from the chair, the sun had long since set, and my house was in complete darkness. I didn't bother turning a light on, and I didn't even have the urge to light candles and pop in a Depression Session mix. But what I did have the urge to do was to call Jane.

There was no way I was going down without a fight. Maybe she just ran away because she was scared about the marriage thing. If so, I would tell her I was just being stupid and I rushed into it too quickly. I would tell her to come back home, and we could take it as slow as she wanted.

So, as I picked up the phone and dialed, I was determined to say the perfect words to get things back to the way they were. Unfortunately, I wouldn't get the chance at the perfect words—she didn't answer my call. She didn't answer any of my calls. Every time her voicemail came on, I would just hang up. On my sixth and final call (that night), I left a message. I don't remember what I said exactly, but I do know it was far from the perfect, magical speech that I intended. It more like the perfect talk-out-my-ass type of babbling message.

14

"FAKE PLASTIC TREES" – Radiohead

As much as I wanted to skip my coffee date with Joanna, I didn't. I was never that great at hiding my emotions, and that morning wasn't any different. Within moments of me sitting down, Joanna knew something was up. Before I even took my first sip of coffee, I had divulged everything to her. I even recited word for word the contents of Jane's note. Yes, I had it memorized. I reread it seventeen fuckin' times.

Joanna was sweet and sympathetic, and despite feeding me the classic cliché lines (Everything will work out… It's always darkest before the dawn…etc), I really was appreciative of her support. I have to admit, by the time we left the coffeeshop, I felt the tiniest bit better. It was nice to let it all out and vent to her. I only hoped that Pete and Doug would be that supportive when I told them later that night. My fingers were crossed, but needless to say, I was absolutely dreading telling them.

As luck would have it, I didn't have to wait until my shift. Not long after Joanna and I had coffee, Pete messaged, asking if I wanted to meet up for a quick lunch. Although I wanted to come up with an excuse why I couldn't make it, I didn't. I figured I might as well get this over with.

When I got to the restaurant, Pete was already there.

"Hey, what's up," Pete said as I sat down.

"Not too much," I lied. "How was your trip?"

"Pretty boring and non-eventful. God, I wanna quit."

"Yea, I'm sorry," I said. "When did you get back?"

"Late last night," he replied, and then gave me a weird kind of look.

"What?" I asked.

"You sure you're okay?"

That was my opportunity to open the flood gates, but instead, I stood strong and lied.

"Yea, I'm fine. Why do you ask?"

Pete shot me a long look of disbelief and then said, "I know that Jane left."

Fuck! We weren't even in the world of social media yet, and my news was already spreading like wildfire. If Facebook was around then, I would have had to do the obligatory status change. I would have had to change it from *Engaged* to *Unengaged*. Or maybe *Single again*. Or more appropriately, *Still Stupid & Still Single*. Of course, that would be followed by my friends responding with sad or angry emojis or commenting shit like, *Oh no! So sorry, Josh*. Or *Keep your head up, bro*. Or *Trust me, it's her loss*. Thankfully, there wasn't any social media at that time, so I didn't have to deal with any of that shit.

"How did you hear?" I asked.

"Michelle told me when I got back last night. Apparently, Jane stopped in on her way out of town to explain everything to Michelle."

"I'm sorry," I said. "I know you guys were counting on her to watch the girls."

"Seriously? Josh, I couldn't give a shit about that right now. I'm really sorry, man. I was gonna come over or call you last night, but I figured you needed a little space."

"Thanks," I quietly said.

"I wish I knew the right words to say to cheer you up."

"And I wish I knew the right words to get her back," I sighed.

After we placed our order, I asked Pete if Doug knew yet.

"I don't think so. I tried calling him earlier to see if he wanted to join us, but all I got was his voicemail."

"He's gonna give me so much shit, isn't he?" I said.

"Nah."

I met Pete's response with a look of disbelief.

"Well, maybe a little bit of shit," he smiled.

"Exactly," I said.

Pete ended up getting a phone call and needed to get back to the office, so we cut our lunch short. I did get a chance to fill him in on the exact contents of Jane's note, and he again offered his sympathies. I was still devastated and in disbelief, but I was thankful of his support. I was even more thankful that he held off on spewing out the same tired, positive clichés, like the ones Joanna used.

After lunch, I made the mistake of going back home before my shift. For two fuckin' hours, I wandered around the house reminiscing. At times, it felt like I was a tour guide, filling in my imaginary tour group on everything that once was Josh &

Jane.

"Here's the table we used to eat dinner at. Here's the mug Jane preferred to use when she had tea. Now, if I can focus your attention on the kitchen wall… That grease stain is from when we had a food fight with mashed potatoes. On a side note, I won the food fight. If you guys make your way into the living room, you'll see the couch we used to spoon on. The couch we used to watch American Idol together. And yes, the couch that we had sex on exactly five days ago. If you all listen carefully, you probably can still hear the shrill sounds of orgasmic ecstasy. Also, on a side note, this is the very same couch that Jane used to suck my…"

Anyway, I think you guys get the picture. I ended my imaginary tour guide at the pièce de résistance—the window sill. The ring and note were both still there, as if to give my pretend tour group the full effect.

You guys are probably thinking I need some professional help. You wouldn't be wrong.

After I ended my imaginary tour, I showered and headed into Hoohahs. I wasn't in the mood to work, and I certainly wasn't looking forward to telling Doug about Jane. Whether it was right off the bat, or later in the night, I knew there would most definitely be an *I told you so* comment from Doug.

As it turned out, I wish *all* he had to say was I told you so, because what he ended up revealing to me had me on the verge of punching him dead in his face.

When I arrived at work, they told me Doug was in the back office. I figured I might as well get this over with before my shift, so I headed back.

"Hey man, how was your big three-day weekend with your fam?"

I said nothing, just shrugged. By the way, the silent shrug is guy code for *My weekend wasn't that great.*

Doug noted my silent shrug and said, "Uh oh, what happened?"

I followed his question with another shrug and then said, "Eh, I don't really wanna talk about it."

This was guy code for *If you ask me what happened a second time then I'll spill it.*

"Seriously, dude, what happened?" he repeated for a second time.

"Fine," I sighed, and then spilled everything to him.

"Holy shit. She just packed up and left you a note? She didn't even tell you to your face?"

"Nope."

"Personally, I thought you were rushing way too fast into this engagement thing, but, shit, man, I can't believe she didn't tell you in person. A note is kinda cold."

I nodded and said, "Obviously my proposal has her scared and overwhelmed. Way more than she let on. But… but she didn't have to pack up and bolt outta town. I know if we can just talk, I'll be able to fix things. I've tried calling her like thirty times since last night, but all I get is her stupid voicemail."

This caused Doug to laugh and say, "I knew that was a given. I warned her about that one."

It took a second for it to resonate, but when it did, I shot Doug a look and said, "What do you mean you warned her about that one? Did you know she was leaving me?"

"Not exactly," he said.

"What the fuck does that mean?"

"It means she came by the bar Friday night for a drink and we talked."

"You talked? You fuckin' convinced her to ditch me, didn't you, ya fuckin' backstabber!"

By now, I was right in Doug's face.

"First of all, get thc fuck out of my face and chill!"

I backed up slightly but continued to glare at him as I clenched my fists.

"I didn't stab you in the back, asshole! And I certainly didn't tell her to leave you high and dry the way she did. The only thing I said was —"

"All you said was what?" I said, moving back into his face.

"Dude, you need to seriously relax and back the fuck up."

"Ya know what, save your fuckin' bullshit explanation. I know you were behind this whole thing. You're just jealous."

"Jealous?" he laughed.

"Yup. Jealous that once Pete and I are both married, you'll be the odd man out."

Doug continued to laugh then said, "Yea, you got me all figured out. I'm so jealous of marriage. I can't wait to wake up every day to a giant Honey-Do-List! And I certainly can't wait to only have sex maybe once a month! Ya know what, I'm not gonna waste my night off listening to your stupid shit. I'm outta here!"

With that, he brushed past me and left the office. A few minutes later, he left the bar all together. Needless to say, I spent the rest of the night fuming. He had no right talking to Jane and telling her… and telling her… well, whatever the fuck he told her. No right at all! And believe me, when Pete showed up that night, he got quite an earful from me.

"Whoa, whoa, whoa," Pete interrupted. "Slow down. First of all, I need a beer."

I sloppily poured him a draft and placed it less than gently in front of him, glaring at him the whole time. He shook his head, took a long sip, then calmly spoke.

"Look, I have no idea about this Jane and Doug conversation. None. Zero. I told you, I got in late last night, and besides, I still haven't even talked to Doug since I've been back."

"I swear to God, Pete, if Doug convinced Jane to break up with me and leave town, so help me, I'll kill him."

"Relax, killer. Do you really think Doug would do that to you?"

I was close to quickly blurting out, *Fuck yes, he would*! But I paused. Doug had never filtered his thoughts when it came to the women in my life. And yes, there were a few times he confronted them and said what was on his mind. And yes, I was mad at him for it. And yesssss, his comments always came from a good place. Usually, the only time he'd say something to them was if he thought they were treating me like shit or something. As I continued to pause at Pete's question, he threw another one my way.

"And seriously, Josh, even if Doug said what you think he said, do you really think Jane would listen to him?"

Fuck! Have I ever mentioned, I hate when my friends make sense—especially when I'm trying to be pissed off? Again, Pete's question caused me to pause.

"Look, Josh, I'm not sure what was said between them, but maybe Doug just pointed out what Jane already knew—what we all kind of already knew."

"Which is what?" I said, perturbed.

"Which is she really, really cares about you, but…"

"But what?"

"I know you guys have been having fun together, and I

know that's led to you guys rekindling things, so to speak."

"So to speak?"

"I just think Jane still looks at this place as her vacation spot, not her permanent home."

"Well, you'd be wrong!" I snapped. "This time was different. I could tell. She wanted this to be her permanent home."

"I'm sure she wanted to want that, but—"

"But what?" I asked. I could tell Pete was holding something back. "But what?"

"Last week, one of Jane's old co-workers offered her a job out in San Francisco. I don't know exactly what it entailed, but apparently it had Jane all excited."

"You fuckin' knew this and didn't tell me?"

Before I could rant about how both my friends were backstabbers, Pete cleared the air.

"I just found out from Michelle this afternoon. Jane mentioned it to her on her way out of town."

I had no words to reply. I felt like such a fool.

"This whole summer was a sham," I mumbled. "I'm such an idiot."

"You're not an idiot, Josh, and this summer was definitely not a sham. It was obvious to all of us just how much Jane cares about you. And like I said, I'm sure she wanted to *want* to settle down here, but I just don't think it's in her blood. I mean, do you really think being in this little town working as a babysitter for us was her goal? She's always needed more than this place had to offer. It has nothing to do with you or her feelings for you."

I let Pete's words sink in for a moment then replied, "If it had nothing to do with her feelings for me, then why didn't she ask me to go with her? I would have, ya know?"

Pete gave me a half-laugh before saying, "I know you would have. But I think we both know, it wouldn't take long before you were missing home. And more importantly, Jane knew the same thing. I'm sorry, Josh, I really am."

I was officially left with nothing to say. As much as I wanted to rant and rave, I couldn't. I knew what he was saying made a lot of sense. On his way out, Pete offered me a bit of advice.

"Look, I know you're hurt and upset, and I can't believe I'm actually saying this, but you might want to take it easy on being pissed at Doug. I'm sure whatever was said between him and Jane was with your best interest in mind. And before your imagination gets too carried away, which it has a tendency to do, you might wanna find out what was actually said between them."

As Pete stood up to leave, I responded with a slight shrug, which is guy code for *Yea, I know you're right, but I'm not ready to vocally admit that yet.*

15

"THE REASON WHY" – Rachael Yamagata

Doug had the next two days off, so I figured I'd wait until he returned to apologize for snapping at him. That plan really didn't last, however. After I closed up Hoohahs that night, I headed straight over to Doug's place. I'd like to say I went over because I was eager to apologize, but the truth was, my curiosity got the best of me, and I needed to find out what was said between Doug and Jane.

Luckily for me, Doug was still awake. Also luckily for me, Doug was taking the night off from entertaining the female species. I offered my apologies for blowing up at him, and I told him I really, really needed to know exactly what was said between them. Doug knew how important it was to me, so he obliged by filling me in on their conversation—word for word.

So, without further ado, I give you word for word, Doug's recollection of their chat.

"Jane, what are you doing here?" asked Doug.

"I'm hoping you'll pour me a red wine, that's what I'm doing here," she smiled.

"No, I meant why aren't you with Josh? Isn't he visiting his sister out in the Berkshires for a few days?"

"Yea, but I had already promised Michelle I would watch the girls for her. With Pete being out of town on business, and her juggling school and whatnot, I knew she was pretty desperate for me to stick around. I actually just left her house now."

"Huh, she could have asked me. I would have watched the girls."

"She wasn't THAT desperate," smirked Jane, taking a long sip of wine.

Apparently, Jane and Doug bantered back and forth with small talk for a while before turning the conversation a bit more serious.

"So, how are the girls?"

"Kayla and Lindsay? They're good. They're so damn adorable."

Doug laughed then shook his head.

"What? You don't think they're adorable?" she asked.

"I totally do. That's not why I'm laughing. I'm just thinking you must be going stir crazy around here. Admit it, you miss your career and the bright lights of the big city."

"A little bit, I guess," she shrugged. "I definitely don't miss the company I was working for."

"So, if it was for a different company, you'd go do it again?"

asked Doug.

"Maybe," she shrugged. "Depends on the type of photography I'd be doing."

"You have something lined up, don't you?" Doug said, slightly accusatory.

"No," she quickly defended. "I don't have anything lined up, but…"

"But what?" he asked.

Hesitantly, she said, "One of my old co-workers is forming a new company out in San Francisco, and he kind of asked if I would partner up with him."

"What did Josh say about that?" Her expression said it all. "You haven't told him, have you?"

"There's nothing to tell. It's not like I accepted the offer."

"Are you gonna take it?"

She took a long pause before saying, "Umm, no, I don't think so. I mean, San Francisco is one of my all-time-favorite cities, but… I'm kind of happy right where I am now."

Doug stared long and hard at her before speaking.

"Kind of happy right where you are? Dude, you babysit kids and work a shift or two here. How happy can you be?"

All Jane could offer was a shrug.

"Seriously, Jane, what are you doing to Josh?"

"Excuse me? What does that mean?"

"It means, it doesn't surprise me that he's continued holding a torch for you all these many, many years, and it doesn't surprise me that you guys still enjoy hanging out together, and it doesn't surprise me that you guys still have hot sex together. I mean, he's never given exact details or sketched any of it on a napkin, but he always hinted that you are an animal in bed."

At that point, Jane's cheeks matched her red wine.

"Anyway," continued Doug, "it also doesn't surprise me that he went temporarily insane and bought you a stupid engagement ring. But… but what shocks the shit outta me is the fact that when he proposed to you, you—"

"I didn't actually say yes," she interrupted.

"But you didn't say no. And we both know, to Josh that *is* a yes."

Jane knew she couldn't argue that point. She just stared deeply into her wine then sighed and said, "I think we both know, I've spent most of my adult life traveling around place to place and never letting grass grow under my feet."

"Gypsy Jane," smiled Doug.

"Yea, Gypsy Jane," she repeated. "And because of that, my relationships have suffered. Don't get me wrong, that's not the only reason they've suffered. I've also been known to date a loser or two… or five. But through all my traveling, and through all my dating, Josh has always been there for me. He's been my best friend through it all, and whenever we're together, he makes me feel special, like really special."

"But you don't love him, Jane. At least not the way he loves you… not in the 'let's walk down the aisle, 'til death do us part' sorta way."

Again, Jane shrugged then said, "But maybe I can learn to love him that way."

Doug looked at her deadpan then said, "Jane, I say stupid things all of the time. As a matter of fact, I've spent most of my life saying stupid things, but that… that is the most idiotic and stupid thing I've ever heard. You can't learn to love someone. You either do or you don't."

Jane knew in her heart that Doug spoke the truth. All she

could say was, "If you were in my shoes, what would you do?"

Doug thought a second then said, "Either break his heart now with your honesty, or agree to this sham of a marriage thing and REALLY break his heart later on. If I was you, I'd be honest with him now and tell him exactly how you feel, and then I'd take that job offer and get the hell out of Maine. And I'm not saying that because I don't want you around, I say it because you being here only gives him false hope. Also, if I was you, I wouldn't tell him your new address, and I would definitely not take his calls."

"Doug, I could never do that."

"I'm not saying forever, but we both know, he's gonna call you like 37 times a day, hoping that if only he could say the right words…"

Knowingly, Jane sadly nodded.

"If he knows where you live, he's liable to quit the bar and move closer to you to win you back. Jane, he loves this area, and for the most part, he loves this bar—and I'm not saying this because I'd miss him, or for selfish reasons, I'm saying it because—"

"I know, Doug," she quietly said. "He's always loved this area… and his friends. I know what you're saying is true, but it's just so hard. How am I supposed to look into his eyes and crush his heart… yet again?"

Sympathetically, Doug shrugged.

Jane finished her wine then said, "Do you think he'll ever be fine with us being just friends?"

Again, Doug shrugged and said, "Maybe. Maybe not. At least not until he finds a new someone. But of course, if the new someone is just a someone and not 'the one' then, well… I don't know, ya know?"

"Surprisingly, I think I know exactly what you mean. You know, Doug, you're a good friend to him."

"I know," he said matter-of-factly.

Jane put her hand on his hand and said, "Thanks for the drink—and the talk."

"Of course. That's what a bartender is for, right?"

Before Jane walked away, Doug said, "Remember Jane, be strong. Don't let his babbling and puppy-dog-eyes keep you from doing the right thing. And change your phone number!"

She smiled, rolled her eyes, then started to head out. She stopped short of the door and turned back around and said, "Hey, Doug, make sure you —"

"Don't worry, Jane, we'll take care of him. We always do."

Again, she sadly smiled then exited the bar.

As you probably can guess, after Doug finished giving me all the details, I felt like a giant piece of shit. Doug wasn't the reason Jane ditched me, and he certainly wasn't a backstabber. I had no right accusing him of that and getting all up in his mug. I let his words sink in, and then I raised my beer to him and gave him an apologetic nod. Yup, guy code for *I'm sorry, dude.* He returned my nod then proceeded to crank up the Beastie Boys "Intergalactic" – guy code for *Apology accepted.*

16

"COME AROUND" – Rhett Miller

Suffice it to say, after Jane left me high and dry, my bounce-back-ability lessened quite a bit. As a matter of fact, it would be a solid ten weeks before I even thought about moving on. It was a long, long ten weeks for me, and I suppose an even longer and more annoying ten weeks for my friends and co-workers. Admittedly, I had fallen back into old habits and had once again become a sad fuck.

I suppose the good news was my phone calls to Jane were fewer and far between. By October 1st, I was only leaving one or three messages a week on her voicemail, and by November, none at all! You'll also be happy to know, my imaginary tour guides slowly ended as well. And no, the ring and the note were NOT still sitting on the sill. I'm not that glutton for punishment.

I actually took care of them a few days after the original discovery, and by took care of, I mean I packed them away in my Jane Memorabilia Box. Yes, I had one of those, and yes, it said Jane Memorabilia Box in black marker—and yes, it was a big fuckin' box.

By November, I was doing much better. Although tempted, I didn't once pick up the phone and call her. Not once! I even threw away the blouse she left behind. You know, the one that smelled exactly like her. And by threw away, I mean I tossed it in the Jane Memorabilia Box. Hey!! Cut me some slack here!! The fact that I was no longer taking a whiff of her stupid shirt on a nightly basis was huge. Huge, I tell ya! It's all about baby steps.

At one point, I placed the box in the center of my sacrificial burn pile, but I just couldn't do it. I had the lighter fluid clutched tightly in my hand, but I just couldn't strike the match. Like I said, baby steps.

To make matters worse, Jane's breakup and subsequent departure wasn't the only thing to break my heart that fall. The mother-fuckin' Red Sox were one game away from making it to the World Series, until Aaron fuckin' Boone hit a home run off Tim Wakefield in extra innings. Yup, salt in my wounds.

In those ten weeks after Jane left, the biggest change in my life was Hoohahs. Originally, when it first happened, Doug told me to take some time off to clear my head. At the time, I had no desire to be at the bar, so I was very thankful for his offer. Unfortunately, as time went on, I was never able to regain that desire. Although I worked a few shifts here and there, I eventually came to the decision that I was done. Done, done.

Sadly, I told Doug I wanted out of the partnership. It wasn't personal. I just needed a big change, I guess. Doug made it clear if I ever wanted back in to just let him know. Luckily for me, I still had a good amount of money in my savings, so I planned on taking the rest of the winter off while I figured out my next move. As it turned out, I wouldn't have to wait the entire winter to figure that out. More on that later.

So, what did I do with all of my free time? Surprisingly, I was quite productive. I decided to use my Jane debacle as fodder for a new screenplay. Come November 2003, not only had I slammed out a new screenplay, but I had come up with a brand-new idea. Little did I know at the time, the idea would one day be a game-changer for me. At that point in my life, I had written more than a handful of screenplays, but I felt I was no closer in getting them turned into movies. That's when it hit me!

One night, as I lay in bed, I remembered a line from Anna's letter years earlier. She had encouraged me to sit down and write my first screenplay. She also pointed out that if the movie thing didn't work out, then maybe I should turn it into a novel. So, it was at that very moment, with a sad smile on my face, that I decided to do just that!

One by one, I was going to turn my screenplays into novels. Best of all, I also decided I was going to combine my "Elise screenplay"(*The Empty Beach*), my "Anna screenplay" (*Between Hello and Goodbye*), and my new (untitled) "Jane screenplay" into a trilogy and call it The Soundtrack to my Life trilogy!

For the most part, I stayed away from Hoohahs. I spent most of my mornings moving from one coffeeshop to another, pouring my heart out with a pen and paper. Because of this, I guess I sort of lost track of what was going on in my friends' lives, especially Pete and Michelle.

Pete was still working at his job, and yes, he was still miserable. Michelle had not only finished her classes, but she had just recently landed a job at a small law firm in Portsmouth. For the first month or so after her school was over, she had sent out dozens of resumes to no avail. She hadn't held a real job in seven years, so her resume was quite bare. Not to mention, she had zero experience in an actual law firm.

Luckily for her, one of her old friends was very close friends to the owner of a law firm, and she put in a good word for Michelle. A week later, she was hired.

One would think that seeing as she was finally done with classes and had a job in her field that her stress level would have lessened. Unfortunately, that wasn't the case. She knew she got the job as a favor, so she was determined to work her ass off to prove her worth. This meant working extra hours, and extra hours meant less together time with Pete.

When she was working, Pete did his best to stay home and watch the girls. When Pete needed to be at the office, she did her best to be at home with the girls. When they both needed to be at work, they relied on babysitters or daycare. Either way, Pete and Michelle rarely saw each other, and when they did, they were either too tired to hold a conversation, or the conversation revolved around bills or the upcoming week's schedule.

Pete did his best to avoid these types of conversations. He did this by hanging out at Hoohahs late into the night, claiming he had to work late. I'm sure Michelle could tell by the alcohol on his breath where he was, but she was probably too tired from her own day to say anything. Either way, their disconnection was growing by the day.

My mornings were spent in coffeeshops, but my nights

were usually spent at home alone, watching classic movies, listening to sad music, and yes, pouring more of my thoughts onto paper. My writing not only kept me busy, but it proved to be quite cathartic.

My biggest cathartic moment, however, came on Thanksgiving eve. That's when Jane finally reached out and called me. Our phone conversation lasted three hours and eleven minutes. It was honest and raw, and at times, a little uncomfortable, but it was long overdue and definitely needed.

She let me know just how terrible she felt for leaving the way she did and for not calling or not returning all my messages over the last three months. Jane tried to give me the old *it's not you it's me* speech, but I think we all know that adds little consolation to a broken (crushed) heart.

Although her new job offer wasn't the main reason for her leaving, she made it a point to let me know just how much she loved it. She went on and on about it, and at one point, she called it her "ultimate dream job."

I have no doubt she loved it, but I think she was laying it on a little thick in attempt to ease my pain. I think she thought if she would have left me behind for just an average job, then it would have hurt me more. But if she let me know it was her ultimate dream job, then I would look at it as fate, and maybe I would hurt less knowing how happy she was.

It was a sweet gesture on her part, but unfortunately her perfect little job didn't take the sting away from me any less. She also offered to pay me for the ring. It was another sweet (guilty) gesture, but I turned the offer down. I would have felt like even more of a shmuck accepting it.

Bottom line, Doug was right, she just didn't love me the way I loved her. That, my friends, was the cold, hard truth. I still didn't like how things went down, but I suppose, in my heart, I knew she was only doing what she thought was best. Forced with the same dilemma, I have no idea what I would have done myself. I'm not sure if I would have bolted like that, but we all handle situations differently, I guess.

I will say this, I think by the end of our phone call that night, we were in a better place. To be honest, even before her phone call, I had pretty much come to terms that Jane and I were not destined to be together after all. That being said, I was glad she called, and I was glad I was finally able to hear her voice again.

My writing over those few months, along with her phone call, provided me with exactly what I needed to pick up the pieces and to finally move on!

17

"TRUST" – The Cure"

On that following Saturday after Thanksgiving, I was feeling rather social, so I organized a breakfast date with Doug, Pete, Michelle, and the girls. I chose the Friendly Toast, which in retrospect, didn't turn out to be the best idea.

I had just spent the last few months keeping to myself and just plugging away with my writing. I wasn't being anti-social, but I definitely had fallen out of the social loop. So much so, that I didn't realize just how bad things were getting between Pete and Michelle, and the fact that I chose the Friendly Toast for breakfast, didn't help things either.

It had been months since Pete designed Hoohahs new sign and logo, but sometimes, I still caught him just staring up at it, admiringly. And why shouldn't he, something he created had made its way into the world for all to see. To be honest, Pete's sign was a huge inspiration to me. Whether it was thought of seeing one of my screenplays on the big screen or seeing one of my novels sitting in a bookstore, I couldn't wait for the day where I too could stand back and admire one of my own creations.

Unfortunately, as proud as Pete was, Michelle didn't really share in it. It wasn't that she was being mean or unsupportive, but it was just that she was so focused on getting her own career going. Pete knew this, and eventually just started keeping all his thoughts to himself.

One of the biggest qualities I used to admire about Pete and Michelle was their communication. They always had such great rapport with each other, so it was absolutely heartbreaking to see them like this. That morning at the Friendly Toast was the perfect snapshot of how their communication, and ultimately their relationship, was quickly disintegrating.

Even though Cat's new graphic design company was picking up steam, she still waitressed one or two shifts a week. And as you probably guessed, that particular morning was one of them. Also, that particular morning would be the first time Michelle would officially meet Cat. It would also be Kayla and Lindsay's first time at the Toast, so needless to say, they were wide-eyed and excited about all the cool stuff on the walls and ceiling.

We were originally told it would be at least a forty-five-minute wait, but Cat pulled some strings and got us seated within fifteen minutes.

"Well, hello, girls," Cat said, handing them crayons and a paper placemat. "You must be Lindsay, and you must be Kayla?"

"How'd you know that?" Kayla asked shocked.

Cat smiled then said, "Because your dad talks about you all the time. You girls are kinda famous around here."

Lindsay giggled, and Kayla proudly beamed.

"I'm kinda famous here too," Doug whispered to the girls.

"You're more infamous here," Cat joked. "There's a difference."

Neither of the kids got the joke, but they giggled anyway.

"And you must be Michelle?" Cat said, reaching out her hand. "Pete talks about you girls so much, I feel as though I already know you."

Maybe it was the semi-fake smile Michelle wore on her face, but I think I knew right then and there, we were in for a long breakfast. After Cat headed off from taking our drink order, Michelle looked over to Pete.

"She's quite friendly, huh?"

Before Pete could say a word, Doug jumped in and said, "To be fair, Michelle, this *is* the Friendly Toast." He then looked over at Kayla and Lindsay and said, "Not the Unfriendly Toast."

Both girls giggled at Doug's comment. Michelle, not so much.

"So, who is she again?" asked Michelle.

"I've told you about her before. She's the one who just started her own graphic design company."

"Oh yea," Michelle said, scanning the menu.

The first half of our breakfast was mostly small-talk. Everyone talked about how their Thanksgivings were, and at one point, I even mentioned that Jane had called me a few nights earlier. I asked Michelle how her new job was going, and she eagerly filled me in. It was nice to see how excited she was about her new career. I also revealed to everyone about my big idea about turning my screenplays into novels.

I asked Doug how Hoohahs was going, which led him to tell one story after another. Due to the fact that there were little girls present, the stories lost some of their luster because he was forced to make them G-rated.

We were all enjoying our breakfast, so I made it a point to NOT ask Pete how his job was going. I figured opening that can of worms would only bring the vibe down. Unfortunately, that can of worms eventually found its way open.

Towards the end of breakfast, Cat came over to check on things. While she was there, she admired the drawings that Kayla had done.

"Wow, those are great, Kayla. If you want, I'll hang one up by the register."

Kayla's blue eyes widened. "Really?"

"Of course," Cat said, taking the drawing from Kayla's little hands.

"What do you say?" said Michelle to Kayla.

"Thank you, thank you, thank you!" Kayla shouted.

"Thank you, thank you, thank you," echoed Lindsay, holding up her own drawing.

Cat smiled and took both pictures. "I'll hang these up side by side." After glancing at the drawings again, Cat said, "Looks like you girls get your drawing talent from your daddy, huh?"

Pete gave a slightly embarrassed smile.

"Seriously," Cat said to Michelle, "your husband is super-talented. He should take some graphic design classes. His drawings and ideas are amazing. And you should definitely take me up on my offer, too," Cat said, looking Pete's way.

I had no clue what offer she was referring to, and

apparently, neither did Michelle, because after Cat walked off, Michelle said, "What offer was that?"

Pete shrugged and said, "I guess they do a lot of logos for companies, and they asked if I would help them out a bit. You know, just part time."

"Well that's cool," said Doug.

I kinda got the feeling Michelle didn't share in that opinion.

"Are you gonna do it?" I asked.

Again, Pete shrugged. "I don't know. I told her I'd think about it."

"I'm not really sure what there is to think about," Michelle said. "When are you gonna find time for that? Do you know how expensive daycare is getting? The more days you can be home, the better."

Doug and I looked over at Pete and then to Michelle. We didn't say a word, but Michelle read our minds anyway.

"Look, I'm not trying to come across as the mean wife here. I know you hate your job, but I'm not making the kind of money yet that will allow you to quit, and until that happens, we just have to do what we gotta do. And right now, we need to cut back on daycare."

"Yea, I know," Pete quietly said, not even attempting to say what was really on his mind.

Doug and I lowered our eyes, trying our best to stay out of it.

"I know you guys think I'm being selfish here, but I kinda deserve to be… at least a little bit. I've waited a long time to have a career of my own."

"Michelle, seriously, you don't have to defend yourself to us," I said.

"I think it's great that you designed a cool logo for Doug's bar, I do, but coming up with a little design for your friend's bar and working as a real graphic designer are two different things. Unfortunately, we just don't have the time or money for you to pursue your little hobby."

I've known Michelle a long time, and she definitely isn't a mean-spirited person, but the way she just came across was extremely condescending. Her comment left all of us in silence… an uncomfortable silence. The kind that seemed like it would go on forever. Fortunately, Doug spoke up and ended the silence. Unfortunately, his comment only made things worse.

"I have a brilliant idea," he announced. "You should quit your job and come work with me. It just so happens, I could use a new business partner." Doug looked over at me and specified, "Don't worry, Josh, if you ever want back in, we'll make it work as tri-partnership."

Doug's offer was met with an intrigued smile from Pete and a blank glare from Michelle.

"Seriously, think about it. You can work as many nights a week you want, and that way can you be home during the days with the girls, saving greatly on daycare," he said in Michelle's direction. "Not to mention, you'd still probably have some free time to work a little with Cat. It's a win, win, win," he said, pointing at Michelle, Pete, and himself.

I've come accustomed to Doug being the master of talking out his ass, but I have to admit, his new idea was a good one, and by the look on Pete's face, I could tell that he thought it was as well. Michelle, not so much.

Pete spoke up and said, "I actually think that's a pretty good idea."

"You're kidding me, right?" said Michelle.

"No, no I'm not," smiled Pete.

"You're gonna quit the job that you've been at forever, the same job that gives us health insurance and retirement, just so you can draw somc logos and work at some bar at night?"

Doug was quick to jump in. "He wouldn't just be working— he'd be co-owning!"

Doug happily offered Pete a fist bump, which Pete happily returned.

Doug then turned to Michelle and said, "And he wouldn't be co-owning just 'some bar,' he would be co-owning the one and only…"

Doug pointed to the girls, and they responded loudly in unison, "Here Hey Hoohahs!"

"I taught them that," he proudly said as he gave high-fives to both girls.

Pete and I laughed, but all Michelle did was shake her head at Doug.

"Oh, come on, Michelle," said Doug. "You have to admit, my idea is really good."

"I'm stressed out enough trying to get my feet wet at my new job, the last thing I need is the added stress of new business ventures."

Doug wouldn't let it go. "It's really not a *new* business venture. My bar is pretty well establi—"

"Jesus, Doug, give it a rest! It's not gonna happen. Just mind your own business, okay?"

Before Doug could go back at her, I shot him a look that said he needed to zip it and let it go. After that, we all just sat there in silence. Yup, another uncomfortable silence, but this one was way more uncomfortable.

"How come you're yelling at Uncle Doug, Mommy?" asked

Kayla.

Before Michelle could answer, Doug said, "She wasn't really yelling at me, kiddo. She was just joking around."

"She didn't sound like she was joking," mumbled Kayla.

"Well she was," Doug said, ruffling up her hair. "Do you girls wanna go look around at all the cool stuff on the walls?" he asked.

Both girls excitedly nodded their heads. Doug took them by the hands and led them off. When they were out of earshot, Pete looked over at Michelle and said, "You didn't have to snap at him like that. He was just trying to help."

Michelle looked from Pete to me then back to Pete. "That's right, I'm the bad guy here," she said as she shook her head and laughed to herself. "I'll be out in the car." With that, she stormed off.

For as long as I could remember, I was always jealous of their relationship—the way they got along, the way they joked with each other, the way they communicated. But that morning at the Friendly Toast might have been the first time I was NOT envious or jealous of them. Not at all actually.

18

"IF WE NEVER MEET AGAIN" – Reckless Sleepers

For the next week, I pretty much kept to myself and just concentrated on my book. Not only was my writing going well, but my life in general seemed to be getting back to normal. There was still a part of me that was saddened and affected by the events of three months ago, but my mood and attitude were definitely trending upwards. Little did I know, it was about to get even better.

A couple of weeks after Thanksgiving, I decided to head over to Hoohahs for a few drinks and some socializing. It was a little strange being on the other side of the bar again. Even though I was enjoying my time off that winter, there was a part of me that missed the place. As I sat there drinking my beer and listening to one of the playlists I had made, I reconsidered coming back to the bar. Maybe Doug was right, maybe I just needed to recharge my batteries a bit. Although it pains me to admit when Doug is right, I decided to mention to him about us rejoining forces again. Before I had the chance to broach the topic, I felt a hand on my shoulder.

"Hey, stranger."

I turned around to see Joanna standing there.

"Hey, you," I smiled.

"I haven't seen you at Breaking New Grounds in a while. You're not cheating on us, are you?" she joked.

Guiltily, I shrugged. "I may have gone to a couple of other coffeeshops this week. You know, just to try out a new atmosphere."

"Uh huh. You're such a coffeehouse whore," she smirked.

"I kinda am," I laughed. "You here by yourself?" I asked, looking over her shoulder.

"Actually, I'm meeting my date here in a few."

Doug overheard her and laughed. "You and your online dating. I can't believe you're still at it."

I nodded my head in agreement.

"Technically, this one isn't from a dating site," she said.

"Good for you," I said. "How'd you guys meet?"

With a slightly embarrassed look, she hesitantly said, "Well, technically we haven't met yet. He's the son of one of my mom's friends."

"Ha! Good luck with that," laughed Doug. "You couldn't pay me to go on a blind date."

"Technically, it's not really a blind date. I've seen a picture of him. He looks pretty cute."

Doug rolled his eyes and said, "Pictures can be deceiving. Ya know, technically."

"I know," she sighed.

"Yea," I added, "like that dude you thought was super-cute and then you found out about his hobby."

"Oh God, don't remind me," she said, covering her face.

"What was his hobby?" asked Doug. "Watching porn?"

"I wish," laughed Joanna.

"He collected ear wax and used it to create artwork," I laughed, filling Doug in.

"You're shitting me, right? He used his ear wax for artwork?"

"Not just *his* ear wax," Joanna specified. "He happily solicited it from whomever he came across. He even asked me for a sample during dinner."

"Are you serious? What did you do?"

"I looked at the waitress and said, 'Check, please.' "

I arched my eyebrow at her and said, "Why don't you tell Doug what *really* happened."

As soon as Joanna shot me an embarrassed glare, Doug knew what had happened.

"You gave him some of your ear wax, didn't you?"

Joanna covered her face then said, "I didn't want to be impolite."

"So you dug around in your ear and gave him a sample? Dude, the guy is probably like an ear wax serial killer. He probably went home and combined your wax with his and sculptured a mini-figure of your likeness. I bet he has a giant diorama filled with wax mini-figures of all of his failed romances… AKA – his future victims. I can see the headline now – *The Ear Wax Picasso Killer strikes again.*"

Joanna and I both laughed. She then scanned the place for an available table to sit at. There were a few empty ones towards the back, but ultimately, she chose to sit up at the bar.

Both Doug and I gave her a look.

"Safety in numbers," she smirked, then sat a few seats down from me. "Best behavior, by the way," she said, looking from me to Doug. "No embarrassing me."

"We'll pretend we don't even know you," said Doug.

I nodded in agreement. I was glad she sat up at the bar. Mostly, because now I could be within earshot and finally witness one of her infamous dates firsthand. As it turned out, her date with Jonathon did not disappoint. Well, it didn't disappoint Doug and I. Joanna was a different story.

Upon first glance, Jonathon looked very clean-cut, normal even. He wore a tucked-in white button down shirt and khakis. Both were crisply ironed. He politely shook her hand, and during their initial small-talk, he was great at maintaining eye contact with her. He asked her about her job, and he genuinely seemed interested in her life as a barista. It wasn't until she turned the tables and asked him about his job that things really got interesting. And by interesting, I mean amusing.

"So, what do you do for work, Jonathon?" she asked.

"I'm actually a student again. About a year ago, I decided to go back to school to pursue my true passion and calling."

"Wow, that's wonderful. What do you want to do?" she asked.

"A teacher," he replied.

"Aww, I love that! Good for you."

"Thank you. Actually, I consider myself more of a messenger than a teacher," he said, pulling out the Bible.

Yup, I shit you not, he pulled out the Bible. Apparently, the dude was a theology major. The look on Joanna's face was priceless. Doug and I fought back our laughter.

Jonathon spent the next thirty minutes or so getting all

biblical and shit on her. To her credit, she sat there with a fake, curious smile, and every so often she would nod in agreement. Although Doug and I were eavesdropping, we made it a point not to make eye contact with them. The one time I did look over and make eye contact, Joanna's eyes were screaming – *Help me*!

"Dude, we've gotta do something," I whispered to Doug.

Doug thought for a second then gave me a devious smile. It was the type of smile that you didn't bother asking what was up his sleeve, you just went with it. It didn't take long for his plan to reveal itself. I watched as he slowly approached Joanna and her date. He gave her a long, curious look and then it was game on.

"I'm sorry, I don't mean to interrupt you guys, but I've been racking my brain all night trying to figure out where I know you from," he said to Joanna. "And it finally just hit me. You work over at Kittens! It's Candy, right? I mean, I know that's just your stage name, but... wow, I knew I knew you! I guess I'm not used to you with clothes on."

All I could do was fight back my laughter as Doug continued laying it on thick.

"You're a lucky man," Doug said, shaking Jonathon's hand. "Not only does this girl know how to work the pole, but she gives the best lap dances ever!"

By now, Joanna's face was bright red in embarrassment. On the contrary, her date's face was pale white in shock. At any second, I expected Jonathon to pull out a cross and start chanting, *Repent! Repent! The power of Christ compels you*!

"Well, I won't interrupt you guys any longer," said Doug. "I just wanted to say hi and let ya know I'm a big fan."

Before turning away, he topped his performance off with a

wink in her direction. As Doug walked by me, we gave each other a mental high-five, and then he headed off towards the office in the back. His work there was done, and less than five minutes later, Joanna's date was as well.

By the time Doug returned behind the bar, Joanna was seated next to me. Her face was still red, and she kept shaking her head back and forth as she smirked at Doug.

"I can't believe you said all of that!" she said, reaching across the bar, smacking his arm.

"A simple thank you would suffice," he said.

Joanna looked over at me, but I just nodded in agreement with Doug.

"It's true," I said. "It might have been a little over-the-top, but he did rescue you from Jesus Christ Superstar."

She thought about it for a second and then began laughing. "Can you believe he brought a Bible to a date?"

"On the bright side, he's a step up from your ear wax Picasso," joked Doug.

Joanna put her head in her hands and sighed, "My dating life sucks so bad."

"It really does," laughed Doug.

With all the excitement of eavesdropping on Joanna's date, I didn't get a chance to tell Doug that I was thinking about coming back to the bar. As it turned out, that was a good thing, for I was about to get a career offer I couldn't refuse.

"I feel like I haven't seen you in a while," I said to Joanna. "How are things going? You know, besides what we just witnessed," I joked.

"Ha, ha," she sneered. "Actually, I have some very exciting news."

From behind the bar, Doug yelled, "You've accepted Jesus

Christ as your Lord and Savior?"

Joanna shot him a look but couldn't help but laugh at his comment.

"Are you going to be here for a while?" she asked me as she stood up.

"Yea, why?"

"I'm gonna hit the bathroom, but when I come back, I'll fill you in on my big news. And… I also have a huge proposition for you."

Again, Doug yelled from behind the bar, "Proposition? Does it involve a stripper pole or a lap dance? If so, I'm thinking I should get first dibs. Especially considering I'm the one who rescued you from the clean-cut cult leader."

Joanna rolled her eyes then headed towards the bathroom. When she was out of earshot, Doug said, "What do you think her proposition is? Do you think she wants to… you know…"

At that point, Doug resorted to middle school sign language for sex. Yes, he formed a finger-circle with his left hand and began profusely fingering it with his right index finger.

"Can you not do that, like ever again?" I said, looking around at everyone laughing at his antics. "And I'm positive that's not her proposition. We're just friends."

When Joanna returned, she informed me that she was seriously thinking of quitting her job and opening up her own coffeeshop.

"Aw, Joanna, I think that's great. Good for you," I said.

"Thanks," she smiled. "So, here's my proposition to you – I want you to be my business partner."

"Me?"

"Well, yea. I remember a few occasions you mentioned wanting to maybe own your own coffeeshop or café. And I also remember how cool some of your ideas were of what it would look like."

"Wow. I'm kinda speechless. You really wanna open a place with me?"

"I do. I've actually wanted to ask you for a while, but I knew you were tied to this place. As soon as you told me you were stepping away from here and taking some time to figure things out, I knew that was my chance. I don't know what your money situation is, but my dad said he'd help us get started."

She was right, I had mentioned a few times how cool it would be to own a coffeeshop. And technically, I still had a good chunk of savings left. I really was kind of speechless.

"I'm sorry. I know I'm springing this on you. I tell you what, tomorrow I'm going to look at a few spaces for lease, why don't you just come with me. No commitments," she smiled.

"I suppose I can do that," I replied.

I ended up going home that night and thinking heavily on her offer. I was thoroughly enjoying my time off, and I wasn't sure if I was ready to jump back into business, especially a brand-new business from the ground up. I decided to honor my word and go with her to look at some spaces, but as my head hit the pillow that night, I was pretty sure I was going to pass on her partnership offer.

Long story short, we both absolutely fell in love with the third place we looked at. The rustic woodwork combined with the old brick walls were absolutely perfect—so perfect, that my mind immediately was racing with one idea after another.

Was I enjoying my job-free winter? Yes.

Was I loving all my free writing time? Yes.

Did I accept Joanna's offer to open up our very own coffeeshop? Yes, yes I did.

19

"THE STORY" – Brandi Carlile

Joanna and I spent the rest of the winter getting our new place ready to open. When you partner with someone, there are bound to be occasions where you just don't see eye to eye. Fortunately, Joanna and I seemed to be on the same page with most everything. She concentrated on setting up the actual coffee area: the counters, the display cases, the coffee and espresso machines. I concentrated more on the atmosphere of the place. We wanted it be cozy, relaxing, and most of all, eclectic.

We had a giant wall that was designated for displaying local artists and photographers. The rest of the walls were adorned with pictures and posters of classic bands or movies. It wasn't as wildly eclectic as the Friendly Toast, but it still had its share of pop-culture. In one of the corners, we even had a small section of vinyl records and classic cassette tapes for sale. In the opposite corner, I built a small stage in case we ever did an acoustic open-mic night or a poetry night or whatever. And yes, Joanna had no problem letting me be in complete control of the music. And yes, the music was as eclectic as the shop itself. Jazz, classical, reggae, the 80's, and even some 90's dance music, we had it all. And yes, I had plenty of alternative songs and depression session stuff as well.

On March 1, 2004, The Eclectic Café & Coffeehouse officially opened its doors, and although it would take a while to get the word out, it was very exciting times. When I partnered up with Doug, Hoohahs was already established, so I never really got to experience my own business from conception to realization. When Joanna and I opened our doors for the first time, the feelings we had were indescribable.

Considering most every waking moment that winter was spent getting the place ready to open, I didn't have much time for my writing. I didn't completely abandon it, however. I did squeeze in a few late-night writing sessions here and there. By the time our café opened, I pretty much had finished turning my *Empty Beach* screenplay into a novel. I figured I'd take the next couple of months to edit and fine tune it, and then I would tackle book two – *Between Hello and Goodbye*. The coolest thing was I now had my very own coffee shop to sit and write at.

Overall, my life was going pretty damn well. It had been months since I had heard from Jane, but it didn't really bother me. Between my new business and my writing, the wallowing over Jane had completely subsided. As a matter of fact, I felt so good and so confident in my life, that I was more than ready to jump back into the dating scene. I did, however, have no intention in using any sort of online dating services. I was still determined to meet someone the old-fashioned way. Even Joanna had slowed down her use of online dating services.

My luck was going so well that I didn't even have to look far for my next romantic interest. One morning, while I was doing some writing at *my* shop, I noticed a cute woman sitting up at the counter drinking a coffee by herself. This in itself wasn't that strange, but what caught my attention was her demeanor. She kept checking her phone and looking around. I noticed on a couple occasions Joanna engaging with her.

At one point, I motioned Joanna over and asked, "Hey, what's the deal with that cute chick at the counter? She looks a little frazzled."

"Poor girl. She was supposed to meet her date here, but it looks like he's a no-show."

"Let me guess, she met him online?"

Joanna nodded. "The poor girl is all paranoid that he showed up, caught a look at her in real life, and then bolted."

"What? That's crazy," I said. "She's wicked cute."

Joanna smiled then said, "Why don't you go tell her that?"

Normally, I would have just rolled my eyes at Joanna, but like I said, I was feeling rather confident in my life. So much so, that I did just that. I walked over, sat next to her, and basically told her it was one hundred percent his loss for not showing up. I then gave her the typical, but honest line, "I still don't know why someone as cute as you would need an online dating service."

Her name was Hayley. We continued to talk and laugh for a while longer, and before she headed off, I semi-smoothly asked her on a date and promised there was no way I would stand her up. So, just like that, I had myself a date, and I did it the old-fashioned way.

My life was most definitely trending upwards, but unfortunately, the same couldn't be said for Pete and Michelle. While Michelle was putting in more hours at her job, their communication was becoming less and less. I found out through Doug, that Pete was secretly doing some side projects for Cat's new company. I get that Pete hated his job and that he was just looking for a creative outlet, but keeping secrets from Michelle was not like him. Not at all.

I kept meaning to get together with Pete to see how he was doing, but between my new business, my writing, and my subsequent dates with Hayley, I just didn't have time for my friends. Looking back on it, I should have found the time. I should have made the time, especially for Pete and Michelle. I'm not sure it would have changed anything, but still, I should have tried. Maybe it would have prevented what we witnessed a month later on the night of April 13th.

20

"BLUE MONDAY" – New Order

Before I delve into the night of April 13th, I should probably tell you about the night of April 11th. For me, life was still going great. We were starting to see a little increase in business, and things were good between Hayley and I. She was a nurse over at Portsmouth Hospital and worked long hours. Due to both our busy schedules, we had only been on a handful of dates, but I definitely enjoyed her company, and I'm pretty sure she enjoyed mine.

Although I was still editing my *Empty Beach* novel, I had already started writing the follow-up - *Between Hello and Goodbye.* Music had always been such an integral part of my life; it added to the good times, and it rescued me and helped me cope with the bad times. As it turned out, my writing proved to be just as effective, especially working on my Soundtrack to my Life trilogy. Whether it was sad moments like Anna, or the many humorous moments with my friends, writing things down proved to be very liberating for me.

Okay, back to the night of April 11th. It was just after midnight when my phone rang. I had just written a kick-ass scene and was quite pleased with myself. My happy mood was about to come to a grinding halt. On the other end of the phone was Jane. It had been a couple-few months since we last talked, so naturally, I was excited to hear from her and to fill her in on my new business.

"Hey, Jane."

"Hey, Josh. Is this a bad time?"

I could tell by her voice that something was up.

"Nope, not at all. I was just doing a little writing. How's life on the west coast?"

When my simple question caused her to pause, I definitely knew something was up.

"Everything okay, Jane?"

"I just really need to tell you something," she said. "I've been wanting to tell you for a while but I just didn't know how…"

"Oh my God, Jane, are you okay?"

I knew there must be something wrong with her health. When she hesitated again, I jumped in with, "Whatever it is, I'll be with you every step of the way."

Naturally, my mind went to the worse-case scenario. I assumed it must be cancer or some incurable disease.

For the moment, she eased my mind with, "Thanks, but it's not what you think."

I was relieved, but before my mind could create a top 3 list of what her news was, she blurted out, "I'm getting married…

at the end of the summer… in York Beach."

For a super-brief second, I wished for the incurable disease thing. I know, I know, it was absolutely horrible of me. I really didn't wish that on her, of course I didn't! I guess I just wasn't expecting or prepared for her saying those words.

"I was supposed to come back to Boston to see my sister last month, but I had to cancel because of work. I really wanted to tell you in person, not on the phone."

It was my turn to be hesitant and speechless. Jane went on to tell me how they met. They work together blah, blah, blah. He's a traveler/gypsy just like her blah, blah, blah. They've been dating since last Halloween blah, blah…

"Wait, what??" I said interrupting her. "Wait, so when you finally called me last Thanksgiving eve after ditching me two months earlier, you were already dating this dude??"

"Umm, yes," she quietly said. "That phone call was hard enough on both of us as it was. I didn't think it was appropriate to throw in the fact I was dating someone. Besides, with my track record, I just assumed it wouldn't last very long anyway."

Do to the obvious awkwardness, our conversation only lasted another five minutes or so. I honestly had no idea how to respond to any of what she was saying. Jane knew she had blindsided me, and she knew I would need some time to process it. I hung up the phone and did just that—process it.

"Are you fuckin' kidding me?" I yelled at my John Cusack *Say Anything* poster. "Getting married? To some dude she's only known for six months? We have a ten-year history together, and she's gonna choose a dude she just met?"

With his boombox above his head, my John Cusack poster stood expressionless, staring back at me. I know you guys are probably thinking I'm a hypocrite. You're thinking in the movie *Say Anything*, Lloyd and Diane only dated for one summer, yet they knew they were meant to be together. And you're thinking, how can I be a huge fan of that movie and of their romance, and yet question the validity of Jane and her fiancé?

Those are fair and valid points. But this is Jane fuckin' Wheeler we're talking about!! And *Say Anything* is just a movie!

I was tempted to throw my beer at the poster, but I thought better of it. After all, Lloyd Dobler didn't do anything to deserve that. In my heart, I knew I had no right to be this upset, especially considering I actually had a girlfriend at the time. This led me to wonder: Does this make me a bad boyfriend to Haley? I'd like to think not, but what probably made me a bad person and friend is I never actually said congratulations to Jane. I'm sure that phone call must have been hard for her to make. I never even hinted that I was happy for her. I thought about calling her back, but I didn't. I simply turned off the lights and went to bed—after watching *Say Anything* again.

21

"LOVE WILL TEAR US APART" – Joy Division

I didn't bother telling Hayley about Jane's phone call. I mean, she knew about our history, and about the ring, but I didn't really see the point in telling her about Jane's engagement. Fortunately, it would only be two days before I was completely sidetracked from the Jane situation. Well, fortunate for me, but not for Pete and Michelle, especially for Pete.

The morning after the call, I ended up telling Joanna about Jane's engagement. Although I tried to play it off like it didn't bother me, Joanna knew better. She also knew she needed to bring in the big guns to help cheer me up. That following night, on April 13th, she and Doug took me out drinking in downtown Portsmouth. Pete was supposed to join us, but he was at home watching his girls while Michelle worked late.

I spent the first part of the night yapping about Jane and feeling sorry for myself. By the time we hit our second bar (State Street Saloon), my alcohol intake had increased and my pity-party had slowly decreased. Doug's storytelling was in full-effect that night, and he made it impossible to remain in a bad mood.

He started off by telling the bartender that I should be drinking for free because I was going to be a famous author. I was embarrassed, yet flattered—mostly embarrassed. Luckily for me, Doug's next story turned the embarrassment onto himself.

"Hey, Joanna, any crazy online dating stories lately?" he asked.

"Nope. I'm taking a little break from the dating scene."

"Well I've got a crazy story for you guys. It's not an online dating thing, but it was fucked up!"

When most people have an embarrassing, fucked up story, they usually lower their voice to tell it. Not Doug. Even if the story is self-deprecating, he tends to raise his voice for everyone to hear.

Doug began his story by telling us how he went out drinking the other night with a couple of his cousins. They ended up going to Ruby's bar and grill on Rt. 1 in York. The local favorite band Johnny Wad and the Cash were playing there and the place was packed. Doug went on to tell us how they were all drinking and dancing all night. He also informed us about a "smoking hot twenty-one-year-old chick" that was "all over him."

"Not only were we making out inside the bar, but she took me outside and blew me on the little grassy knoll in the back parking lot. I'm telling ya, this chick might have been young, but she was fuckin' wild. She had a body like an angel… but a tongue like a fuckin' hooker."

Doug ordered another round of drinks for us, and then continued his story.

"She told me her roommates were gone for the night and that we should go back to her place so she could 'rock my fuckin' world.' Her exact words. We weren't at her place five minutes and she was already naked on her bed using a vibrator on herself. One of her *three* vibrators, I might add."

Doug pounded down his drink and excitedly (and loudly) told us about all of the lotions and toys this girl owned.

"Dude, it was like her top drawer was a God damn porn shop! She had things I had never even heard of. At one point, she ordered me to tie her up and put these nipple clamps on her."

"You've never heard of nipple clamps?" Joanna asked.

"I've heard of them, I've just never used them on a chick before. She kept ordering me to punish her, telling me that she'd been a bad girl."

"I'm not gonna lie, Doug," I said, "I don't really see a problem here."

"No, there was no problem. It was fuckin' amazing! She was having me do positions I had never even heard of. I mean, I had done some of these before, but I didn't know their slang name. I didn't want to seem old and out of touch, so I just went along with whatever she suggested."

"Like what?" I asked.

"Like the Viennese Oyster, the Pinball Wizard, the Reverse Cowgirl, the Irish Garden. Oh, and then there was the Octopus position. I nearly pulled a muscle on that one."

"The only one of those I've ever heard of is the Reverse

Cowgirl," I said.

"Exactly! Me too," exclaimed Doug.

"Really?" said Joanna, a bit surprised.

"How the hell have you heard of them?" I asked.

"The Urban Dictionary," she said matter-of-factly.

Neither one of us had a clue what she was referring to. Like I told you earlier, back in the early 2000's I wasn't much of an internet kinda guy, but don't worry, I would eventually become very familiar with the Urban Dictionary. Anyway, back to Doug's story.

"I still don't see a problem with your story," I said. "Especially if you were enjoying these positions."

"I was enjoying them. I was very much enjoying every kinky thing she was suggesting. So much so, that I started to agree with everything she suggested, even if I had no clue what she was talking about."

"Uh oh. That's probably not a good idea," exclaimed the bartender.

"No, not at all," Doug sadly said.

"What did she suggest?" smiled Joanna.

"She asked if I was feeling adventurous, and I might have said Adventurous was my middle name."

By now, there was a handful of people gathered around us, anxiously awaiting what Doug was going to say next.

"She said she really wanted to… to… peg me."

Both Joanna and I nearly spit our drinks out.

"Please tell me you didn't say yes?" asked Joanna.

Doug looked around at all the faces that were surrounding him. As soon as he covered his face in shame, we all burst out laughing.

"Sorry if I'm not up on my Urban Dictionary terminology,"

snapped Doug.

"Dude, even I know what pegging is," I laughed then clarified, "Not from personal experience though." Doug remained with his head in his hands. I then asked, "What the hell did you think she meant? That she wanted to peg you in the head with a dodgeball or something?"

"I don't know what I thought!" he yelled defensively. "I was still recovering from a position called The Rusty Trombone, so I wasn't thinking very clearly."

"So what happened next?" asked a random girl, standing next to Doug.

Hesitantly, Doug continued his story.

"Well… she gave me a big smile and walked over to her magical porn drawer and pulled out this giant strap-on cock. She then tossed me a huge tube of lube. Seriously, it was like industrial-sized! It was like she bought it in the Costco of porn shops."

At this point, Joanna literally had tears in her eyes she was laughing so hard.

"She told me to get ready and that she would be right back. As soon as the bathroom door closed, I put two and two together and realized what the fuck pegging was."

"What did you do?" asked another curious bystander.

"What the hell do you think I did? I grabbed my clothes and got the fuck outta there! Doug doesn't peg!" he proclaimed as the crowd burst out laughing.

The phrase *Doug doesn't peg* would be repeated several times that night by strangers as they toasted their drinks to Doug.

When their laughter subsided, Doug then said, "I tell ya what, up until that night, I never knew what the hell Meatloaf was talking about, but now I do."

"Meatloaf? What?"

"You know, the singer? Up until that moment, I never knew what he meant when he sang, 'I would do anything for love, but I won't do that.' Yup, now I finally know what *that* is. The poor bastard. Meatloaf's girlfriend was probably like, *if you really loved me, you'd let me peg you.* I bet Meatloaf bolted out of the house just as fast as I did."

"Like a bat out of hell?" I joked.

"Yes!" Doug exclaimed, catching my joke. "See, the pegging incident inspired Loaf to write not one but two songs!"

Again, the whole bar erupted in laughter.

Fun Fact: For Doug's next birthday, I bought him a tee shirt that said *Doug doesn't peg!* Of course, it would have been even funnier if I had put it on the ass of his pants.

Needless to say, between the alcohol and Doug's stories, I was able to temporarily put Jane's engagement out of my head. After we laughed and drank our way through a couple more bars, we decided to call it a night. Well, we called it a night after stuffing our faces with chili cheese fries from Gilley's.

Joanna was our designated driver, so we staggered behind her as she headed towards her car (the whale-wall parking lot). For whatever reason, Doug and I were loudly and drunkenly singing "Mr. Jones" by the Counting Crows.

"Guys, enough!" Joanna jokingly scolded.

As we entered the parking lot, our singing came to a halt. It wasn't because of Joanna's warning, it was because of what we saw—what we witnessed. About thirty feet ahead of us we saw a couple making out next to their car.

"Looks like someone's gonna get lucky tonight," I whispered to Doug.

Before Doug could offer a comment, the couple pulled

apart, and the woman got into her car. It was at that point, we stopped dead in our tracks. It wasn't just a car, it was Michelle's car. And it wasn't just a woman, it was Michelle. Panicked, and unsure what to do, all three of us ducked behind an SUV.

As soon as she pulled away, I turned to them and said, "Please tell me I've had too much to drink and that I'm hallucinating. Please tell me that wasn't Michelle."

Slowly, Joanna nodded her head and said, "It was her. It was definitely Michelle."

"Oh my God. What do we do?"

"I'll tell ya what we do," Doug said, stepping out from behind the SUV. "We go fuck that guy up."

By now, the guy was getting in his car on the opposite end of the parking lot.

"We're not fucking him up," I said, grabbing Doug's arm.

Still in shock, we stood there as the guy started his car and drove away.

Joanna was first to speak. "I can't believe she's cheating on Pete."

"I'm telling you, we shoulda kicked his fuckin' ass."

Joanna dismissed Doug's comment then said what we were all thinking.

"What are you guys gonna do?"

That was certainly the big question. Do we go straight to Pete and tell him? Do we confront Michelle first? Do we give her the choice that either she tells Pete or we will? Or do we say nothing and simply mind our own business?

22

“WHEN YOU LOVED ME” – Juliana Hatfield

Michelle was like a sister to us, and although we were tempted to confront her first, we didn’t. Whether it was because of the guy code, or simply because it was the right thing to do, we went straight to Pete and told him. It was one of the hardest conversations we’ve ever had.

Originally, Pete thought we were just busting his balls and playing a stupid joke on him. He didn’t believe us at first, or maybe he didn’t want to believe us. When he finally realized we were dead serious, he didn’t say a word. He didn’t yell, or scream, or even throw things. He just slumped in his chair with this sad and devastated look on his face. It was a look I had never ever seen from him before.

It took him a couple of days, but when he had her all alone, he finally confronted Michelle. She was caught off guard and tried to deny it, but Pete knew her too well. He could tell she was lying. When he pressed more, she finally crumbled and admitted to everything. And by everything, I mean she admitted to not only making out with that guy, but to having an affair with him as well. The guy turned out to be one of her co-workers.

Michelle told him it had only been going on for less than two weeks and swore it meant nothing. At that point, I think Pete was less concerned with how long, and more concerned with what exactly went on in those two weeks. Stupidly, he pushed for details. Details like: How many times? Where? Did they ever do it in their house—in their bed?

Don't get me wrong, if I was in his shoes, I probably would have pushed for details as well, and it would have been just as stupid. Michelle refused to get into specifics, but did assure him, they never ever had sex in their house.

If you guys remember, back in the day, Pete used to have quite the short temper, especially down at the basketball courts. To our surprise, however, he never *lost it* with Michelle. Oh, he was angry and pissed, and I'm sure he raised his voice, but to our knowledge, he never yelled or screamed at her. We assumed he'd be punching holes in the walls, and we definitely thought for sure he'd immediately drive over to her work and kick the ever-living shit out of her co-worker, but he didn't.

It was obvious that Pete was beyond angry or pissed. Like I said, I had never seen him that hurt and devastated before. The situation was so serious that even Doug knew better than remedy it by suggesting a trip to the strip club.

So, just like that, their seemingly perfect little family had crumbled down to nearly nothing. Pete packed his things and moved in with Doug. There was no mention of divorce, but there was certainly no mention of a reconciliation either. Probably the hardest part of the situation was the girls. Lindsay was only four, so I think she was too young to completely understand what was going on.

Kayla, on the other hand, was nearly eight, so it didn't take long for her to start asking questions. Questions like: why her daddy didn't sleep at home any more? They played it off by telling Kayla that Pete had an overnight job. I was the same age as Kayla when my parents got divorced, so I knew exactly what she was going through. I also knew she suspected more than she let on.

Besides a few brief words when he picked up the girls, Pete and Michelle didn't talk—at all. Michelle desperately wanted to work things out, but Pete wanted nothing to do with her apologies or pleas. As a matter of fact, every time she attempted to talk to him, she was met with nothing but sarcastic and hurtful comments.

Doug and I did our best to be Switzerland. We were always there if Pete or Michelle needed to vent, but we rarely offered advice, we usually just listened.

It didn't take long for Pete's hurt and devastated mood to change into an *I don't give a fuck* attitude. One month after he moved out, he finally quit his job, and not only did he continue working with Cat on side-projects, but he made sure Michelle knew it. He also made sure Michelle knew that he had been secretly working with her for a while. This upset Michelle, which I guess was the point. The whole situation had become a shit-show.

Knowing that I wasn't going to return to Hoohahs, Doug again offered Pete to be his business partner. Pete strongly considered it, but due to the uncertainty of his future and his marriage, Pete decided against it. He did pick up a handful of shifts for Doug, but between that and his part time work with Cat, he was still making way less than before. He was much happier than before but was definitely making less money.

Because of their money situation, Michelle ended up keeping her position at the firm—with her co-worker—the co-worker she had an affair with. I know, right? This absolutely didn't set well with Pete, and to be honest, it didn't set well with me either.

Michelle swore the affair was 100% over. She said she had applied to multiple firms, but until something came through, they needed the money too much to just up and quit. I believed her when she said the affair was over, and I even believed her when she said it was the biggest mistake of her life and that it meant nothing. I knew ever since Pete quit his job that they were having money problems, but still, if you really wanted to fix your marriage, you should probably stop working with the guy you were once having an affair with. Like I said, the whole situation had become a shit-show.

In direct contrast to that, my life was going great. Word of mouth was spreading about our coffeeshop, and business was growing by the day. It was such a rewarding feeling watching your business grow from the ground up. I can only assume this must be how Doug felt about Hoohahs. Not to mention, it was also super-cool to sit and write in a place which I owned.

Speaking of writing, I was killing it! Book two of my little trilogy was coming along swimmingly. I'll be honest, I hadn't really put much thought into how I was going to actually publish them. I had a short-list of potential publishing companies I planned on submitting to, but at that point in my life, I was more focused on just getting the books written.

Between my writing and owning the best damn coffeeshop in the seacoast, I had little time to concentrate on dating. Oh, you're probably wondering about that Hayley girl from a couple of months earlier. Although we went out on a handful of dates, and although she was a great girl, it just didn't work out as a boyfriend/girlfriend thing. It didn't end badly, it just wasn't meant to be, that's all.

***

By the time August rolled in, tensions were high all the way around. Jane's wedding was fast approaching, and although I had spent the entire summer repressing my feelings, they were inevitably being forced to the surface. Jane made another attempt to call me, but I never returned it. I had a feeling her call was to follow up on the wedding invitation. Yup, that's right, back in early July, she mailed me an invitation. I knew it wasn't meant to be a slap in the face, and in her heart, she just wanted me to be there, but come on, there was no fuckin' way I was going to attend. I think she knew this, which is why she was probably calling me.

Most of that summer, I dealt with my feelings by writing, working a ton, and just keeping my thoughts of Jane to myself. I didn't mope around or act depressed, and I didn't even listen to sad music—not much. I suppose I had become the master at repressing.

Within the first week or so of August, I had even started to see someone. No, not like a shrink or anything. Although, I probably could have used one. I actually started seeing a woman I met at my coffeeshop. By the way, it never gets old saying *my coffeeshop*. Her name was Krystal and she was twenty-seven. She was originally from Dover, NH but now lived in Kittery. She wasn't my usual *type*, but we had a lot of fun together. And yes, by fun I mean we had great sex. We had just started seeing each other, but it was clear that she was completely and totally uninhibited. I could only assume it wouldn't be long before we were having wild and crazy sex. Maybe this time, Doug and Pete would watch as *I* was the one sketching sexual positions on a napkin.

Seeing as Krystal was seven years younger than me, I wanted to make sure I was up to speed with today's lingo. I spent hours online surfing the Urban Dictionary for as many slang terms for sexual positions as possible. If Doug had taught me anything, it was that it was better to be safe than sorry. There was no way I was going to agree to a sexual position without fully knowing what it entailed. I certainly didn't want a pegging incident like Doug. Nope. No way! I would do anything for love, but I also won't do that!

Unfortunately, due to conflicting schedules, we didn't see a lot of each other. But still, Krystal proved to be another great distraction from Jane's fast-approaching wedding. At one point, I had this fleeting thought that I would attend the wedding and Krystal would not only be my date, but would be all over me, and maybe even give me a hand job out on the dance floor in front of the happy couple. Relax! I did say it was just a fleeting thought. I would never ever do that. Besides, I have stage-fright. I can't even pee with people watching me, never mind get a hard on.

Anyway, as we entered mid-August, Pete and Michelle were going on their fourth month being separated. More importantly, their fourth month without facing the problem head on. Michelle knew she had screwed up, and she was willing to do whatever it took to make things better. Pete showed no interest in working things out, he was quite content living and working with Doug and doing his own thing. I should say, he *appeared* quite content.

It was clear to everyone that burning deep inside of him was anger, resentment, and total and utter heartbreak. I guess I wasn't the only one repressing my feelings that summer. The big difference was how we dealt with our repression. I completely kept my feelings about Jane's upcoming wedding to myself. Pete, on the other hand, had no problem offering up his thoughts on Michelle. Unfortunately, they weren't healthy thoughts. It seemed whenever her name came up, he never missed an opportunity to offer a snide, uncalled for remark.

We knew how much he was hurting, and what Michelle did was terrible, but his sarcastic digs were getting old fast. I didn't see Pete that often, so I only experienced this in small doses, but because they were living and working together, Doug wasn't so lucky. He knew Pete was just masking his true feelings, and he felt for him, but still, he was getting fed up with Pete's caustic attitude.

The whole situation was horrible for all involved, but my heart went out most to Kayla and Lindsay. August 9th was Kayla's birthday party, and it was uncomfortable, to say the least. There were classmates, and cake, and presents galore, so the girls were pretty much oblivious to the awkwardness surrounding the rest of us. Between Michelle and Pete's relatives, you could cut the tension with a knife. Don't get me wrong, everyone was polite enough with each other, but the uneasiness of the situation was definitely prevalent.

Luckily for all involved, Pete kept his snide comments to

himself. To his credit, I don't think he had ever said anything mean about Michelle in front of the girls. He saved that for his friends. Lucky us.

Speaking of us, on more than one occasion, Pete shot us a hot glare because we were being "too friendly with the enemy." His words. He didn't really like that we were still friendly with Michelle. We had known Michelle for nearly fifteen years, so despite her terrible indiscretion, we were still friends. Pete looked at it as us taking sides against him. I will say this again - the whole situation was a shit-show.

The worst part of the birthday party was the end, when everyone started to filter out. We were one of the last to leave, so we were there to witness Kayla's reaction to Pete's goodbye.

"Aren't you gonna stay and play with my new toys with me?" she hopefully asked.

Pete looked over at Michelle and then back to Kayla. "I'm sorry, sweetie, but I have to get going. I promise I'll play with you next weekend."

"But I wanted to watch my new movie with you and mommy tonight," she sadly said, holding up her new *Finding Nemo* movie.

"Yea, Daddy, stay and watch it with us," Lindsay sweetly uttered. "Mommy can make popcorn!"

My heart felt for Pete and Michelle, but my heart was absolutely breaking for poor Kayla and Lindsay. Pete might have done his best to avoid the whole situation all summer, but he knew it was really starting to affect his girls. That truly became evident the following Sunday when Pete and I took the girls to York's Wild Kingdom.

***

For the most part, we all had a fun day. As many times as I've been there, and as much as it's completely run down, it takes on a new life when seen through the eyes of children. From riding on the elephant to feeding the silly deer, the smile and light never once left Lindsay's face. We must have been there for thirty minutes feeding those frickin' deer. We stood there patiently as Lindsay named each and every one of them. Kayla was also having a good time, but as the day went on, I could tell there was something off about her. I couldn't help but notice that Pete was on the quiet-side as well.

While the girls sat eating their giant piece of fried dough, I approached Pete.

"Everything okay? You seem a little off today."

"Yea, why wouldn't I be? I'm here with the girls while Michelle is probably off banging the rest of her co-workers."

See, these are the type of snide comments I was telling you guys about. I knew Pete and Michelle had an annual family tradition of taking the girls here to the Wild Kingdom, and I knew this must be hard on him to do it without Michelle, but still, his wise-ass remarks weren't helping anyone. I didn't really think he believed what he was spouting, so I didn't bother saying a word. I simply put my hand on his shoulder in a show of support.

Despite drinking a 32oz. Mountain Dew and pounding down a piece of fried dough, by the time we finished riding all of the kiddie rides (13 times each), I was completely exhausted. After we left the amusement park, we made our way over to the playground by the basketball courts. It was there that both Pete and I noticed how *off* Kayla was.

We weren't there but five minutes, and Lindsay had already

found some other little girls to play with. While they ran around the playground screaming loudly, Kayla sat on the swing. She wasn't swinging, but just kicking at the sand with her feet. Pete and I made our way over to her.

"You don't wanna go play with your sister and the other girls?" asked Pete.

Kayla shook her head no.

I approached the swing and said, "Do you want Uncle Josh to push you high?"

All she offered was a sad shrug.

"What's wrong, sweetie? Didn't you have fun today?" asked Pete.

"How come Mommy didn't come? We always go there together as a family."

"Mommy wanted to, but she just had to work, that's all."

The look on Kayla's face said she wasn't buying Pete's white lie. And with her next comments, she showed just how much this situation was affecting her.

"Are you and Mommy gonna get a divorce?"

Hearing Kayla say the D word caused Pete's eyes to widen and caused his tongue to go speechless. Ironically, Kayla might have been the first person to mention the D word to him in the past few months. It was one of those words that Doug and I had avoided using. I have to admit, it made me uncomfortable hearing her say it, so I know it must have freaked the shit out of Pete.

"Divorce? Who told you that?" he asked Kayla.

She shrugged then said, "Are you mad at Mommy because she made a big mistake?"

Again, his eyes widened and his lips quivered as he gave Kayla a puzzled look.

"I heard her talking on the phone with Auntie Susan."

Pete scrambled for words. "Umm, it's just complicated adult stuff, honey."

"If Lindsay or me make a big mistake will you divorce us too?"

My heart sank as I'm sure Pete's did too. I could tell he was fighting back tears. I watched as he scooched down in front of his daughter.

"Oh, pumpkin, is that why you're so sad today? I'm gonna love you girls no matter what mistakes you make. I'll always, always forgive you."

"Then why can't you forgive Mommy?"

It was official, Kayla had left both of us completely speechless. Luckily, we were saved by Lindsay and her new friends. They rushed over and asked Kayla to go on the merry-go-round with them. Reluctantly, she agreed and headed off with the other girls.

"What the fuck has Michelle been saying to her sister?"

I shot Pete a look and said, "Pete, come on. Just because you've been avoiding the topic, it doesn't mean it's not affecting everyone else."

Normally, Pete would have snapped at me, but he was still reeling from Kayla's comments.

"Can you believe that Kayla said that?"

"They might be young, but you'd be surprised how much they can sense what's going on."

Pete sadly shook head as he watched his girls on the merry-go-round.

23

"BULLET WITH BUTTERFLY WINGS" – Smashing Pumpkins

While Pete dropped the girls off to Michelle, I walked over to Hoohahs for a drink. I filled Doug in on what Kayla said. We were both in agreement that Pete needed to start facing this situation straight on rather than just ignoring it.

"I should get someone to cover Pete's shift tomorrow night and all three of us can go out. It's been awhile."

"Yea, it has. Let me get back to you on that. I'm not sure if I'm doing something with Krystal or not."

Doug simply rolled his eyes at me.

"What? You don't like Krystal, do you?"

"Nope. Not at all."

"Why, because she doesn't laugh at your jokes?" I asked.

"That's one of the reasons."

"Oh, just one of them? What are some of the other ones?"

Doug shrugged and said, "I just don't like her, that's all. You shoulda stuck with that Hayley chick. She was cool."

Doug was right, Hayley was cool, and I did have more in common with her than Krystal. There just wasn't that spark between us. You know, that "it" factor. I don't think she felt the spark either. I think that's why when it ended neither one of us were devastated or angry.

Krystal and I had only been seeing each other a couple of weeks, so I'm not saying she had that spark or the "it" factor either, not yet anyway. But so far so good.

I'd been down this road with Doug before, so the fact that he didn't like a girl I was seeing, didn't really bother me. We both dropped the subject of Krystal and went back to talking about Pete.

"Didn't you say he was coming back here after dropping the girls off?"

"I thought so," I answered.

"You think he and Michelle had a blowout?"

"Nah, not in front of the girls. Besides, I don't even think they've officially had a blowout since the affair."

"I was thinking the same thing. You know what that means, don't you? It means Pete is a ticking timebomb," said Doug.

No sooner did I nod in agreement, Pete stormed through the front door. I hadn't seen his face that flushed with anger since he had his hand on the throat of that hip-hop punk down at the basketball court years earlier.

Doug was the first to initiate. "Everything okay, big guy?"

"Of course. Why wouldn't it be? I have a wife who cheated on me, yet my girls seem to think I'm the fuckin' bad guy!" With that, he stormed into the bathroom.

"Kaboom goes the timebomb," said Doug, in full effect.

I slowly nodded. We both knew something big must have just went down. I turned to Doug and whispered, "You take Pete, I'll take Michelle."

We cared deeply about both of them and knew they were both going through a lot. At this point, it wasn't about taking sides, it was just about being there for them.

Later that night, Doug and I compared notes, and from everything Pete and Michelle had told us, this is how things went down earlier that day:

When Pete dropped the girls off, he asked them to go play upstairs in their rooms, so he could talk to Michelle in private. He then proceeded to tell Michelle about the conversation he had with Kayla at the playground.

"Kayla really said that?" said Michelle. "This is affecting them way more than I thought."

"Maybe you should have thought about that before you let what's-his-face stick his dick into you."

"Oh for Christ sake, Pete! How many times do I have to say I'm sorry? It was a stupid, stupid mistake, but I promise you, it meant nothing."

"It means something to me. And don't you think it's weird that you're constantly apologizing to me, yet you still work with him? Fuckin' twisted, if you ask me," he said a bit louder.

"Until I get accepted at another firm, I can't exactly quit now, can I? Besides, it's not like your new, little career choices are setting the world on fire."

Pete just shook his head and started for the door. Michelle felt guilty about her comment and switched gears, in hopes of working things out.

"I really wish you would reconsider counseling. Especially seeing how this is affecting the girls."

Pete stopped and turned back around and said, "Let me get this straight, you fuck around on me, and I'm the one who needs counseling?"

"Not just you… us," she clarified.

"Why don't you see if your little boy-toy will go with you. I'm sure that little wife-fucker needs it more than I do."

"Your sarcasm isn't helping here, Pete. And besides, what about you? You've always seemed very friendly with your little tattooed waitress."

"Are you fuckin' kidding me? Cat and I have never once crossed the line! Friendly conversations are all we've ever had. Period! Conversations I might add, that don't involve swapping spit or any other bodily fluids!"

"Yea, right. I'm sure by now she's offered to show you all of her hidden tattoos and piercings, huh?"

"Hey, don't reflect this onto me. I've never once cheated on you. Ever! Oh, by the way, I'm just curious, when you guys were doing it, did he leave those expensive shoes on?"

Michelle glared at him and said, "Sarcasm—still not helping."

"No? Well it's better than me driving over to his office and shoving my 7 iron up his fuckin' ass for coming onto my wife!"

"It wasn't like that," she said. "It wasn't his fault. It just sorta happened. You wouldn't understand."

"Oh, please, enlighten me, Michelle."

"This is not the time or place," she said, motioning upstairs towards the girls' rooms.

"Trust me, now is as good as it's gonna get because I'm sure as hell not doing this with a counselor."

Michelle didn't want to get into it, but she knew this conversation was long overdue.

"Fine," she said. "When I talk, he hears me."

"And I don't?" asked Pete.

"You listen, but you don't always hear. And yes, there's a difference. We're just able to have different conversations than you and I."

"What the fuck does that mean?"

"Pete, don't get upset. You asked me to explain, and I'm trying to. It just felt like the last year or so, we've been like two ships passing in the night. And no, I'm not saying that's your fault. It's just the way our schedules worked out. But when we were alone together, it felt like all of our conversations revolved around the girls, or bills, or house repairs, or how stressed I was with my classes, or how you hated your job… things just got so predictable."

"And that was my fault?"

"I didn't say that! I just don't think you realize how important it is for me to finally have a career. It feels like I pretty much went straight from college to marriage to kids… and no, I'm not complaining about that at all. I love being a Mom and a wife, but I just want something for myself too. And with David, we were able to talk about all kinds of different things, things that you and I haven't talked about in years. I guess I just liked the attention he was giving me, but obviously things went too far."

"Well, there you go, Michelle, looks like you finally found your soulmate."

"Pete," Michelle sighed in frustration.

It was at point, the timebomb known as Pete was about to go off.

"Let me tell YOU a few things," began Pete. "Things have gotten predictable for me too, ya know. And I'm sorry I don't talk about world events or lawyer type of stuff. But to be fair, I don't really get stimulated by your conversations either. You know, the ones you hit me with after a long, shitty day at work? '*Here's a list of things you need to do around the house. Here's a list of times you need to watch the girls. Here's a list of reasons why I'm too tired to have sex with you.*' I'm sorry I hated my career so much that I had to quit, but just so you know, I was miserable with my job long before I actually told you! I knew how important school and your career were to you, so I figured I'd just keep my mouth shut and suck it up. And I'm sorry you don't approve of my new job choices, and I'm sorry I'm not as accomplished or as well-dressed as your fuckin' David!"

Pete threw his hands up in the air and once again headed towards the front door.

"That's right, walk away and avoid things. Go have a few drinks at Hoohahs, just like you have been doing this past year."

"Don't even!!" Pete yelled, turning back around. "You're the one who fuckin' cheated on me, remember?!? And you're crazy if you think a stupid counseling session will ever wipe away the image I have of you and that asshole fuckin' behind my back!!!"

With tears forming in Michelle's eyes, she pleaded, "So, what are you saying? You're not willing to at least try and save our marriage?"

Coldly, Pete stared at Michelle and slipped off his ring.

"Who are we kidding, Michelle? We have no fuckin' marriage anymore!"

With that, Pete angrily whipped his ring across the room and then left, slamming the door behind him.

By the time I got to their house, Michelle was still in tears and on her hands and knees searching for Pete's ring. At first, I had no idea what to do or say, so I just stood there. It wasn't until she accidently knocked over a lamp that Kayla came downstairs and saw her mom frantically searching for something on the carpet.

"What are you looking for, Mommy?" she asked.

Michelle did her best to wipe away her tears and said, "Just a ring that Daddy lost."

"Want me to help you look?" asked Kayla.

"No, Kayla. Just go upstairs and check on your sister. She should be getting up from her nap soon."

"But I'm a really good finder-of-things," said Kayla, joining her mother on the floor.

"Kayla, I said go upstairs, NOW!"

Hearing her mother's anger, Kayla froze.

"Come on, kiddo," I said, "I'll go upstairs with you."

After I got Kayla settled in her room, I came back downstairs. Michelle had abandoned her search and sat in tears with her head in her hands. We made our way into the kitchen and sat. She poured herself a wine, and for the next hour we talked. Well, she did most of the talking, I mostly listened. I felt I was in no position to offer advice. I knew what she did was wrong, completely wrong, but my heart broke for both of them. So, the best I could do was nod and listen to her cry and vent.

"I know you and Doug are in a bad position, and I'm sorry for—"

"Michelle, it's okay. We care about both of you, and I just wish I knew how to make things better."

"I just want things to go back to the way they were," she

said.

"Me too," I said sympathetically. "Me too."

***

Usually, Doug was never at a loss for words, and he certainly never lacked advice, but even he found himself doing more listening than talking when it came to Pete. What happened between Pete and Michelle was horrible, but unfortunately, over the next week, ALL of our lives would take a turn for the worse.

Up to that point in our lives, usually only one of us at a time was in a crisis mode. This always allowed the other two of us to be rocks of support. That particular week, however, there were no rocks of support. We were all sinking fast, and with no one to throw us a life-preserver, our friendship would be tested greatly.

24

"I'M ONLY HAPPY WHEN IT RAINS" – Garbage

After Michelle and Pete's big fight, Doug strongly suggested that Pete take a couple of days off and spend it with Kayla and Lindsay. Pete knew his girls were caught in the middle of this mess, so he appreciatively took Doug up on his offer. He ended up taking his girls to Santa's Village and Storyland in the White Mountains.

At our coffeeshop the following morning, I filled Joanna in on Pete and Michelle's big blowup.

"As much as I complain about my dating life," she said, "I can't imagine being in their situation. And those poor kids being stuck in the middle."

I nodded and said, "Speaking of your dating life, how's that going?"

"I'm actually going on a date tomorrow night, and if it

doesn't work out, I think I'm gonna call it quits with the whole online dating thing."

"Smart move," I smiled.

"You and Krystal should totally double date with us. It'll take the pressure and awkwardness off a bit."

"I suppose we could do that," I said.

"How are things going with you guys anyway?" she asked.

"Eh, okay, I guess. We've only been seeing each other for a couple of weeks. The sex is really good though."

"Way to rub it in," she said. "I vaguely remember what it's like."

"Aww, I'm sorry, Joanna. Maybe this new guy will be the one."

"Maybe," she said. "But probably not."

***

Later that morning, while listening to one of my kickass 80's mixes, "White Wedding" by Billy Idol came on. Apparently, my expression caused Joanna to approach me and say, "The big wedding is coming up, huh?"

"What wedding?" I asked, playing dumb.

"Jane's wedding," she humored me.

"Oh… yea… that wedding. Ten more days."

"You're really not going?"

I didn't really want to get into this again, but I did anyway.

"I know everyone thinks I'm not going because I'm still hung up on her… but I'm not. In my heart, I know we're just not meant to ever be together. She made that crystal clear when she ditched me and left the ring."

Joanna gave me the all-too-familiar sympathetic look.

"But just because I realize we're not meant to be together, it doesn't make it any easier to watch her walk down the aisle with someone else."

Joanna put her hand on my hand and said, "I get it. I do."

"Well you're the only one who does. I keep getting shit from everyone for not going."

"You gotta do what's best for you," she said. "I promise, no more talking about it from me. Besides, we have a double-date to focus on, right?"

I gave her a nod and an appreciative smile. As much as I'd like to say that I put the impending Jane marriage out of my head, I hadn't. And like I told Joanna, even though I had long since come to terms with Jane, it didn't mean I was ready to see her walk down the aisle with someone else—someone she just met less than a year ago.

***

By the time our double-date night arrived, I was very much looking forward to it. A distraction from my over-active brain was very much welcomed. Not to mention, I was excited to see Krystal again. It had been a few nights since we were "together." I was also intrigued to see first-hand what Joanna's latest online date was like.

Unfortunately, I didn't get to experience any of those things that night. Even at age 34, life still had a way of kicking me in the nuts. Krystal called and told me she was sick in bed with the flu, so I was forced to cancel with Joanna. I was disappointed, but I think Joanna was even more so. I knew she was at the end of her rope with the whole internet dating thing.

I thought about hanging out at Hoohahs with Doug, but I

made the mistake of staying home alone instead. For the longest time, I just sat on my couch staring at Jane's wedding invitation. Did she really think I was going to go? Or was the invitation just one of those polite gestures people do? Considering the RSVP deadline was weeks earlier, I'm sure she realized that good ol' Josh Wentworth would not be attending.

I'm glad she didn't call and question me on my decision. It would have probably made for an awkward phone conversation, and more than likely, I would have caved under pressure and ended up telling her that I would go.

Thankfully, she never called to push the issue. Wait… why didn't she call and push the issue? She should have been beside herself with sadness that I never RSVP'd.

Before my twisted, fucked up mind over-analyzed this any further, I threw down the invitation and literally yelled out loud, "What the fuck am I doing?!?"

It was at that moment, the classic Stephen Stills song, "Love the One You're With" began playing in my head. "*If you can't be with the one you love, honey, love the one you're with.*"

That's exactly what I needed to be doing. Now I'm not saying I was in love with Krystal, because I wasn't, not at all. But the general gist of the song rang true. I needed to stop thinking about Jane and start concentrating on what I had—and at the moment, that would be Krystal! It's a sad day when a Stephen Stills' song is the thing that motivates me (no offense, Mr. Stills).

Either way, I got off my ass and headed over to Krystal's house, but not before picking up some supplies. At the grocery store, I bought a variety of cold & flu medications, a box of tissues, and a pint of Ben & Jerry's (New York Super Fudge Chunk). Next, I swung by the video store and rented The Lion

King and Beauty and the Beast. Definitely not my cup of tea, but what can I say, she was a huge Disney fan. Finally, I stopped at a local restaurant and bought her a steaming hot bowl good old-fashioned chicken noodle soup.

Operation - "Love the One You're With" was in full effect. So much so, that I found myself humming the song the whole way over to her apartment. As I walked up to her front door, that song was replaced with Nelly's "Hot in Herre." Not because I started humming it, and certainly not because I liked it, but it was because the song was loudly blaring from her apartment. So loud, in fact, no one even heard me knocking. I couldn't believe her idiot roommate was being so insensitive to her.

I remembered Krystal telling me her roommate was heavily into hip hop music and was an aspiring rapper. She often complained about him; about he would always leave his dirty dishes and dirty laundry strewn about the place. Or how she was disgusted by his lack of aiming skills when it came to the toilet. Unfortunately, she was also too shy to ever call him out on his cleanliness. Luckily for her, not only did I come bearing gifts, but I was going to give her the gift of standing up to her obnoxious roommate.

With cold remedies, ice cream, and piping hot soup in tow, I headed around towards the back door, and just as I suspected, the idiot roommate had left the rear sliding doors unlocked. I was never much of a confrontational type of guy, but I had been feeling a bit bold lately. Wannabe Eminem had no idea what he was in for. I was about to go all Ice Cube on his ass!

As I entered their apartment, it quickly became apparent that homeboy was "entertaining" a lady friend. (So, yea, he was banging her.) All I could see was his white-as-snow ass with her legs wrapped tightly around him. I was in quite the quandary here. I mean, even though I was feeling bold and determined, I didn't really want to interrupt him right in the middle of sex. There's gotta be a guy code for that somewhere.

As 50 Cent's "In the Club" came on, I decided to discretely head into poor Krystal's bedroom and deal with Puff Daddy later. Unfortunately for me, I only took one step before I heard him loudly moan.

"Oh yea, baby!" he said. "I fuckin' love being so deep in you, Krystal."

I stopped dead in my tracks. The proverbial needle scratched across the record, and all went quiet. For a brief moment, I thought (hoped)((prayed)) his girlfriend was *also* named Krystal… just a weird, strange coincidence, that's all.

"I want you so deep that your balls are in me," she yelled in pleasure.

Her familiar voice caused me to drop the bag of remedies—which caused him to stop mid-pump—which caused her to peer around him at me.

Nope, not a weird, strange coincidence, it was indeed *my* Krystal.

Her face went white (as white as his ass), and she embarrassingly exclaimed, "Josh?!?"

This caused me to drop the other bag, which contained the soup. The impact caused the soup to splash up on my bare leg. I did mention the soup was piping hot, right?

Needless to say, I was feeling neither bold nor confrontational. I just wanted to get the fuck out of there. For a reason which I can't explain, before I left, I bagged up the scattered remedies (minus the soup) and then bolted.

25

"LOSER" – Beck

I could have easily gone home and wallowed in my misery for the rest of the night, but I didn't. I decided to go straight to Hoohahs and wallow to my friends.

Well, if we're still doing this honesty thing, I *might* have made a quick pit stop to my house, and I *might* have lit a quick sacrificial fire.

Seeing as there wasn't that much to burn, I only used a quarter of a bottle of lighter fluid. I tossed in the cold and flu medications and then the box of tissues. I even tossed in the two stupid Disney movies. Yes, I was fully aware the video store would make me pay full price for them, but trust me, it was well worth it. I was even going to burn the fuckin' pint of Ben & Jerry's, but, well… New York Super Fudge Chunk was one of my favorite flavors, so I decided to eat it as I watched the fire burn out.

As soon as it was totally out, I headed over to Hoohahs. Usually, I would just sit there, staring at my beer and frequently sigh (loudly). This would cause Doug and Pete to ask me what was wrong, to which I would sigh again and say, *Nothing*. It was usually after they asked for the third or fifth time that I finally revealed what was on my mind.

On that night, however, there were no sighing or hesitation games to be played. As a matter of fact, before Doug could even slide me a beer, I was blurting out the events of my night. Once I started, I couldn't stop. I filled them in on every detail of my miserable night. I was so self-consumed, that I didn't even bother to ask Pete how his trip was to the White Mountains with his girls, nor did I ask how things were going with Michelle. But to be fair, why would I? I had just seen a girl I thought I was dating, getting banged by some dude with bad taste in music. My eyes were still burning from seeing things I couldn't unsee. My ears were also burning from hearing his crappy music… and their moaning… and… their dirty talk.

Doug sympathetically put his hand on my shoulder, paused a moment then said, "Dude, did she really ask him to go balls deep into her?"

All I could do was slowly nod.

"We're sorry, bro," said Doug.

"Yea, we're sorry," echoed Pete.

I was glad I showed up at Hoohahs and vented to my friends. It was a much better choice than having a giant depression session in my darkened house. It was also a good choice to suggest that we all go on a long, overdue walkabout. Sadly, that's where my good choices ended.

Less than ten minutes into our walkabout, I mighta, sorta compared my situation to Pete's. I believe my exact words were: "I guess I know exactly how you feel, Pete. Both of our women cheated on us. Although, I actually walked in on the act… that's probably worse."

And I believe Pete's exact words were: "Are you fuckin' kidding me? Our situations are nothing alike! Michelle and I have been together over ten years, and you and what's-her-name just met a few weeks ago!"

"Cheating is cheating, right?" I stated.

"No, not right. Not by a long shot," he huffed.

I needed to try and save face here. For whatever fucked up reason, I needed to show that my life was just as shitty as his. Sometimes I'm competitive in the most fucked up ways possible.

"And you're also forgetting that I'm dealing with my ex-girlfriend getting married this weekend. Right here on the beach… our beach… less than a year after she ended our engagement."

Pete slowed his pace and shook his head and said, "You really are pathetic, aren't you?"

"I'm pathetic?" I repeated.

Just then, Doug interrupted us. "Jesus Christ! Both of you shut the fuck up! First of all, Pete's right, you can't compare your little bimbo cheating to Pete and Michelle."

Pete smiled and gloated, "Thank you."

"And you," Doug said, looking at Pete. "You're just as pathetic."

"What are you talking about?" asked Pete.

"You need to make a decision, my friend. Either forgive Michelle and move on or DON'T. What she did was wrong, totally wrong, but ever since you've moved in with me, all you do is bitch and moan. So, either forgive and move forward or don't and move on! By you constantly giving her guilt trips and sarcastic remarks… well… that's just childish, dude."

"Childish?" laughed Pete. "That's a funny word coming from the poster boy for childish. A different girl every week, never committing to anyone… you have no clue what it's like to be in a real relationship. What's your relationship record, three weeks?"

I chuckled at Pete's spot-on observation.

"What are you laughing at?" he shot my way. "What's your record, three months? Oh, wait, I forgot about your thirteen-year imaginary relationship with Jane."

This time it was Doug's turn to chuckle at Pete's comment.

"You're both fuckin' assholes, do you know that?" I said pissed.

"Hey, I'm just pointing out the facts," said Pete. "The point is, neither of you know what it takes to make a marriage work."

"And obviously neither do you," mumbled Doug.

"I'm gonna pretend I didn't hear that," said Pete.

"I could say it louder, if you want?"

Doug's sarcastic comment cut Pete to the core, which I suppose was the point.

Pete turned to Doug and clenched his fists. For a second, I thought there was going to be a major throw down. Instead, Pete controlled his urge to punch Doug and simply said, "Fuck you! Fuck you both! And don't worry, you won't hear me bitchin' and moanin' anymore. I'll stay at a fuckin' hotel!"

With that, Pete abruptly ended his walkabout and stormed off in the opposite direction. Doug and I hesitantly continued on but not another word was spoken. Not until Doug pointed out, "And for the record, I warned you about that Krystal chick. I told you I had a feeling about her. For the record."

"You can be a real fuckin' dick sometimes... for the record."

That's all it took for me to turn and also head the other way.

We've had arguments with each other before, some more contentious than others, but very rarely were we all pissed at each other at the same time. As far as I could remember, that was the first time one of our walkabouts ended that abruptly, that angrily. And make no doubt about it, I was angry.

I mumbled and murmured to myself the rest of the way back to my car. What was I thinking confiding and venting to my friends about Krystal—or Jane, for that matter? I should have gone straight home and vented to myself—to my Cusack poster—to my music. Yup, that's all I really needed anyway. Fuck my friends and their negative vibes! And for the record, my longest relationship was 107 days, NOT three months!

26

"SOME STREETS LEAD NOWHERE" – Matthew Ryan

Okay, let's recount the last 72 hours, shall we?

1. Pete and Michelle got into a giant fight where he took off his ring and threw it across the room.
2. I walked in on Krystal getting pounded by her hip-hop roommate.
3. I was dealing with the impending Jane wedding.
4. Doug, Pete, and I had a huge blowup and were no longer talking to each other.

Unfortunately, our shitty week was just getting started. The morning after our walkabout disaster, I was in no mood to fully tell Joanna about the previous night. I promised her at some point I'd fill her in on the details, but I left her with these little nuggets: Krystal and I were over, and Doug, Pete, and myself were no longer on speaking terms.

I could tell her curiosity was piqued, but there was no way I was ready to delve into details. I briefly got her sidetracked when I asked her about her date. Joanna was also not in the mood to reveal details. She simply left me with: "He made Ear Wax Picasso seem like a good catch."

"Wow. I'm sorry, Joanna."

"It's okay. It is what it is, right? I tell you what though, if you ever run out of writing ideas, you can always write about my online dating experiences."

"I'll keep that in mind," I laughed.

I think that was the last time I would laugh that week. Less than a minute later, the front door opened. I looked up to greet the new customer, but the words failed to exit my mouth, and all I could do was stand there, frozen. Joanna looked from my expressionless face to the front door, and there, in the flesh, was Jane.

My mesmerized, speechless state was broken when I heard an excited voice from behind Jane say, "Josh!"

It was Jane's younger sister, Molly. She was seven years younger than Jane, and it had been years since I had seen her. Molly rushed over and gave me a hug.

"Molly Wheeler? Wow, look at you. You're like all grown up now."

"I think the last time you saw me I had those stupid braces on. I told you I'd be hot one day!"

"Oh God, Molly, get over yourself," said Jane.

After we all had a quick laugh, Jane hesitantly approached me and gave me a hug. Jane and I had a lot of hugs over the years, but that particular one was in the top three for its awkwardness.

I was briefly saved from the awkwardness when Molly said, "So, this is your new place? I frickin' love it!"

"Yea, it's really great, Josh," said Jane. "I'm really happy for you."

I couldn't help but wonder, did she want me to return that phrase to her? Was she expecting me to tell her how happy I was for her too? I didn't really have the chance to think too long on this because Joanna made her way over, greeted Jane and offered her own congratulations. Jane introduced her to Molly, which was followed by Joanna giving them a visual tour of the place.

Jane and Molly gazed around at all of the cool décor on the walls. From the classic movie and band posters to the small section of vinyl records in the corner—they were all smiles. Their excitement and positive comments briefly provided an escape from the obvious awkwardness. The escape would be short-lived, however.

"So, where's this fiancé of yours?" asked Joanna.

Who the fuck cares where he is, said the little voice in my head. Not out loud, of course.

"Oh, he had to make a phone call, he should be right—"

Before she could finish her sentence, the front door opened, and right on cue, entered Jane's fiancé, Brett. I wanted to throw up. I suppose on the bright side, he didn't look like I had pictured. He wasn't a Pitt/Clooney/Depp combination, not at all. As a matter of fact, he was pretty average looking. Maybe slightly above average, at best. Not that I'm good at judging guys' looks or anything, just sayin'.

Jane started with Joanna first. "Brett, this is Joanna. She is one the owners here."

They shook hands and my heart beat faster, knowing full-well I was up next.

"And this is Josh. He also owns this place."

I quickly wiped the sweat from my palm and shook his hand. I made it a point to straighten up, and I put a little extra grip in the hand shake. Stupid, I know. What was I going to do next, grab a tape and have a dick-measuring contest? Guys can be such idiots—*I* can be such an idiot.

"Nice to finally meet you, Josh. I've heard a lot about you."

What the hell did that mean? What exactly did Jane tell him? Did she tell him we used to date? Did she tell him that I proposed to her and that she semi-accepted? Did she tell him about ditching me and leaving the ring and a note on the sill? Did she tell him about the time we had sex in the bathroom at Applebees? Or the handjob she gave me at the Depeche Mode concert?

Yea, she probably left those out.

Molly interrupted my train of thought when she declared to Brett, "Josh is one of the best and nicest guys in the world."

"Geesh," said Brett, "looks like you've got quite the fan club."

"Aww, you're a great guy too, Brett," said Molly. "Hey, Josh, remember on my sixteenth birthday when I got wasted at my friends party at the beach? I called you and you came and picked me up right before the cops showed up. You took care of me all night until Jane got there. Sorry again for hurling on your car door… and your living room rug."

"And my couch," I smiled. "But who's counting."

"See, Brett, I told you, one of the best guys in the world," boasted Molly.

We all reminisced a bit and made small talk, and as much as

I wanted to hate Brett, I couldn't. Truthfully, he seemed like a nice guy. Not as nice as me, but still, he made it hard for me to hate him. That being said, it was still quite awkward seeing them together. Him calling her hun—his arm around her—holding her hand. Her hand, I might add, that had a huge rock on it. It dwarfed what I originally had given her.

The real awkward moment came when Jane said, "Hey, when I talked to Michelle on the phone last week, she told me you're seeing someone. How's that going?"

Out of the corner of my eye, I could see Joanna trying to signal her not to broach the subject. It was too late, and with all eyes on me, I panicked and did my babbling thing.

"I walked in on her with another guy… a naked guy… listening to 50 Cent. She asked him to go balls deep in her, and I dropped hot soup and burned my leg. So, to answer your question, things aren't really going so well with her."

It was as if you could hear a pin drop. Everyone continued to stare, yet no one quite knew how to respond to that. Finally, it was Molly who joked, "Which 50 Cent song?"

Her comment lessened the mood long enough for Joanna to jump in and ask what they all wanted to drink. She took their order, and I made sure she put it on the house. Brett offered me to join them at their table, but I made up some excuse about having some stuff to get done in the back.

Before I walked off, Brett said, "We'll definitely have to talk more at the reception, Josh. You need to give me as much dirt as you can on Jane. You never know when it'll come in handy."

I politely smiled and looked over at Jane. It was apparent that she hadn't told Brett that I wasn't planning on attending the wedding. I was feeling more and more like a jackass every minute.

27

"SOMETHING I CAN NEVER HAVE" – Nine Inch Nails

Throughout the rest of the day, I could tell Joanna wanted to ask how I was doing. She knew I was having a shit week, and I'm sure she was still curious about what went down with Pete and Doug. She also knew if I wanted to talk about it, I would. I appreciated her giving me space.

Seeing as I still wasn't on speaking terms with my friends, I decided to forgo my nightly beer at Hoohahs. I grabbed a six-pack at Cumbies then picked up some Chinese takeout over at Green Leaves. Cheap beer, Kung Pao Chicken, and the Red Sox on TV; that's all I needed that night.

Unfortunately, the Red Sox were getting blown out 11 – 3, so by the 5th inning, the volume went down and Depression Session (Vol. 13) went up.

As I tipped back my fourth beer, and as "Something I can

Never Have" by Nine Inch Nails played on my stereo, my gaze was focused on my Jane Memorabilia Box. My gaze was rudely interrupted by the ringing of my phone. It would have been way too creepy if it was Jane. And by creepy, I mean, serendipitous. I hopefully glanced at the caller ID.

It wasn't Jane.

It wasn't serendipitous.

It was Doug.

He probably wanted to apologize for being a dick. His apology would have to wait, for I was right in the middle of reflecting—reminiscing—wallowing? Okay, okay, feeling sorry for myself.

I ignored his call and walked over and retrieved the box. The first thing I pulled out was the fuckin' note Jane left me a year ago before she bolted. Yes, I saved the note. What can I say, I'm a glutton for punishment. In the folds of the note, I had carefully placed the ring. Who the hell would be pathetic enough to not only save a note like that, but to tuck the ring in it? That would be me! That fuckin' pathetic person would be me.

I held the ring in my hand and just stared, but once again, my misery would be interrupted by the ringing of my phone. And once again, it was Doug.

"Fine, fine, fine, fine!!!" I yelled aloud. I would let him apologize so I could get back to my wallowing.

"Hello," I said with a slight attitude.

"Hey, bro. How's it going?" he said with more than a slight slur. "I was thinking maybe we could hang out tonight. I could really, really use a—"

It was quickly apparent that he wasn't calling to apologize. I bet Pete still wasn't talking to him either, and he probably just called me to be his wingman, or more likely, he wanted me to be his driver to a fuckin' strip club.

"You could really use a what?" I snapped. "A trip to Kittens? Seriously, dude, don't you think it's about time you grow the fuck up?"

I didn't wait for his drunken, sarcastic response, I simply hung up the phone and returned to my own drinking. Little did I know at the time, but Doug didn't call me to be his wingman or to even take him to a strip club. As a matter of fact, as bad as my last 24 hours seemed, it was nothing compared to Doug's day—or Pete's, for that matter. Soon enough, I would feel very guilty for not hanging out with Doug that night like he wanted.

It wasn't long after Doug's call that I ended up going to bed. I might have been in the midst of a classic depression session, but I knew I had to get up bright and early to open the shop. You can't really call out when you're the owner. It sucks when responsibility gets in the way of my misery. What sucks even more, is when my misery gets in the way of being there for my friends, especially when they need me the most.

28

"THE HARDEST WALK" – Jesus & Mary Chain

The next morning, I reluctantly climbed out of bed and headed into work. As usual, one of my opening girls was twenty minutes late, and as usual, it was a lame excuse. It was Joanna's day off, but she came in around nine-ish. She claimed she just wanted to grab a coffee and do some computer work. Personally, I think she was just checking in on me, making sure yesterday's Jane sighting didn't beat me down too much.

When she said, "I'll be over in the corner doing some work," what she was really saying was, *if you need to vent, let me know*. I didn't end up venting, but I was very appreciative of her friendship. I still found it mind-boggling that someone like her was still single.

When it slowed down, and when our workers had it under control, I grabbed a coffee and joined Joanna. I still wasn't in the mood to talk about Jane, or Krystal, or anything for that matter. We were in the process of expanding our hours to later in the evening. One of Joanna's friends, Kelli, was going to be our evening barista/manager. Kelli was Joanna's age and they had worked together at Breaking New Grounds. Supposedly, Kelli was a barista-extraordinaire. She also had a ton of cool ideas for us to try out. Things were really starting to take off for our business. At least one thing in my life was going well.

My self-pity was about to be put in check, however. Around 10 AM, Pete entered our shop. As he slowly made his way over to us, he seemed to be in a daze.

He forced a slight smile and said, "Hey, guys."

His look and tone told me something was wrong.

"Is everything okay?" I asked. When he hesitated, I said, "Are the girls okay?"

"Yea, they're fine. It's Doug."

"What about Doug?" I asked.

"I guess he went out drinking in Portsmouth last night by himself and proceeded to get totally shit-faced."

"Of course he did," I laughed, shaking my head.

"At some point in the night, he picked a fight with not one, but three dudes at the bar. Apparently, they waited for him outside and ended up kicking the shit out of him."

"Oh my God!" exclaimed Joanna. "Is he okay?"

"He spent the night in the hospital and got released this morning."

"How did you hear about it?" asked Joanna.

Pete let out a guilty sigh and said, "He tried calling me last night, but I was kind of in the middle of something, so I didn't bother answering. And when he tried calling back a few minutes later, I just shut my ringer off for the night. When I turned it back on this morning, there were multiple messages from him, including one from the hospital around 2 AM."

"He called me last night too," I said. "I think he was well on his way to being drunk. I really didn't want to deal with him, so… so I just hung up."

"Josh!" Joanna said, giving me a glare.

"What? He only called us because he probably couldn't find anyone else to get drunk with. This is exactly what Pete and I were telling him the other night. He needs to start growing the hell up, right?" I said, looking for confirmation from Pete.

Pete paused then said, "I think he was just calling us so we could be there for him. Doug found out yesterday that his father passed away."

"Oh no. Poor Doug," Joanna sympathetically said.

I would explain to her later about Doug's dad and about their relationship, or lack thereof. Doug hadn't seen his father in nearly thirty years, and even though Doug was always bitter about this, I'm sure he was still devastated about the news.

"Oh, man, I feel like shit now," I said. "I can't believe I hung up on him. I just thought he wanted to go out drinking or hit a strip club or something."

"I know," nodded Pete, "I feel like shit too."

"You said he's home now?" I asked.

"Yea. When I called him a little bit ago, he said his mom gave him a ride home from the hospital."

"Christ, he must have been desperate to call his mom to come get him at the hospital."

Pete nodded then said, "Do you wanna head over there with me?"

I looked over to Joanna and she sweetly said, "Go. I'll stay for the day."

"You sure?"

"Of course. Give him my best, okay?"

I nodded then quickly headed out with Pete.

***

When we got to Doug's place, he was laying on the couch with an ice pack on his bruised face. His eye was black and blue, and his lip was all busted up and swollen.

"Jesus, dude, you look like shit," joked Pete.

"Ha, trust me, I look a hundred percent better than I did when they brought me in last night."

"I'm sorry, man, we shoulda been there for you. You needed us and we let you down."

"Don't sweat it," he said. "Not a big deal."

"It is a big deal!" I said, raising my voice. "I've been so consumed with my own stupid life that I've lost sight of the people that truly matter. You guys were right, I always make too big of a deal about my silly problems."

Doug removed his ice pack and said, "I was out of line the other night. I know how much you care about Jane, and how you always pictured it would be you that she would marry. This whole wedding thing has to suck for you. I should have been more sensitive to that."

Pete looked my way and agreed with Doug.

"And you were right, Pete, I have no clue what it's like to be married or to be in a serious relationship, for that matter. Hell, I probably never will," Doug said, returning the ice to his face.

Pete slowly shook his head and said, "No, Doug, you were the one who was right. Either I forgive Michelle and we move on together, or I don't and I move on without her." Pete took a long pause then said, "Although... that's kind of the least of our worries now."

Doug and I looked at each other, wondering what Pete was referring to. Doug spoke first.

"Oh my God, dude, you banged Cat, didn't you?"

"What? No!" Pete quickly answered.

After I shot Doug a stern look, Pete again took a long pause before continuing.

"Michelle had a doctor's appointment the other day, and they told her—"

"Holy shit!" interrupted Doug. "She's pregnant?"

"Jesus, Doug! Let Pete finish." I looked over to Pete then hesitantly asked, "She's not pregnant, is she?"

"Pete's face was deadpan as he quietly said, "There were some abnormalities in her blood work, and... they also found a lump."

Both Doug and I sat there stunned, and after a few minutes, I said, "Is it..."

"They don't know yet. They're running more tests. She has hospital appointments all week."

Between Doug's dad passing and hearing about Michelle, my problems were certainly put into perspective.

"That's why I didn't take any calls last night," Pete said to Doug. "Michelle was right in the middle of telling me when you called."

Now I felt like even more of an asshole. At least Pete had a good reason for ignoring Doug's calls. I hung up on the poor guy just because I didn't want to be bothered. It was at this point, the usually stoic Pete, started to get emotional.

"I... I have no idea how to tell the girls. They're only four and eight, for Christ sake. How am I supposed to explain this?"

"Whoa, whoa, whoa," I said. "There's no reason to tell them anything right now. You need to think positive thoughts."

"Josh is right. Just wait for the final test results."

I think Doug sensed the heaviness of the moment because he quickly switched gears and tried to lighten the mood. He filled us in on the details of his bar fight, as much as he could remember anyway. He also claimed one of the nurses was flirting with him all night in the hospital. He said he would have gotten her number, but she said she couldn't because of hospital policy—kind of like the same policy that strippers have, he pointed out. For the moment, anyway, the mood was lightened.

"I'm not sure where you've been staying this week," said Doug, "but you know you're welcome to come back here?"

"Thanks," said Pete, "but I think I'm gonna crash on the couch back at home. I need to be closer to my girls right now."

He didn't specify, but we knew he was referring to all three of his girls.

"Hey, why don't you guys let me run the bar for the next few nights," I said. "I think you both could use some time off."

"Aren't you guys open at night now?" asked Pete.

"Yea, but it'll be fine. I'll take the early morning shifts, and Joanna and Kelli can handle the rest of the day."

"Thanks, Josh, but —"

"There's no buts, I'm doing it."

Both Doug and Pete gave me an appreciative smile.

29

"SOMETIME AROUND MIDNIGHT" – The Airborne Toxic Event

After I left Doug's house, I went back and told Joanna what was going on. She was more than willing to help out in any way possible. So, true to my word, I took over bar duties at Hoohahs for the next few nights. It felt pretty good being back behind the bar, and even better knowing I was helping out my friends. I suppose I shouldn't have been shocked, but on my first night there, Doug showed up around 10-ish.

"Dude, what are you doing here?" I said. "I told you I would handle things."

"Oh, I'm not here to work," he smiled, planting his ass on the stool at the bar. "I was just bored sitting at home by myself."

I shook my head, smirked, then began to pour him a draft.

"Actually, I think I'll just have a ginger ale," he said.

Knowing this was probably a good choice, I poured him a ginger ale. Just as I handed him his drink, Joanna entered and sat next to him.

"Hey," she said, trying not to stare at the cuts and bruises on his face.

Doug broke the ice with, "You should see the other guys."

"Oh yea?" she smiled.

"Eh, not really. I was so loaded that I don't even think I landed a punch."

She continued to smile as she shook her head and said, "What are we gonna do with you?"

"We've been asking that for years now," I joked, handing a Joanna a red wine.

"Hey! No making fun of the customers," said Doug.

Joanna took a sip of her wine then turned to Doug and sympathetically said, "I'm really sorry about your dad."

"It is what it is."

Joanna and I both knew his sarcasm was just how he coped with things. I think we also both knew, that even though their relationship had been non-existent for years, the news of his father's death definitely affected Doug more than he was letting on.

"I meant to ask you," I said, "how did you find out?"

Doug laughed and said, "My step-mother called me. That's right, apparently, I have a step-mother. Who knew?"

"Wow," was all I could say.

"No shit. I guess they got married a few years ago."

"Are you gonna go?" Joanna asked out of the blue.

"Go where? To the funeral? No fuckin' way!"

I was a little surprised that Joanna continued her line of questioning.

"It's none of my business, but I really think you should go. Despite everything, he's still your dad."

"Biologically only," he pointed out.

"Like I said, I know it's none of my business, but I just think if you don't go, you'll regret it one day."

"Yea, yea, yea," he said. "That's what my mom says. Can you believe it, if my mom's health wasn't so bad, she would actually consider flying down to the funeral. Fuckin' insane if you ask me."

For the moment, Joanna sat and quietly drank her wine and relented on any more comments regarding his father. It quickly became apparent that the whole thing was still on Doug's mind.

"Besides," he said, "I'm sure it's not gonna be that big of a deal. I can't imagine he had too many friends. The only people who'll probably be there are his *new wife* and maybe some of his drinking buddies. I'd just feel out of place anyway."

I knew Doug all-too-well. In his heart, I think he really did want to go, but I also believed him when he said he'd feel out of place. So, knowing that he would never go alone, I decided to help my best friend out and volunteer to go down to Texas with him. I figured I could get a hold of Taylor and have her run the bar while we were gone. Before I had a chance to present my offer, Joanna spoke up and beat me to it.

"I'll go with you," she said. "You know, for moral support."

Doug and I were equally stunned.

"You will? Why would you do that?" he asked.

"I lost my mom when I was thirteen. I was lucky enough to have my friends and family help me through it. There's no way I could have gotten through it alone. I know your situation is different, and you two weren't very close —"

"At all!" he specified.

"I just think this is the perfect opportunity to maybe get some closure. And I really, really think you'll regret it one day if you don't go."

Joanna completely stole my thunder and my offer, but she was 100% right, Doug needed to go.

"But… but if Josh is helping out here, won't you guys be short at the coffeeshop?"

"Not at all," said Joanna. "My friend Kelli is amazing, and she would love the extra hours."

Doug looked over at me and I nodded in agreement with Joanna.

"You'd really go with me?" he asked.

Again, she sweetly smiled and said, "Yea, I really would."

For a brief moment, as they both smiled at each other, it sort of felt like there was something there—something more than just a friendly gesture. A spark maybe? Nahhhhh! There was no way. I worked with Joanna every day, and I would know if she had a thing for Doug. And we all know Doug didn't have an edit button, so if he had a thing for Joanna, he would have surely told me, right?

Then again, I was kind of clueless about Jane—and Krystal—and probably a handful of other girls, so maybe I'm not the best judge. But Joanna and Doug??? Noooooo way!

Either way, Joanna was going to accompany Doug down to Texas. As a matter of fact, they ended up flying out first thing the next morning, leaving me to run both businesses.

I'm not going to say the next few days in Texas completely changed Doug's life, but I will say, it was a much needed and important moment in his life. A little later on I'll fill you in on the details of their trip. For now, I was focused on running both businesses while trying my best to be there for Pete and Michelle. I felt pretty helpless though, and besides a quick check on them, I figured it was best to give them space. I made sure they knew if they needed anything to let me know.

So, with Doug and Joanna in Texas, and with Pete and Michelle dealing with their own things, it left me with time to attempt to deal with that girl named Jane Wheeler. I still thought that not going to the wedding was a smart move. I didn't need to put myself through that. I was, however, a little surprised that she hadn't called or stopped by to try and convince me to go. I suppose she had more important things to concentrate on, and it was probably high-time I realized I was no longer on her priority list. The good thing about working so many hours, was it took my mind off of all of these things. Not completely, but still, work proved to be a great distraction.

On the eve of Jane's wedding, Pete swung by Hoohahs. It was the first time I had seen him face to face since Doug left. My first impulse was that he had bad news to share.

After a few minutes of trivial conversation, I hesitantly asked, "Any word on…"

"No, not yet," he said somberly. "We have an appointment first thing Monday morning, so hopefully we'll get some answers. The not knowing is the worst."

"I'm sure," I said. "How's Michelle holding up?"

Pete shrugged and said, "Even though I'm back at home, our conversations are still few and far between - mostly small talk concerning the girls."

Sadness poured out of Pete's face, and I knew the weight of the past year was destroying him.

"Hey, seeing as I we have plenty of help here tonight, why

don't you and I go shoot some hoops?" He remained sullen and stone-faced but managed to slowly nod at my suggestion.

It was just after ten when we arrived at the courts. Besides a couple of horny, immature teenage boys trying to show off for their girls, we had the court to ourselves. And yes, I realize that once upon a time, *we* were those horny, immature teenagers.

As we watched the boys obnoxiously flirt with the girls, there was no doubt in my mind, that at this point in our lives, all three of us guys would give anything to be back in their shoes again.

Young, dumb, wild and carefree—those were the days. And the problems we thought we had back then, absolutely paled in comparison to now. As the girls laughed at the boys' idiotic antics, I knew Pete was thinking the same thing as me. At any moment, I expected one of us to yell out, *Enjoy it all now because one day it'll suck beyond belief!*

Don't worry, we didn't yell or say anything. Besides, they would have just laughed at us—as we would have when we were them. Nothing much was spoken for the first five minutes or so, we just quietly shot around. Eventually, the three boys moved to *phase 2*, as they entered the playground with the girls. As they walked by us, we gave them a little nod. It was as if we were offering them a mental high-five and saying, *Good luck, boys. May the York Beach force be with you.*

When we had the courts to ourselves, things really got heavy. Pete grabbed the rebound of one of my misses, and he just stood there, holding and staring at the ball. Finally, he looked over at me and spoke.

"Where did it all go wrong?"

I had no idea what to say. The easy answer would have been

to say, *When she cheated on you,* but we both knew it went deeper than that.

It was as if he read my thoughts because the next words out of his mouth were, "The affair wasn't the cause of our problems, it was just the effect. Of course, it's the effect that won't let me move past it and forgive her."

I continued to say nothing. I stood quietly by as Pete let it all out.

"There's nothing I want more than to be able to forgive her and just move on with our marriage. The sad thing is, I know I played a role in pushing her to this point, the point she needed to turn to someone else for attention. In my heart, I know how much she regrets what she did, and I know it wasn't based on her fallen in love with him, or her not wanting to be with me anymore. And to be honest, Josh, I kinda get where she was coming from, and I think I can forgive her, I really do, but…"

Again, Pete stared long and hard at the basketball in his hands before continuing.

"But there's a huge difference between forgiving and forgetting, and I don't think I'll ever forget that image I created in my head of my wife fucking someone else. So, until that happens, how in the hell am I supposed to move on?"

All I could offer was a shrug. I literally had no clever words or wise advice for him.

Pete shot the ball, and as I rebounded it, he said, "What if she does have cancer? And what if I still can't forgive and forget? That kind of makes me like a giant asshole, doesn't it?"

By this point, tears were slowly running down his cheek. My heart was breaking for my friend, for everyone involved actually.

"And the girls," he said. "This whole thing is so unfair to them. They're so young and innocent, and all they want is for us to be a happy family again. What if that never happens?"

I walked over to him and said, "I'm so sorry, Pete. I wish I knew the right words to say."

It was almost like he didn't even hear me. He was just standing there, staring out towards the ocean. I could tell his wheels were spinning and that he had more to say.

"I've been sleeping down on the couch the last few nights," he began, "and at some point this morning, I felt these little hands gently trying to wake me up. It was Kayla. I looked over at the clock. It was barely 5 AM. I was like, 'Kayla, what are you doing up so early?' She just stood there smiling at me. 'What are you smiling at, honey?' I asked. She leaned in and whispered, 'I found it, Daddy.' 'Found what, sweetie?' 'I found the ring you lost. The one Mommy has been looking for.' "

Pete clutched the basketball tightly then continued.

"Kayla pulled her little hand out from behind her back, revealing my wedding ring that I whipped across the house last week. She had this sad, yet hopeful look on her face as she said, 'Now Mommy can stop crying, right? And you can come back home for good, right?' It was all I could do not to burst out in tears. I just lay there, frozen, staring at the ring in her innocent little hand. When I didn't say or do anything, she carefully slid the ring on my pinkie finger. She then gave me a hug and whispered, 'Don't lose it again, Daddy. It was really hard to find. Luckily, I'm a good finder-of-things.' She kissed my forehead and scampered back up to bed."

Pete nervously fidgeted with the ball then said, "I wish it were that simple. I wish by me putting my ring back on, it could make it all better."

Over the next few minutes, nothing else was spoken by either of us. A light mist began to fall, and as the fog slowly rolled in, the courts felt eerily quiet. Even the playground was silent. I guess the guys and girls had moved onto *phase 3* (a walk on the beach).

"Well, I think I'm gonna take off," Pete said. "You?"

"I might shoot around a little while longer," I said.

Before Pete left, he turned to me and said, "I take it you're still not going tomorrow… to the wedding?"

I shrugged and shook my head no.

"You do know Michelle and I are both going, right?"

I nodded.

"I can totally bail if you wanna hang out or whatever."

"It's okay, man. You guys have known Jane just as long as I have. You should go. I appreciate it though."

"If you change your mind, let me know. Just promise me you're not gonna pull your shades, light candles, and crank up The Smiths."

"Nah, don't worry about me," I laughed.

Pete got halfway to his car then yelled, "And that includes The Cure as well!"

My friends knew me all too well. I ended up shooting around for another twenty minutes or so, and if I may say, I was on fire. At one point, I think I nailed a dozen 3-pointers in a row—at least five anyway. My hot streak ended when a car pulled into the space directly behind the basket and its headlights blinded my eyes. With a whole empty parking lot at their disposal, why would this moron park there? It wasn't until the car was shut off, and the person exited, that I realized the moron in question was none other than Jane.

"I thought that was you," she said, climbing over the

guardrail. “Ahh, late night hoops. Some things never change, huh?”

I could have listed at least five things that had indeed changed, but I didn’t. I just politely smiled.

“We just finished the rehearsal dinner a little while ago. I’m on my way back to the hotel. We’re all staying at the Union Bluff.”

I did my best to offer small talk.

“How are your parents doing?”

She brushed off my attempt and went straight to what was on her mind.

“I’m sorry we showed up unannounced at your place the other day.”

“It’s okay.”

“And I’m really sorry about that girl you were dating. You deserve better. I hope you know that?”

I took a few dribbles and shrugged.

“And I’m also sorry for —”

“Jane, seriously, you don’t need to apologize.”

“I just don’t want to hurt you more than I already have.”

I laughed and said, “I think I do a fine job of that on my own. Besides, you shouldn’t be worrying about me. Tomorrow is your big day. Brett seems like a great guy.”

“He is, and he treats me like gold. Not that you didn’t,” she quickly pointed out. “It’s just —”

“Jane, you don’t have to explain. I get it. The heart wants what the heart wants. The other morning, I watched how he looked at you, and how you looked at him. You know Jane, over the years, you have given me some pretty great looks, you really have. But I’m not sure your eyes ever quite had the shine that they do when you look at him.”

Jane guiltily smiled and looked away.

"I'm not gonna lie, it made me kind of sad, well, jealous. Sad and jealous. I mean, I always wanted to be the one you looked at that way. But that being said, despite what you might think, I am happy for you, Jane. You deserve it."

Her eyes smiled into mine as she said, "So do you, Josh. So do you. And I know one day you'll find it."

I politely smiled at her sweet, cliché-filled comment.

"You do know it would mean the world to me for you to be there tomorrow?"

I took a second to gather my thoughts then I said, "I meant it when I said I was happy for you, but there's a difference between being happy for you and actually watching you get married, ya know?"

"I understand, I really do, and I know this is selfish of me, but I just can't picture my most special day without you being there." She let out a sigh and continued. "Why do I feel after tomorrow nothing will be the same again between us?"

In my head, I knew things had already changed. Ever since the night she left her ring on the sill, things had completely changed. I didn't bother to point this out, even though in her heart, I'm sure she already knew it.

"You're right," I said. "Things will probably never be the same… but that's not a bad thing. You've got a new best friend now, one who'll walk this world with you."

My comment caused a tear to fall down her cheek. My reflexes kicked in, and I reached over and wiped it away with my thumb.

"Aww, Jane, don't be sad. Tomorrow is going to be the happiest day of your life."

With that, she gave me a long Jane-hug. The kind of hug

you didn't want to end, because when it did, you'd realize it was really over.

When we finally parted, she slowly started making her way back to her car. As I watched her taillights fade to black, I took one final shot then headed back over to Hoohahs to help close up.

I didn't find out until days later, but that particular night was eerily similar for all three of us friends. Whether it was for nostalgic reasons or for some sort of closure, we all sat in our respective places and looked through old photos.

Pete lay on his couch, alone, looking through old photos from the early 90's when he and Michelle first met: photos of their wedding day… photos of their girls growing up.

At the same time, Doug sat in his hotel room in Texas, emotionally looking through an old shoebox his step-mother had given him. Like I said, more on Doug's trip later.

After I left Hoohahs, my night was spent on the couch also going through a box. Mine was much, much larger than a shoebox. You guessed it. It was my Jane Memorabilia Box, containing letters to photographs and everything in between. You're probably assuming I spent the rest of the night going through each and every piece of memorabilia, all the while I cranked up some Depression Session mixes. Well, you would be wrong! Kind of.

I did have a Depression Session playing, but I didn't go through each letter, each photo, each memory. I knew what needed to be done, and I cut right to the chase. I grabbed the box, a bottle of lighter fluid, and my trusty matches, and I marched outside. The only thing I removed was the ring I had given her. I stuck that in my pocket. No, I wasn't saving it for my future Mrs. Right. I just figured no matter how many bottles of lighter fluid I used, eventually, the ring would still be laying there in the ashes afterwards.

I suppose the final piece of my closure would be later that night when I drove up to the Nubble and chucked the ring into the Atlantic. Yes, I know, the wise financial move would be to get something for it at a pawn shop, or on Ebay, or Craigslist even, but this wasn't about the money. It was about closure, and to be quite honest, it felt pretty damn good, and it was long overdue. You're still probably thinking I'm a dumb fuck for throwing thousands of dollars into the ocean. And once again, you probably wouldn't be wrong.

I'm getting ahead of myself though. Before my trip to the lighthouse, I thoroughly soaked the box and set the fucker ablaze. I didn't look at it as a burning of memories, for those would always live in my head, and it wasn't about exorcizing what Jane had meant to me over the years, for that would always be in my heart. It was just a way to start a new chapter.

I'm sure my neighbors thought I was an absolute whacko with my sacrificial burn piles over the years. They wouldn't be wrong. But I always looked at it as me just trying to do whatever I could to move on. So, when the last ember was out, and once the ring had sunk to the bottom of the cold, dark ocean, I knew it was time to do just that—move on.

30

"I HOPE YOU'RE HAPPY" – Blue October

Jane and Brett's wedding went off without a hitch. It was perfect weather with nothing but blue skies for their outdoor ceremony in the park down at the harbor. And I'm sure this isn't going to come as a surprise to any of you, but yes, I attended the wedding.

Just because my sacrificial burning of the box was a success, and just because I had my closure, it still didn't prevent some uncomfortable moments as I watched them become husband and wife. Despite those moments, seeing Jane's face light up when she spotted me in the crowd made it worthwhile. As hard as it was, I knew I made the right decision by attending.

That being said, I only made it through an hour of the reception before bailing. Luckily, I had Pete and Michelle to keep me company. I suppose they were probably glad I was there to keep them company as well. I tried my best to provide conversation to fill the quiet void between my two friends. Doug was way better at that than I was, but I'm sure he was feeling his own quiet void down in Texas.

Watching Jane and Brett say their vows was uncomfortable for me, but I'm sure it was nothing compared to how Pete and Michelle felt. They both must have been reliving their own beautiful wedding day years earlier. There's no way they could have pictured or predicted how things would have turned out.

It's kind of depressing seeing all of these couples on their wedding day. They're all so happy and positive, thinking that they're marrying their soulmate. Yet, 50% of them will end in divorce. Sooner than later in most cases. Watching Pete and Michelle go through some heavy real-life shit, certainly put my own shit into perspective.

As soon as I got to the reception, I walked up to the DJ. No, I wasn't asking him to play a song, I was there to ask him to NOT play a song, well, a band, actually. I knew if he played anything by U2 that Pete would lose it. I quickly explained the situation, and he was happy to oblige my request.

Unfortunately, I also should have unrequested "Pete and Michelle's song," which wasn't a U2 song. It was "(Everything I Do) I Do it for You" by Bryan Adams. Yup, as you might have guessed, about an hour in, the DJ played it. As soon as it came on, it seemed like all the couples were out on the dance floor; all except Pete and Michelle.

I walked over and offered my hand to Michelle. I made it seem like it was less about me feeling sorry for her, and more like she would be doing me a favor. Once again, while we danced, I did my best at small talk, but it was obvious the person she really wanted to be dancing with was sitting across the room. And in Pete's heart, I knew she was the one he wanted to be dancing with as well. Sadly, I also knew in his heart, he might not ever be able to forgive and forget enough to ever have that dance again.

Even though I knew my shop was in good hands with Kelli, I still used it as an excuse for leaving the reception early. Pete and Michelle also followed suit and left when I did. Before we all left, I did have one final slow dance.

"You're not going to leave without dancing with me, are you?" Jane asked.

Wedding code – you can't say no to a dance with the bride.

"Reserve the next slow song for me, okay?" she smiled.

"Yea, of course," I replied.

Secretly, I prayed the next slow one wouldn't be some long-ass song like "Stairway to Heaven" or some shit. I just wanted to get this over with and head out. The song we danced to was Sheriff's "When I'm With You." Luckily for me, it was under four minutes. Our conversation started off with your typical cliché-filled wedding banter.

"It was a beautiful ceremony," and "You couldn't have asked for better weather," and "Your parents looked very happy and proud." I think I even made a comment about the food spread.

And yes, I did tell her how amazing she looked.

And yes, she nearly teared-up as she told me how grateful she was that I showed up.

Most of the time, people never realize when they're doing something for the final time. Like, when Pete, Doug, Scott, and I had a walkabout after Anna's death; that proved to be the final time all four of us would get together to do that.

My dance with Jane was different. As the song faded out, I

had a strong feeling it would be the final slow dance we'd ever have. As time moved on, I'd be proven correct. I guess now I kind of wished it was a longer song. Just like I now wished for a longer walkabout with my three best friends years earlier. Unfortunately, life is what it is. We just need to savor every moment, even if it seems insignificant. I know, I know, way easier said than done.

Anyway, all three of us left the reception together, yet we all went our separate ways. Michelle went to pick up the girls, Pete went to check on things at Hoohahs, and I headed over to my business. The last place I needed to be was at my house having a pity party for myself. Besides, I was out of lighter fluid and shit to burn.

The Eclectic Café provided the perfect escape and distraction. I profusely thanked Kelli for all her help the past few days. She informed me that Joanna and Doug were airborne and would be back in town later that night.

31

"4 AM" – Our Lady Peace

This next chapter is based directly on everything that Doug told me about their trip to Texas.

For the longest time on their flight down to Texas, both Joanna and Doug remained silent. Joanna flipped through magazines while Doug just sat there listening to music.

About halfway through the flight, Doug removed his earbuds and said, "Twenty bucks says this Lorraine chick is a major redneck with missing teeth and everything."

Joanna looked up from her magazine and curiously said, "Who?"

"Lorraine… otherwise known as my step-mother."

"Ahhh."

"Seriously, I really don't know why I'm going to this."

"I think you're doing the right thing."

"Well that would be ironic. I don't think my old man *ever* did the right thing."

Joanna used this as her window to get more information on the situation.

"How old were you when he—"

"When he ditched us? I was five. Five fuckin' years old. I think in the beginning, every time I asked where he was, my mother would lie and tell me he was away on a business trip. I guess after a while, I figured out he wasn't coming back, and I just stopped asking. It wasn't until I was in my teens that she told me everything."

"Which was?" Joanna quietly asked.

"He was a druggie and a drunk. Of course, my mom sugar-coated it by using the phrase, *he had an addictive personality which led him down the path of alcohol and drug use.* Even today, she still sticks to that phrasing. Oh, and to go along with his addictive personality, he was also a degenerate gambler as well. Did you know he ran up so much debt that the bank took our house away?"

Joanna continued to sympathetically listen as Doug opened up to her.

"My mom said he was into those get-rich-quick schemes and was always searching for the next big thing… along with his next big fix. I guess having a wife and kid only slowed him down."

"Did you ever hear from him again?"

"Over the first few months, he called and talked to me a handful of times. I'm sure the real reason he called was to get my mom to lend him some money, and he probably figured while he had her on the phone, he might as well talk to his fuckin' son. Eventually, my mom stopped sending money, and not coincidentally, he stopped calling."

Joanna reached over, grasping his hand.

"Actually, it was so long ago, and I was so young that I barely remember him at all." Doug paused and let out a sad chuckle. "Do you wanna hear something fucked up? One of the only memories I have of him is when we all went to the fair. I just remember being on his shoulders, feeling like I was on top of the world." Again, he chuckled and said, "I even remember I was eating cotton candy—blue cotton candy. I told ya, some fucked up shit, huh?"

"I'm so sorry, Doug."

"Whatever. It doesn't fuckin' matter anyway. We didn't need him in our lives. Not at all."

Joanna knew this was just Doug's defense mechanism kicking in and that it actually did matter to him. She also knew it still had an effect on him today.

When they arrived at the hotel, Doug not only paid for her room, but he made sure it was the nicest one they had. He was extremely grateful for her coming down with him. Seeing as this was both of their first times in Texas, they spent that first day sightseeing.

I think it was easier for Doug to pretend it was a mini-vacation rather than face the depressing truth, and from what both Joanna and Doug told me, it sounded like, at least for that day, they escaped the reality of the situation and had a fun time.

Doug rented a car and they drove all around from one attraction to another. At one point, around sunset, Doug stopped at some ranch and arranged for them to go horseback riding. Doug even bought cowboy and cowgirl hats for them. And if I know Doug, which I do, the whole time they were horseback riding, he was probably spewing out one quote after another from the movie *City Slickers*. Even though it was nearly sunset, they said it was still pushing 95 degrees.

After hearing about all the fun things they did that day, I couldn't help but be reminded of the time I took Anna on that full day tour of Maine lighthouses and forts. For the longest time, memories like that would depress the hell out of me, but now, five years later, it put a smile on my face. It also put a smile on my face knowing that Doug and Joanna got to experience that type of a day. Of course, I was still hesitant believing their day would lead to any sorta romantical type of shit, but I have been wrong before.

As fun and distracting as their day was, the next day was a different story. From what Doug told me, the funeral was awkwardly surreal. He said there was only about thirty people, which was about twenty-five more than he predicted. Most of them were relatives of Lorraine, and a handful were co-workers of Doug's father. Apparently, his dad worked as a mechanic at the local garage in town, and from all accounts, he was very well-liked.

Doug and Joanna sat in the back, and he did his best not to make contact with anyone. The question of *why am I fuckin' here* constantly ran through his mind. As he listened to one person after another saying great things about his father, he felt a twinge of sadness. He hated that he felt that.

It was Lorraine's beautiful and emotional words that really got to him, so much so, that he got up and quietly walked out before the ceremony ended. Joanna followed, but the right words escaped her, and she could only offer her hand on his shoulder.

As people began filing out of the small church, Doug turned

to Joanna and said, "I'm ready when you are."

"You sure?" Joanna asked, looking over at Lorraine exiting the church.

"Yup, I told you, I don't belong here," he said.

"You should probably go introduce yourself and say hi," Joanna encouraged.

Doug glared at Joanna, but before he could reject her suggestion, it was too late. Lorraine was already making her way directly over to them.

"Oh fuck," mumbled Doug.

"You must be Doug?" Lorraine warmly smiled, extending her hand.

Doug half-nodded and hesitantly shook her hand.

"Hi, I'm Lorraine," she said, and then extended her hand to Joanna.

"Hi, I'm Joanna. I'm a friend of Doug's."

"Thank you both for coming."

It was apparent that Doug had nothing to say, so Joanna forced polite conversation.

"We're really sorry for your loss, ma'am."

"Thank you, but please, call me Lorraine."

Doug continued staring at the ground, nervously shuffling his feet. An older couple came over and offered Lorraine their condolences.

Before the couple walked off, they said, "We'll see you back at your house?"

"Yes, I'll be heading home in a few," said Lorraine. She then turned back to Doug and Joanna and said, "We're having a small get-together back at our house. I would love for you to stop by. Nothing major, just some drinks and refreshments."

How appropriate, thought Doug. *Let's have a drink to honor my drunken father.* Doug smartly kept his thoughts to himself, but before he could reject Lorraine's offer, Joanna stepped in and said, "Thank you, we would love to."

There was no hiding Doug's displeasure as he glared at Joanna out of the corner of his eye.

Lorraine must have known how hard this whole situation was on him, so before walking off, she said, "Feel free to follow me back to the house... if you'd like."

Less than ten seconds after she walked away, Doug said, "Why the fuck would you tell her we'd go to her house?"

Joanna was quick with her response, "Look, we've come all this way, you might as well see it all the way through."

As tempted as he was to argue with her, he didn't. He huffed and puffed and sighed his displeasure, but ultimately, he followed Lorraine.

On their ride over, Joanna tried to break the ice by saying, "So much for your toothless, redneck theory. Guess you owe me twenty bucks," she smiled.

He said nothing. He just shook his head and stared straight ahead.

"Oh, come on, Doug. You have to admit, she's nothing like you thought she'd be, and she seems very sweet too."

"I don't care how she looks or how sweet she is, the fact that she was with someone like him is all I need to know about her!"

Joanna knew she was fighting an uphill battle, so she decided to keep her comments to herself. They drove the rest of the way in silence. She was only trying to help, and Doug knew this, and he really was appreciative of her being there with him.

As they exited the car at Lorraine's house, he said, "Don't

go volunteering us to sleep over here tonight, okay?"

It wasn't until she saw his smirk that she knew he was kidding. She also knew his sarcasm was his way of saying, *I'm sorry*—and *thank you.*

The lightened mood only lasted up the walkway. When they were in the house, the mood once again became awkward and heavy for both of them. The uneasiness was immediate. Lorraine was off in the kitchen organizing the food platters, which left Doug and Joanna to mingle in the living room.

I can't imagine how Doug felt when strangers came up to him and asked how he knew the deceased. I'm sure Doug wanted to say, *I didn't. I didn't know him at all.* To Doug's credit, he matter-of-factly said, "He was my father."

A few of them knew that Mr. Andrews had a son, but most didn't have a clue. One woman even said, "Wow, I didn't even know Jim had a son."

Joanna immediately regretted opening her big mouth and accepting the invitation to Lorraine's house. The moment that really pushed Doug over the edge was when a woman hesitantly approached him. She was in her mid-thirties and introduced herself as Lorraine's daughter. She knew exactly who Doug was and knew exactly how strange this whole situation was for him.

She was very kind and sweet, and she offered small talk to Doug and Joanna. She asked how their flight was and if this was their first trip to Texas. She also made a joke about the oppressive Texas heat and how the A/C was their most precious commodity. She asked about Maine and said she would love to visit New England one day. Doug was still reeling from the fact he technically had a step-sister, so Joanna did most of the talking.

After his step-sister excused herself to go help in the kitchen, Doug used that moment to get some fresh air. Considering it was nearly 101 degrees out, Doug would be the only one outside. Joanna gave him a few minutes then joined him with a couple of cold drinks in her hands.

"Lemonade?" he asked. "I think I need something stronger than that."

"Sorry," she smiled. "I actually didn't see anything alcoholic."

"Ahh, just my dumb fuckin' luck. I can't even get a drink in a drunk's house."

"Doug."

"What? This whole thing is fuckin' crazy! I spent the last two hours listening to one stranger after another say nice things about him, and all I kept thinking about was who the hell are they talking about? It certainly wasn't the selfish, drunk asshole who ditched his family."

Just then, they turned around to see Lorraine standing there. Joanna cringed and offered an apologetic look.

"I'm sorry Lorraine, but that's who he really was," Doug stated.

An uneasy silence filled the air.

"I think I'll go grab us another drink," Joanna said, excusing herself.

Lorraine approached Doug and softly said, "It means a lot that you came."

"To who? It certainly wouldn't have meant anything to him!"

"That's where you're wrong," she said. "I can't image what you and your mother went through. You're right, he was a selfish, drunk asshole for how he treated you. He drank, did drugs, lied, cheated—"

"And don't forget gambled away our fuckin' house."

Sadly, Lorraine nodded. "Your father was a very sick man with a lot of demons."

"If this is the part of the speech where you try to get me to feel sorry for him, you can save it."

"No, Doug, I'm not trying to get you to feel sorry for him. What he did to your mother was horrible, and walking away from his only son was inexcusable. I'm not trying to defend him, I'm just trying to tell you how fucked up he was back then. Forgive my language."

Doug glanced down at the ground then said, "So, tell me this, Lorraine, if he was so sick and fucked up, what were you doing with him? I mean, you kinda seem like a nice, normal person."

She let out a small chuckle and said, "Thanks. When I met your father, he was already clean and sober for a year. We met about five years ago in group therapy."

"You dated and married one of your patients? Doesn't that go against codes and shit?"

Again, she let out a chuckle. "I wasn't his therapist, Doug, I was also a patient. Our paths and stories were fairly similar. I never had a gambling problem, but I more than made up for it with other addictions. Heroine being my worst. I lost my marriage, my career, and for the longest time, my relationship with my daughter."

Doug was stunned by her revelation.

"So much for seeming normal, huh?" she smiled.

Doug forced a smile back at her then stared off into the distance. Without breaking his gaze, Doug said, "Answer me this, if he's been clean and sober the past five years, then why hasn't he tried to get a hold of me? Isn't that part of the program? To make amends with the people you fucked over? I mean, you obviously fixed your relationship with your daughter."

She paused a moment then answered, "He did. He did try."

"What?"

"It was soon after we started dating—probably about four years ago. Your father hated the way he had treated your mother, and he always hated and regretted losing contact with you. Jim and I had so many late-night conversations about those regrets. It was like he was haunted by them."

Although tempted, Doug held back his sarcastic comments. He stood quietly and let Lorraine continue.

"His therapist suggested that he write you a letter once a week."

"I never got any letters."

"I know. Your father was never very good at expressing his feelings, especially on paper. The letters never came out the way he wanted, but he was told to keep writing them, and even if he never sent them, his therapist told him it would still be good for him. After a couple of months of watching him struggle with his regrets, I strongly suggested we take a trip up north to see you… face to face. The thought of that scared the hell out of him, but he knew it's what needed to be done."

"Pffft, but he chickened out, huh?" Doug sarcastically scoffed.

"Actually… we did make the trip up to Maine."

The sarcasm faded from Doug's face.

"Besides hating himself for abandoning you, he also hated the way he treated your mother. He knew he needed to make things right with her first. So he looked her up, found her address, and paid her a visit. I hung out at the beach while they talked."

Doug's face dropped. "He visited my mother?"

Lorrainc nodded.

"She never told me," he quietly said.

"He never went into details with me, but he did say their conversation was painful and emotional, but long overdue. He said it was one of the hardest conversations he's ever had, but at the end of it, he was glad he did it. He knew your mother could never fully forgive him, but I think their conversation was good for both of them. Finally facing your mother after all those years was so hard for him, but it was nowhere near as difficult as facing you."

"So he *did* chicken out, didn't he?"

Lorraine offered a slow, sympathetic nod.

"He came close… so close, Doug. Your mother filled him in on you and your bar. It was pretty busy when we got there, so I ordered us a couple of ginger ales and we sat in the back corner. "

"You guys came into my bar? Was… was I there?"

Lorraine smiled and nodded. "You were. We hung out for nearly two hours. Like I said, it was pretty crowded, and your dad kept mumbling how it wasn't the right time, or how you seemed too busy. The truth was, he was just so nervous and scared, and although he had rehearsed his speech a thousand times, he simply froze up. There's no doubt in my mind, he wanted a drink in the worst way possible. He was literally shaking he was so nervous."

Doug continued to look at Lorraine and listened intently.

"At one point, a couple of your friends came in and sat up at the bar. He watched how you interacted with them, talking and laughing. He also watched you flirting with a couple of girls at the end of the bar. Watching you make the girls laugh and blush made your father smile. I'm not sure if you knew this, but your dad was quite the flirt as well."

Doug tried his hardest not to, but his lips curled into a slight smile. His smile was short-lived as he looked at Lorraine and said, "That was it? He just watched me the whole time? He never had the guts to approach me?"

Sadly, she shook her head no.

"After watching you interact with your friends and customers, and seeing how successful and happy you looked, he said he just couldn't bear to bring you down by digging up the past. He said you were better off without him in your life. I disagreed and tried my best to coax him, but I also knew he needed to do this on his own terms."

Doug still couldn't believe his mom never told him any of this. When she never heard anything from Doug, she just assumed his dad had lost his nerve and failed on the reunion with his son. I guess she also knew that Mr. Andrews needed to come to Doug on his own terms when he was ready. I'm sure his mom was tempted, but she never said a word about his father's visit.

"Once again," said Lorraine, "I'm not making excuses for him, but he was fighting these demons long before he met your mother. I'm not sure if you knew this, but your father's parents were both alcoholics. They also moved around a lot, and by the time he was seventeen, he was already on the streets and on his own. Those early years with your mother were the longest he had ever put roots down anywhere. Unfortunately, he fell into doing the only thing he ever knew… to drink and run."

"He was certainly good at that," Doug reminded her.

Lorraine continued. "On the plane ride home, I could tell he was sad and regretful, but he was also relieved. He was relieved that despite all the shit he put you through, you turned out to be such a great young man. He was so proud of the fact you were such a hard worker and that you owned your own business."

"Pfft, like he'd know anything about being a hard worker."

"Exactly my point, Doug. He spent most of his life in a drunken haze, conning and cheating to get what he wanted. That's why it made him so proud to see that you turned out nothing like him. Despite what you might think, Doug, he did love you. He just lost his way and never figured out how to get back… and he never figured out how to tell you just how sorry he was. Every single day I knew him, the weight of his guilt never left his shoulders, and the thought of his little boy never left his heart."

A tear rolled down Lorraine's cheek as she told this to Doug. Doug, however, remained stoic, just standing there taking it all in. Soon after their conversation, Doug and Joanna headed out, but not before Lorraine handed him a small shoebox. It would remain unopened until later that night.

Back at the hotel bar, Doug and Joanna had dinner and drinks and ended up talking there most of the night. It wasn't until Doug went back to his room that he finally brought himself to open the box.

Inside the shoebox were the letters his dad had written years earlier. Scattered underneath the letters were a handful of old Polaroid pictures. There was a picture of Doug as a newborn being held by both his parents. Most of the other pictures ranged from newborn to three or four years old. Doug had no memory of them.

The final photo, however, sent chills throughout his body. Doug was five years old and was sitting on his dad's shoulders at the fair. In the picture, Doug had the biggest smile for the camera, all the while his face was covered in cotton candy—blue cotton candy.

It was at that moment, sitting in his hotel room, that Doug finally broke down and let it all out. All the years of anger, sadness and resentment were finally released.

Like I mentioned earlier, at that very same moment, all three of us friends sat in our respective locations and flipped through old pictures and dealt with memories, each in our own way. I'm not here to say whose sadness was greater, because if it's one thing I've learned in life, it's impossible to quantify and judge someone else's sadness.

32

"DRUNK IS BETTER THAN DEAD" – Push Stars

When Doug entered Hoohahs, I was in the process of pouring five shots of Jäger. Denise, one of Doug's employees, took them over to the group of guys in the back. I poured two more and slid one to Doug. He gave me a smile and sat up at the bar.

"Welcome home," I said as we clinked our glasses and downed our shots.

"Good to be back," he said.

I had Denise and Jessica take over, and I grabbed a couple of beers and joined Doug up at the bar.

"How'd it go?" I asked.

It was at that point, Doug filled me in on everything you just read in the previous chapter.

"Anyway, it was weird and uncomfortable, but I guess I'm

glad I went," he said, finishing his beer.

He motioned to Denise for two more, and after he took a sip, he asked, "How are things with you? Attempt to stop any weddings today?"

I laughed and shook my head no.

"What, no boombox over your head? No truck full of roses, or marching bands, or skywriters?"

"Ha ha ha," I laughed.

Over the next hour, we proceeded to have more beers and a few more shots, and our voices and laughter became louder with each one. It was at that point, I suggested a walkabout.

"You read my mind," smiled Doug.

We attempted to call Pete, but his phone was shut off. We even thought about calling Scott, but we thought better of it. We knew he'd only offer one of his many reasons why he couldn't.

During our walk, I blurted out, "Well, in the past week, I walked in on my sorta-girlfriend getting pounded by her rapper roommate, and then I watched the so-called love of my life get married on the beach... the very same beach we first met. Ironical, don'tcha think?"

Doug looked at me and said, "Whoever said that God doesn't have a sense of humor, obviously ain't gotta a clue. God can be one funny fucker, I tell ya."

I laughed, knowing it was certainly hard to argue with that.

As we stumbled up the beach, Doug turned to me and said, "Seriously, man, I know today must have been hard on you. You okay?"

"Yea, I'm fine. I'm drunk, but I'm fine. I guess deep down inside, I always knew we wouldn't regain what we once had. But you know me, good ol' Captain Hopeless Romantic. And

I stress *hopeless*. No more of that shit though," I said, pulling out another beer from my backpack. "A toast, to the new me!"

"The new you?"

"Yup. No more living in a fantasy world. No more rushing into things. No more flowers or sweet gestures, and certainly no more surprise soup deliveries. Basically, no more Mr. Nice Guy! From now on, I'm gonna play it cool. Cooler than cool… like ice! Actually, from now on you can call me *The Ice Man*."

"The Ice Man," he laughed.

"Yup. Dude, we can be partners in crime again and be each other's wingmen. You'll have to brush me up on some of those cheesy lines you use, but it'll be great!"

"And you call me an idiot?" he said.

"What?"

"You can't change who you are just like that. All the crazy and romantic shit you do, or the way you trust people so easily, or the fact that when you give your heart, you give it a hundred percent … I could never do those things. Truth be told, there are times I envy those qualities about you."

"Yea, right!" I drunkenly laughed. "Like you'd ever trade in your smooth lines for my clumsy babbling? I'm the one who should be envious. I don't know how you fuckin' do it, dude, but you're always so smooth around chicks."

"Yea, chicks I'm not emotionally invested in, which is most of them. But when it comes to approaching a girl I really like, I'm not as smooth as you think. Maybe I'm afraid of rejection, or maybe just afraid of getting hurt… but I tell you what, Josh, there are definitely times that I'm jealous of your whole heart-on-your-sleeve attitude."

I continued to laugh and roll my eyes at Doug.

"Seriously, Josh, even when that heart on your sleeve gets

ripped off, stomped on, and kicked around, you still find a way to put it back on. That takes balls… big balls, bro."

***

Our walkabout concluded back at my place, where we proceeded to drink some more beers and chow down on Hot Pockets and Funyuns. And yes, we had plenty of great tunes cranked on in the background.

As the Counting Crows sang "Sullivan Street," Doug somberly said, "I keep thinking about my dad's letters. I mean, at some point in his life, he must have had hopes and dreams… for my mom… for me… for himself. There's no fuckin' way his plan was that one day he'd wake up and nearly thirty years would have passed, and those hopes and dreams, along with us, would just be a faint memory. There's no way he could have intended that."

"I'm sure he didn't," I said. "I'm sure he didn't."

A little while later, during "Good" by Better Than Ezra, I found myself staring over at the window sill. When the song ended, I said to Doug, "Every time I look at this stupid window sill, all I can see is…" I paused then continued, "Finding her note and the ring here that night was definitely one of the lowest points of my life. I still kind of get sick to my stomach thinking about that night. Don't get me wrong, I think I finally have my closure, and I'm happy that she's happy, but—"

"But you still wanna rip the fuckin' window sill out and burn it in your fire pit, don't ya?"

I laughed and nodded yes. Don't worry, we were super-drunk, but there was no window-sill-ripping or burning that night.

It was nearly 3 AM when we both finally passed out. I was so drunk and knocked out cold, that I didn't even hear Doug's sonic snoring.

***

With me on the couch, and Doug on the floor, neither of us heard the knocking on the door the following morning. And neither of us heard the door open and someone entering. We did, however, hear Bono loudly singing "Beautiful Day."

"Jesus Christ, Doug, turn off the fuckin' music!" I yelled with my head buried under my pillow.

"I didn't fuckin' turn on any music!" he moaned.

Just then, the volume lowered and Pete's voice said, "What the hell went on here last night?"

I slowly poked my head out from the pillow, shielded my eyes from the obnoxious sunlight, and spotted Pete. He stood there looking around at all the empty beer bottles, bags of Funyuns, and multiple Hot Pocket wrappers. Pete reached his hand in the box of Chicken in a Biskit and began tossing them at our heads. After the 4th or 5th one, Doug finally sat up and snapped.

"What the fuck are you doing, dude!?!"

Pete just laughed.

"What time is it?" I mumbled.

"Eightish."

"Oh, sweet baby Jesus! Let us sleep!" pleaded Doug.

Pete threw two more Chicken in a Biskits at him.

"I'm gonna kick your fuckin' ass, dude!" warned Doug.

"I'm not even sure you could walk right now, never mind kick my ass."

Doug hazily stared long and hard at Pete then finally conceded. "Yea, you're probably right." He then reached over and began eating the Chicken in a Biskits off the floor.

Pete continued to look around the room. "Seriously, what are you guys, twenty-one again?"

"No," I said, sitting up, "I don't think my head hurt this much at twenty-one."

"Don't you have a coffeeshop to run?"

"Nope! I'm taking a well-deserved few days off! And I don't have a bar to run either. You two clowns are on your own now."

"Don't worry," laughed Pete, "I'm good to go. Obviously, the same cannot be said about this guy," he said, kicking Doug's lifeless body.

"Relax, fucker. I'll be good to go by tonight," said Doug.

"Eh, don't sweat it, bro. Why don't you take another night off." said Pete.

By now, Doug and I were both sitting up and curiously looking at Pete.

"What the hell are you so upbeat about?" I asked.

"Especially at early-o'clock in the morning," said Doug.

Pete just laughed as he disappeared into the kitchen. A second later, he returned with three cold beers. He handed one to me, and I looked at him like he was nuts.

"Do I look like I need a beer right now?" I said.

Without hesitation, Doug said, "I'll take one!"

Pete smiled and handed one to Doug and then both their eyes fell on me.

"Fine! Give me the damn beer!" I smirked.

He handed me the beer then plopped himself in the corner chair and began happily eating the rest of the Chicken in a

Biskits.

"Seriously, dude, why are you in such a good mood?"

Pete took a long swig of beer, paused a second, then announced, "Michelle is gonna be fine. It's not cancer."

"Aw, Pete, that's great news!"

"You both must be so relieved."

Pete nodded and said, "There's still some abnormalities in her bloodwork, but they've completely ruled out cancer."

If you're going to be woken up from a drunken stupor, news like that is certainly worth it! As we sat drinking our early-o'clock beers, Pete filled us in on more of the medical details. He then asked Doug how his trip was. Doug told him everything he had shared with me then proceeded to add one more detail of his trip—a detail that he had conveniently left out with me.

"You and Joanna hooked up, didn't you?" asked Pete.

I laughed at the ridiculousness of his question, but before I could express just how funny his question was, Doug answered, "That we did. Well, kind of."

"Whoa, whoa, whoa!" I said. "You're joking, right?"

"No."

"Why didn't you tell me this last night?" I said.

Doug shrugged and matter-of-factly said, "You didn't ask."

Pete laughed and repeated, "Yea, you didn't ask. I saw this coming from a mile away. You really didn't?" he asked me.

"No, I really didn't. When did you guys hook up?"

"The last night at the hotel. After I went through my dad's shoebox, I went back down to the bar for a nightcap. Joanna was there. We drank and talked. We talked and laughed. We went back to her room and we kind of hooked up"

"What do you mean kind of?" I asked.

"No sex. We made out a little and ended up just cuddling and spooning and shit."

"Nice. Good for you, man," said Pete.

"Hold on a second," I said. "First of all, I can't believe you didn't tell me this last night, and second, how come whenever I tell you guys that I didn't have sex and that we just cuddled, you guys laugh and call me gay? Huh??"

Both of my idiot friends clinked their beers and laughed at me. I knew how much Joanna had been searching for a boyfriend, and I also knew how she was NOT looking for just a random hookup. Did Doug drop his stupid lines on her? Did she hookup with him because she felt bad for him? There's no possible way she could think Doug wanted anything more than just a hookup, right?

I love Doug, I really do, and his little one-night stands rarely affect me, but this was Joanna—my business partner—and more importantly, my good friend. I hated the thought of her being the victim of Doug's one-night prowess. I didn't want to bring the vibe of the room down, but I needed to voice my displeasure with Doug. I needed to tell him what he did was kind of a dick move. I needed to tell him—

"I actually asked Joanna out on a date tomorrow night," Doug said, interrupting my thoughts.

"Like a date, date?" asked Pete.

Doug pondered then said, "Yea, a date, date. As a matter of fact, Josh, I was hoping you could give me some good date ideas. You know her better than me, and you *are* the master date planner."

Did I mention how much I fuckin' love this guy??? I knew all along that Doug wasn't in it just for a random hookup. Of course I did.

After we polished off our celebratory beers, Doug proclaimed, "Do you know what we should do?"

Pete and I looked at each other and said in unison, "No, Doug, we're not going to a strip club!"

"Pffft, settle down. I was talking about throwing a party. Like one of our old school parties. Although, a strip club would be pretty nice too. Kittens is actually open right now. They run a legs-n-eggs special."

Pete and I just shook our heads.

"I'm serious about a party though, and we can have it right here."

"Why my house?" I said.

"Your place is more party-friendly than mine."

"What about Pete's house?" I asked.

"Pete's house is definitely not party-friendly. Way too kid-friendly. Stuffed animals and Barbie dolls everywhere. Not to mention, all of the childproof locks. I can't even get into their liquor cabinet, for Christ sake!"

He wasn't wrong. Those child-proof locks might as well be called adult-proof locks.

"And just think, Josh, if we have it at your house, you can play DJ and make some cool new party mixes."

Doug certainly knew the right buttons to push.

"Fine. My house it is."

"And just think," added Pete, "You already have a big bare spot for a bonfire."

"Yea," Doug chimed in, "we can make it a BYOLF—bring your own lighter fluid!"

Have I ever mentioned that my friends were fuckin' idiots?

33

"IT DOESN'T MATTER" – Depeche Mode

It was settled, the following Saturday, which was Labor Day weekend, there would be an old-school party at my house. Unfortunately, most of our old-school friends had long since left York. This didn't slow Doug down in the least. He invited his workers from Hoohahs and extended invites to everyone at our coffeeshop. Of course, I had to be the responsible adult and only allow the workers who were over twenty-one. He also invited people from Hoohahs. Not just his workers but actual customers. I was excited for the party, but I prayed that the whole frickin' town wouldn't show up.

With regards to Doug and Joanna's date; I had a million ideas for him, but I ultimately offered no advice. Joanna liked Doug for a reason, so I figured he certainly didn't need me to help him plan a fun date. I was confident, whatever he chose, they would have a fun time.

By the time the night of the party arrived, I had only invited a few people throughout the week. I left most of the invitations to Doug and Joanna. Just like our old parties, I was a little nervous and anxious. Part of me always had the fear that nobody would show up.

I used to have the same fear when I DJ'd at Goodnight Ogunquit. The clock would hit 10 PM, and there'd only be a dozen or so people mulling about the club. I would start to panic and shit my pants in fear of no one showing up.

Of course, every week was the same; by 11

PM, not only would the club be full, there'd be a line around the building waiting to get in. Yup, it was the same pattern every frickin' Sunday for five years, yet I still stressed myself out beforehand.

So, on the night of our big party, there was still that neurotic part of me that was nervous no one would show up. But seeing how Doug and Joanna were in charge of the invites, a bigger part of me was worried that the whole damn town would be at my house. Luckily for me and my anxiety, the perfect amount of people showed up.

Usually, when Doug and my friends suggested a party, they would always vow to help set up, and more importantly, help clean up the next day. It was fair to say that 99.7% of the time, it was empty promises. This party was a little different. Doug originally told me all I needed to worry about was providing the music. He claimed that he and Joanna would take care of the rest. Guess what? They did! More credit probably goes to Joanna, but either way, those two nailed every party detail. From the food, to the drinks, and even right down to the Tiki torches, they covered it all. And you can bet your sweet ass, I had the music covered as well.

Throughout the week, Pete didn't involve himself much with the party planning. He was fully concentrated on spending time with Kayla and Lindsay. And coming on the heels of Michelle's health scare, he knew he needed to make some big decisions with regards to his marriage.

Doug and I were very confident our party would provide them with a fun night together, in hopes of it being like it used to be—like they used to be. Surely, they would find their way back to each other. Doug and I hoped this would be the case.

I think for all involved, the party would provide a chance at new beginnings. For Joanna; she would finally have an official second date with someone. In Doug's case; hopefully he'd realize that spending a whole party with someone he cares about is more fulfilling than scouring the party all night for just a one-night fling. Pete and I had our fingers crossed for this. That being said, Pete and I also had a wager on how long it would take before Joanna busted him staring at some girl's ass.

The party would be a new beginning for myself as well. Even though it was only a week removed from Jane's wedding, I was surprisingly in a great frame of mind. I had truly and honestly come to terms with it and was more than ready to move on. For the time being, I decided to stop worrying about my relationship status or trying so hard to find my future Mrs. Right.

34

"I KNOW IT'S OVER" – The Smiths

The weather couldn't have been more beautiful on the night of the party. It was the perfect summer's night. After Joanna and Doug got everything set up, she headed back home to shower and change. This left Doug and I to sit back with a beer or two and relax. I popped in one of our favorite guy flicks, *Beautiful Girls*, starring Timothy Hutton, Matt Dillion, and a very young Natalie Portman.

"What? You guys couldn't wait until I got here to start the movie?"

Doug and I turned around to see Pete standing there holding a beer.

"Have a seat," I said. "We figured you and Michelle wouldn't be here until later."

Pete sat in the chair in the corner and said, "Michelle's not coming tonight."

"Really? You guys couldn't get a sitter?"

He paused a second then said, "We're both extremely relieved that she's going to be okay, but…"

We could tell by his "but" and long pause that our high hopes for them getting back together that night weren't gonna come true after all.

"I swear I'm trying, but I just don't know if I'll ever be able to forget what she did. I know she claims it meant absolutely nothing, but unfortunately, I can't stop my imagination from painting a different picture. A more vivid, sexual, disgusting picture of what went down. Whether it's fair of me or not, it's what my mind thinks."

Seeing as I walked in on my girlfriend *actually* having that type of vividly disgusting sex, I knew his imagination probably wasn't far off from what really went down (Don't worry, I didn't tell him that). I didn't say anything at all and neither did Doug. We just sat and listened.

"Ever since the affair happened, I started to doubt everything about our marriage—our whole relationship actually. I kept thinking—was any of it real or was it all just a lie?"

Finally, I spoke up. "I think we all know I'm the King of looking at the glass as half empty, not to mention, over-analyzing things, but what you just said, Pete, is—"

"Fuckin' ridiculous," added Doug.

"I know, I know," sighed Pete. "But I just couldn't help thinking that way. But then, when I thought she might be sick, like really, really sick, those vividly disgusting thoughts were replaced by thoughts of how it used to be… how *we* used to be. It was like my mind was replaying a movie of our life together. It was like one of those montage scenes, ya know?"

I knew exactly what Pete was talking about. My mind creates these montage scenes all the time, usually with a cool song playing in the background. As a matter of fact, my mind did a montage scene last week during my sacrificial burning of Jane's Memorabilia Box. The montage song in my head was "I Know It's Over" by The Smiths. I was tempted to ask Pete what song was playing in his montage, but I thought better of it.

Pete continued. "It was like these quick images were flashing in my head. Images of our first summer lifeguarding… our first date… our first kiss… the first time she laughed at one of my jokes, which was probably the only time she laughed at one of my jokes."

We all smiled, knowing it was true. Pete was just not a naturally funny guy.

"And then, last week, at Jane's wedding, all I could see was a montage of *our* wedding day… how nervous I was… how beautiful Michelle looked in her wedding dress…"

"How you chose Josh as your best man and not me," mumbled Doug.

Pete was deep in thought, so I don't even think he heard Doug's comment.

"I just remember how happy we were that day. And how magical it was when the girls were born… and holding them for the first time…"

Pete slowly snapped out of his zone and looked over at us.

"Anyway, all of those thoughts and memories made me realize that it wasn't all a lie… and that it was very much real. We just lost our way somewhere, that's all."

Doug and I sadly nodded as he continued.

"Those are the types of thoughts I want in my head. I don't know if we can get back to where we once were, but I do know, I at least have to try. So that's why I agreed to start going to counseling with Michelle."

A smile broke from both our lips.

"Good for you, bro," I said.

"Yea, good for you guys," said Doug.

"If you don't mind, I still think it's best if I stay with you for a bit longer though. I'd rather prepare the girls for the worst rather than get their hopes up."

"Yea, of course," said Doug. "Stay as long as you want."

Doug and I had high hopes that not only would Pete and Michelle be at the party together, but that they would be back together period. I suppose the good news was they were both willing to at least work on finding their way back to each other.

"Don't worry," smiled Pete, "I'm not gonna bring the party-vibe down tonight. Believe it or not, I'm in a better place than I've been in a while. I don't wanna get too sentimental, but I just wanna say thanks… for being such great friends, and I'm sorry if I've been a moody, wallowing prick the last few months."

"Dude, if we had to apologize every time one of us was a moody, wallowing prick, then Josh would be apologizing non-stop."

Before I could tell Doug to suck it, he said, "Just kidding, Josh. Just kidding."

Although it was at my expense, Doug's sarcastic comment was just what we needed to lighten the mood. From there on out, we were all in full party-mode.

The next thing we knew, people were filing in, and our 2004 Labor Day party was well under way.

***

"Hey you."

I turned to see Joanna standing there holding out another beer for me.

"Why, thank you," I said.

"How's it going?"

"Things are good. Seems like everyone is enjoying themselves, and it seems like the perfect amount of people too. Even if I don't know who half of them are."

"Yea, I think Doug went a little too crazy with the random invites at Hoohahs."

"Yea, he's definitely a little crazy… and unpredictable." I smiled and continued smiling as I looked at Joanna.

"What? Why are you smiling like that?" she asked.

"I still can't believe you and Doug."

"Does it bother you?" she asked.

"God no! I just didn't see it coming, that's all."

"Yea, me neither. I guess he just sort of grew on me. I always thought he was cute and funny, but seeing his track record with girls and hearing some of his one-night stand stories, I just figured it was best not to pursue him. Besides, I've had enough shitty first dates from online, the last thing I wanted was to be a one-night-romp for one of your friends."

"Well, I think it's safe to say, Doug definitely doesn't look at you as a one-night-romp. You're probably more like a two-night-romp for him."

"Ha ha," she laughed, smacking me in the arm. "Although, with my luck, you're probably gonna be right."

"Nah. I was only kidding. He's really into you."

"Oh yea? Why, what did he say?"

"He didn't say anything. I can just tell."

"Seriously, what did he say?"

"I'm being serious," I laughed.

"Pfft, you wouldn't tell me anyway. You and your guy codes," she smirked.

We both laughed then began people-watching. Joanna focused in on Pete. He was across the yard talking to a few people.

"No Michelle, huh?"

I sadly shook my head no.

"Do you think they're gonna make it?" she asked.

"I don't know. I really hope so, but I just don't know."

"It's crazy to think that two people can share so much history together… marriage… kids… and yet, one stupid mistake can erase it all."

"I'm not sure it erases it all, but it's certainly hard to rebuild trust once it's broken."

Joanna nodded then looked over at me and said, "It feels like I haven't seen you all week."

"Yea, we've been pulling opposite shifts."

"Between my last-minute trip to Texas and now this whole Doug thing, I really haven't had a chance to see how you're doing."

"Surprisingly, I think I'm doing pretty good, considering. Going to the wedding was hard, but I'm glad I went. I think once and for all, I can put the idea of me and Jane in the rearview mirror and finally move on."

"That's good," she said. "And what about the Krystal situation?"

"Truth be told, I really wasn't that into her. She was kind of a pain in the ass."

"So Doug's observations were correct?" she asked.

"Of course they were, but I wasn't about to tell him that."

Joanna rolled her eyes. "You'd rather be with a girl you don't really like, just to prove Doug wrong?"

"Yea, pretty much."

"You guys really are idiots."

"Yea, pretty much."

***

I was psyched that Frank Clines and his wife were in town and were able to attend our party. Even more psyched that he brought his trusty guitar. All we needed now, was for Mike and Andy to streak through my yard.

As the party got going, there was a large group of people sitting and standing by the fire listening to Frank strum away. Even though there were a ton of faces I didn't recognize, it still reminded me of some our old parties. What reminded me even more, was hearing Doug belt out one tune after another with Frank. And yes, by belt out, I mean, off-key and making up his own lyrics.

Directly across from me, I noticed a very cute brunette standing with a couple of her friends. I had no idea who they were, but I did find myself continually (& discretely) checking her out. Actually, to be quite honest, I think she was checking *me* out as well.

Doug wanted Joanna to video his big performance of "Glycerine," but it was too dark. That's when they decided to move into the living room for better lighting. About half of the group followed them inside to witness Doug's big performance.

"You coming in?" asked Joanna.

"Yea, I'll be there in a few," I said.

I grabbed a few logs and tossed them onto the fire. Within seconds, the fire was roaring. It's amazing how big and warm a fire can get when you use actual firewood rather than letters and pictures. The three girls off to my left also began to disperse, but rather than follow her friends, the brunette made her way over to the empty chair next to me. Game on!

"Do you mind?" she asked.

"Not at all," I said.

"Is this your party?"

"Well, it's my house, but I think it's more Doug's party than mine," I laughed.

"Doug was the one singing?"

"If you can call it that," I joked.

"Yea, he was the one who invited my two friends tonight. Apparently, they were at his bar the other night and he announced the party to the crowd."

"Great," I said, shaking my head.

"Don't worry," she smiled. "They said it was a slow night at the bar."

I gave the fire a poke and asked, "You from around here?"

"I'm from Wells."

"Ah, cool. I'm Josh, by the way."

"I'm Wendy," she said, and then gave me a peculiar smile.

"What?"

"You don't recognize me, do you?"

Fuck. Why is it anytime a female asks that question, my heart stops and I get all nervous with internal questions? Questions like: Did we have a one-night stand once upon a time? Did I say I would call, but didn't? Was *she* the one who said she'd call, but didn't? Was she good in bed? Was I good in bed?? I was an anxious wreck.

"Ummmm, did we…"

She burst out laughing. "No, we did not! You can breathe now."

I took her advice and let out my breath.

"You used to be the Sunday night DJ at Goodnight Ogunquit, right?"

My heart rate and breathing returned to normal as I responded, "Ohhh yea, that was me. You used to go?"

"Every Sunday night with my friends. Well, for one summer anyway. I moved to the west coast for a while."

"Ahh, gotcha. Yea, that was some fun times for sure. Feels like a lifetime ago though."

Again, she gave me a weird smile and said, "You really don't remember me, do you?"

Aw fuck, there goes my heart rate again. "I thought you said we didn't—"

"We didn't!" she laughed and blushed. "I probably shouldn't say anything, it's kind of embarrassing."

"For you or me?" I asked.

"For me!" she said.

"Well, now you've gotta tell me."

By now, her cheeks were red.

"I really should learn to keep my big mouth shut," she joked.

I pondered then said, "Were you the one who puked on the dancefloor?"

"No!"

"The one who came up in my booth and puked on my vinyl copy of the Clash's "Train in Vain"… while it was playing?"

"Ewwww! No!"

"The one who got caught having sex in the bathroom with one of the bouncers?"

"God no!"

"This can probably go on for a while, so you might as well tell me."

"Fine," she relented. "One night towards the end of the summer, I climbed up into your DJ booth and asked for a request."

"That's it? A request?"

"No," she laughed, "that's not it."

"What song did you request?"

"It was 'The Killing Moon' by Echo and the Bunnymen."

"Ahh, nice. I love them. What's so embarrassing about that?"

"Umm, because I also asked if you would dance with me to it."

"You did?"

Embarrassingly, she nodded.

"Did I?" I hesitantly asked.

Again, she nodded.

"I don't know why you're so embarrassed," I said. "Did we talk or just dance?"

"Both," she laughed. "When there was about thirty seconds left, you said you had to go back up and switch songs. You thanked me for the dance… and that was it."

The way she said, *and that was it*, made me wonder if she was expecting something more.

"What do you mean *and that was it*?"

"Forget it," she giggled, blushing brighter. "That was the first and last time I ever asked a guy to dance. I guess I was just hoping… you know…"

"That I would ask you for your number and ask you out?"

"Something like that," she smiled.

I was speechless. Totally speechless.

"I'm sorry," she said, "I'm not trying to give you a guilt trip, I swear. Let's just say it was a learning experience for me. I got to see what it was like being in the guys' shoes. Asking a stranger out is nerve-wracking! Not to mention, how much rejection sucks," she laughed.

"To be fair," I said, "you technically didn't get rejected, because you technically didn't actually ask me out. You asked me to *dance* with *hopes* of *me* asking *you* out."

"Which you didn't," she playfully smiled.

"Can I just say my mind is blown right now? My first instinct is that Doug put you up to this little story just to fuck with me."

"I swear this story is one hundred percent true. I've never even had a conversation with Doug."

Wendy and I had only been talking for a little while, but I could tell she had zero bitch-like qualities, and not to mention, she was totally easy on the eyes. Why *didn't* I ask her out back then???

I looked at Wendy and said, "I can't believe I don't remember this, and I certainly can't fathom not asking you out back then."

"To be fair," she said, "I think you were in hot pursuit of someone else."

"I said that to you?"

"No, but after you rejected me, one of my friends asked the bartender what the deal was with you."

"Hey, I didn't reject you!"

"Relax. I'm just kidding," she laughed. "Anyway, the bartender said you were interested in some hairdresser chick or something. Ha, I can't believe I actually remembered that."

"Oh my God. I can't believe I actually know who you're talking about."

The hairdresser in question was Ashley Robinson. I had completely forgotten about her. I don't even think I've seen her since that summer. I think it was only a two-week crush. I just remember being so infatuated with her, and I also remember it being a giant waste of my time.

I didn't bother going into details about Ashley with Wendy. Ashley was what we like to call, the typical "Morrissey-crush." As in, the Morrissey song, "The more you ignore me, the closer I get." Because that's how it was, the more Ashley ignored me, the more I wanted her.

On the plus side, I don't think I ever made Ashley a mixtape or ever gave her flowers. Well, maybe I made her a mixtape, but I know for a fact, I never actually gave it to her!

It kind of pissed me off to think because of that stupid-waste-of-time infatuation, it prevented me from asking Wendy out that night. It pissed me off even more to think because of that stupid-waste-of-time infatuation, it caused me to not even remember Wendy asking me to dance. Don't you just wish life gave you a few *Do-over* cards? If so, I would certainly use one of those cards on that night at the club!

What the fuck am I talking about?!? Maybe life *does* give you a *Do-over* card, and maybe this party is my *Do-over* moment." And maybe, just maybe, that age-old theory is coming true—the theory that says: it's when you stop looking for it, and when you least expect it, that's when love comes walking in. You know, like some kind of alien, it waits for the opening then simply pulls the string, love comes walking in.

Okay, maybe some of that age-old theory was from Van Halen, but you get my point. Either way, was this really it? Was this the moment I finally meet my Mrs. Right (even though I technically already met her but just didn't remember)?

What if all of my crushes, and infatuations, and heartbreaks, and my mixtapes had led me to this very moment? All I knew, was this time, there was no way in hell I would let the moment pass me by! My *Do-over* card was about to be redeemed!

"So, what is the statute of limitations on asking you for your number? I can even go put some Echo and the Bunnymen on, if you want?" I smiled in hopeful anticipation.

She also smiled, but it wasn't as hopeful. It was more… sympathetic? Empathetic?

"I'm sorry, Josh, I should have told you—I'm engaged."

Pathetic! That's what it was, pathetic! I had the prefix wrong, that's all.

She hesitantly raised her hand, revealing her ring. As her diamond glistened in the reflection of the flames, a few thoughts crossed my mind.

1. How did I not notice the ring earlier? That's Flirting 101! Always check a woman's finger. Always! And if there's a ring, either bail, or proceed at your own risk.

2. I just wasted a *Do-over* card on this?? Fuck!!

3. I should go buy up every bottle of lighter fluid and throw *myself* into the fire!

4. Why would she tell me that story if she didn't want me to ask her out now? Pffft, women!

Luckily, the awkward moment (and yes, it was awkward) was interrupted by everyone returning to the fire.

"The lighting was better inside," stated Doug, "but I think my lyrical creativity thrives outside by the fire."

As Frank strummed away on his guitar, and as Doug ad-libbed his own strange version of "Here Comes Your Man" by the Pixies, I started thinking about that famous quote that says: *Those who fail to learn from their mistakes are destined to repeat them*, or something like that.

In my past, the awkward rejection that just occurred with Wendy would have ruined the rest of the party for me. But as I sat by the roaring fire with everyone around me enjoying themselves, I was determined not to let this affect me.

The whole thing was kind of comical. So much so, that I decided to share it with everyone. Although they all cracked up laughing, I didn't really feel like they were laughing *at* me. Well, maybe a little bit at me, but it was earned. Yup, the whole situation was pretty damn funny. As expected, Doug was the first to comment.

"Dude, how did you not see her ring? I noticed it right away!"

This caused Joanna to playfully glare at him.

"Sorry," he smiled. "Old habits die hard."

The mood was lightened even more when we all started reminiscing about Sunday nights at Goodnight Ogunquit. As it turned out, Wendy shared another memory she had from the club. This one didn't involve me. Well, indirectly it did, but Doug would be the star of this memory (or the moon of this memory).

We were talking about how we used to shoot super-soakers out at the crowd through the open window up in the DJ booth. This is what triggered Wendy's memory.

"Oh my God," laughed Wendy, "Speaking of the window,

I remember one night there was some drunk guy who climbed up in your booth. He must have bumped into your turntable because there was this loud scratching noise, and that was followed by him mooning the crowd out the window."

Hearing this, Pete and I cracked up. Doug, not so much. I proceeded to fill everyone in on the story behind the story.

Pete and Scott thought it'd be funny to pull one over on Doug. About halfway through the night, they asked Doug if he heard about the contest the club was doing. When he said no, they told him that whenever I played KLF's "3 AM Eternal," the first person to rush up into the booth and moon the crowd would win two hundred bucks.

Even though he was already drunk, he had his doubts whether they were just fucking with him. He ended up coming into my booth and asking me if it was true. In my best straight-face I confirmed that it was indeed a real contest.

"Really?" he said. "I just assumed Pete and Scott were fucking with me. They're always fucking with me," he slurred.

"Yea, they're always fucking with me too," I lied. "We should turn the tables on them. How about we rig the contest so that *you* win the money?"

Doug widely smiled at me.

"When you hear me play 'Rhythm is a Dancer' that's your clue that the contest song is up next."

Again, he widely and deviously smiled at me. He could practically taste the money. Long story short, when I played "Rhythm is a Dancer", I watched Doug discretely and drunkenly make his way under my booth. As I've said before, the DJ booth was about ten feet in the air overlooking the dance floor, and the only way up was a wooden ladder.

As soon as the contest song came on, Doug rushed

(drunkenly) up the ladder and began to drop his pants. In the throes of his excitement, he bumped into the turntable, causing it to scratch. Now, with the whole crowd looking up at us, he proceeded to stick his ass out the open window. Did I mention he was drunk? So much so, that with his ass out the window, he lost his balance and nearly fell out.

At this point in my story, Wendy looked over at Doug and excitedly chimed in, "Oh my God, I was on the dance floor directly underneath the window, and when I looked up, not only did I see a bright white ass, but hairy, ugly balls hanging out as well."

Everyone laughed except Doug. He wasn't enjoying this story at all.

"Not that balls are ever attractive," she clarified.

Again, everyone except Doug laughed.

"I've never heard that story before," said Frank, clutching his guitar and laughing. "I must not have been there that night. So, I'm assuming there was no contest… no cash money?"

"Nope!" said Doug, shooting Pete and I a hot glare.

"We just wanted to fuck with the drunk bastard to see if he would actually fall for it."

Doug shot back, "Ha, ha, ha! I guess the joke's on you then! I would have done that shit for free!"

Joanna looked at him and pointed out, "Um, you did do it for free."

Doug pondered a second then shrugged. "Aw, fuck it! It was a good time! We fuckin' had some good times there!"

We all laughed and raised our drinks to the good times.

"In my defense," Doug said, looking at Wendy, "back then, I hadn't yet discovered manscaping. My balls look much better now," he proudly said.

I turned to Joanna, who had buried her head in embarrassment. “You signed up for this,” I joked.

So just like that, my awkward Wendy-moment was replaced by Doug making an ass of himself, literally. After recounting that classic Doug story, my party mood was back on track. Frank played a few more songs and there were some more classic stories told. I’ve said this before and I’ll say it again, if cell phones and YouTube existed back in our day, we would be internet sensations. And by we, I mean Doug.

Soon after our stories, Wendy and her friends headed out and moved on to the next party or bar or whatever. As some people left, more were filtering in. There were probably a couple dozen people there at all times. By 10 PM the party was just getting going—as were the surprises.

35

"BARE" – The Cure

I knew there was a lot going on in Pete's mind that night, but for the most part, I really think he was enjoying himself. I'm sure there were many times he thought of Michelle, especially when we were retelling old stories. She was such a huge part of his past, and we all had our fingers crossed that she'd remain that in the future.

We tried our best to keep our eye on him at the party, and any time he looked in deep thought about Michelle, Doug and I would head over and pump his spirits up. Ironically, in the past, it was usually Pete and Doug doing that for me.

It was such a such a beautiful night, and most of the people were either out by the fire or out on my back deck. At one point, we found Pete sitting in the living by himself just staring at the TV. The TV was off.

"Hey," I said, sitting next him. "What's the over/under on Doug and Joanna's relationship?"

It took a second, but Pete finally smirked and said, "I give it ten days."

"Ten, huh?" I said. "I'm definitely gonna go with the under."

"Are you guys serious?" said Doug, pretending to be offended. "You're wagering on the failure of my relationship?"

"Dude, you guys do it all the time with me," I said.

"That's because you're always a sure bet," laughed Doug. "Speaking of which, Pete, you still owe me twenty bucks for the Josh and Krystal bet."

Pete nodded and then started to hand Doug a twenty, but at the last second, he pulled it back.

"Actually," said Pete, "I won the Josh and Jane bet, so we're even."

"Ah yes," smiled Doug. "You're right. We are even."

"What Josh and Jane bet?" I asked, slightly offended.

"I bet that you would attend the wedding," smiled Pete.

"And I assumed you'd be right here," said Doug, "cranking out sad-ass tunes and talking to your John Cusack poster over there."

"Talking to my Cusack poster? Pffft, that's ridiculous," I said.

"And by the way, you're definitely gonna lose your bet on me and Joanna."

"Oh really?"

"Yup! Things are going great, thank you very much. As a matter of fact, I'm taking her out again next Saturday."

"Speaking of dates," I said, "I've got a bone to pick with you, Doug. When you guys had your first date the other night, you took her to a comedy club?"

"Yea, down in Boston. We had an awesome time."

"Michelle and I went to one years ago," said Pete. "It was fun."

"Are you guys kidding me?"

"What?" they both said.

"Over the years, every time I was thinking about ideas for a first date, whenever I suggested a comedy club, you both shot it down!"

"I don't know what you're talking about," said Doug. "A comedy club is a great first date."

Pete nodded in agreement.

"Then why did you two idiots tell me it was a dumb idea?"

They both looked at each other and then Pete asked, "Did you ever end up taking a girl to a comedy club on the first date?"

"Well, no, because you guys said…"

"Well then, you're the idiot for listening to idiots!"

There was no point in arguing. They had a valid point.

"Whatever," was all I could say. "So, where are you taking her next weekend?"

"Dunno yet. Any suggestions?"

"The Sox are in town," I said.

"Eh, that's a horrible second date idea," he said as he smirked at Pete.

I knew they were just trying to get under my skin, so I held my tongue and kept my mouth shut. Personally, I've always thought a Red Sox game would be a great date. As long as she was also a Sox fan—and as long as the weather was nice—and as long as you don't have to pay 500 bucks for tickets—but other than that, it would be a great date! Fuck my friends!

"Actually," I said, "Joanna has been clamoring all summer about going to see *Cats* at the Ogunquit Playhouse."

"Pfft, fuck that!" scoffed Doug. "Why would I want to pay all that money just to take a two-hour nap? Don't worry, I'll come up with something good."

Once again, I just held my tongue and drank my beer. Even if I had responded to him, it would have been short-lived, because in about ten seconds I would be getting a huge surprise. One that would leave me as white as a ghost and completely speechless (at least for a few minutes).

From behind the couch, I heard the sliding door open from the back deck. It was followed by Joanna's voice.

"Hey, Josh, look who's here. It's Kelli."

I turned around, and before I could say hi to Kelli, I saw HER.

And just as I saw HER, Joanna said, "And she brought a friend with her."

"Hey, Josh" said Kelli, "this is my old friend—"

"Elise?" I said in my head. Or was it out loud? Loudly in my head maybe? Either way, I was in complete and utter shock.

"You two know each other?" asked Kelli.

By the look on Elise's face, she was equally in shock. The uneasy moment seemed to last forever. I think it quickly became apparent to everyone that there was a history between us—an unsettled history between us.

It was Doug who broke the silence, and of course, he did it in true Doug fashion.

"Holy shit! The infamous Elise makes her triumphant return to York Beach. How the hell have you been?" When no response was elicited, he continued. "You remember me, don't you? Josh's best friend, Doug. Doug Andrews. You still talk to your friend from that summer? How's she doing? What was her name again?"

Finally, Elise succumbed to Doug's multiple questions.

"Nikki," she softly answered.

"Yea. Nikki. She was cool. A cutie too. Not that it matters… I'm kinda seeing someone now," he said, glancing over at Joanna. "We *are* seeing each other, right?"

Joanna chuckled and nodded yes.

At that point, words finally found their way out of my mouth.

"What are you doing here? And how do you guys know each other?" I asked, looking over at Kelli.

"Elise and I went to elementary school together but haven't seen each other since."

You went to school in Vermont?" I asked Kelli.

"Yup. We moved to Portsmouth when I was ten. That's the last time I saw Elise. When she came in to get a coffee this morning, I recognized her immediately. She said she just moved to the area, so I invited her to the party."

If it seems like Kelli was doing all the talking for Elise, she was. I think Elise was still in shock. She obviously had no clue that I owned the coffeeshop, nor did she know whose house and party Kelli was taking her to.

"How do you guys know each other?" asked Kelli.

Before either of us could answer, Kelli said to Elise, "Oh, that's right, you said your grandparents used to have a place here in York."

"We actually worked together for one summer," I managed to say.

"Wow, definitely a small world," Kelli replied.

By now, Joanna realized this was the same Elise I had

mentioned on a couple of occasions, so she did her best to diffuse the tension.

"You girls want a drink?" she said, escorting them into the kitchen.

No sooner did they exit the room, Doug smacked me on the back.

"What are the fuckin' chances?" he whispered then laughed.

Pete joined me in shooting Doug a look.

"Oh, come on guys, you have to admit this is pretty funny. A week ago, you had to witness the 'love of your life' getting married, an hour ago some chick reveals she had a crush on you years ago, making you feel guilty about not asking her out, and when you finally do ask her out, she tells you she's engaged… and now, Elise! Jesus, how long has it been? Ten years?"

"Nine. Nine years," I specified.

"I mean, the last time you saw her was when she embarrassed herself… and you at that big party, right?"

I pondered and slowly nodded. "Yup, it was at Freddy's end of the year bash… nine years ago… *exactly* nine years ago tonight."

This caused Doug to laugh louder and say, "I'm sorry, bro, but this is hilarious! Shit like this can only happen to you!"

Doug's laughter was excessive and annoying, but he wasn't wrong. Shit like this could *only* happen to me.

"Don't get me wrong," he continued, "there's plenty of shit that could only happen to me, but something like this—this is most definitely classic Josh."

Like I said, he wasn't wrong.

The inside of my house and my yard weren't that big, so the chances of Elise and I being able to avoid each other all night were pretty slim. We did make it forty-five minutes without running into each other. Forty-two, to be exact. If our past was any indication, I assumed any form of conversation that night would need to be initiated by me, not Elise.

My chance finally came when Elise, Kelli, and Joanna were out talking on the back deck. I watched Kelli head inside for another drink, which left Joanna and Elise by themselves. It took a second, but I got Joanna's attention and gave her the "look." The look that said, *beat it, I have some serious babbling to do.* Joanna cooperated by excusing herself to also go get another drink.

As soon as Elise was alone, I took a deep breath and made my move. I had no idea what I was going to say. I had been thinking about it for the last forty-two minutes… well, the last nine years and forty-two minutes… but either way, I had no idea what to say.

Despite what you all might think, I wasn't still pissed at her. As a matter of fact, I don't think I ever was. I was definitely hurt and depressed, and I was left with a ton of questions, but I wasn't pissed. And I certainly didn't hate her. I just wanted answers, that's all.

By the time she noticed me approaching, it was too late for her to escape. I could tell she was panicked, and I'm sure her heart was in her throat. Hell, I was panicked, and my heart was practically coming out of my mouth.

I did my best to cut the tension. I simply shook my head and said, "Elise Carlile. In the flesh. On my back deck. I thought for sure I'd never see you again."

It wasn't intended, but I could tell by her guilty and uncomfortable expression that she took my comment as a dig at her.

"How are you?" I asked.

"Good, thanks," she quietly said.

"You look great. It's like you haven't aged a bit."

Her lips curled into a smile as she shot me an incredulous look.

"Well, maybe you've aged a little, but not much," I smiled. "I still can't believe you went to school with Kelli. She's one of our best workers. Must be a Vermont thing, huh?" I joked.

"Congratulations on your coffeeshop. It was very cool in there."

"Thanks."

"I always knew you'd have your own place one day. You were a good boss," she said, sadly looking away.

"Ha, thanks. Seems like forever ago, doesn't it?"

"Yea," she said, gazing over at the people gathered by the fire. "Do you ever see any of the old crew?"

I filled her in on as much as I knew about everyone. She was pleasantly surprised that Todd had been running and owning the place since that summer. She was saddened and surprised by the news of Mr. Murphy's passing. She was not surprised at all about Freddy moving to New York and doing theater. Just the mention of Freddy made her giggle.

Holy fuck, I missed that giggle. Her cuteness from nine years earlier had transformed into a more mature attractiveness. An adult-cuteness, if you will.

We continued with small talk, but make no doubt about it, there was most definitely an elephant in the room regarding our past. As much as I wanted some answers, I didn't want to bring down the conversation. It was nice. Slightly awkward, but nice.

"Did I hear correctly, you just moved here?" I asked.

"Yea. The Portsmouth area."

"You live in Portsmouth now?"

"Actually, I work over in Portsmouth, but live just over the bridge in Kittery."

"My first apartment was in Kittery," I said. "Are you still doing the social worker thing?"

"The last four years I worked as an adult metal health counselor over in Montpellier. The job I just got here is strictly working with mentally troubled kids. It's definitely the type of job I wanted to do from the beginning."

"Good for you," I said. "I see your grandmother sold her place a while back?"

I immediately regretted asking that, just in case her grandmother had passed away, and that's why it was up for sale.

"Yea," she said. "Her physical and mental health took a turn for the worse. She lives in a senior center back in Vermont."

"I'm sorry."

"It's okay. It's for the best, and besides, it's a really nice place. She originally hated the idea, but now I think she loves it there. Sadly, I think she has more of a social life than I do."

"Ha. Yea, my grandmother was in one of those places too. It was like a geriatric version of teenage summer camp. Activities, sing-a-longs, movie nights…"

"And don't forget bingo nights," Elise smiled.

"Ah yes, bingo nights."

"Although, the place she's at now is a little wilder than bingo night."

"Gin Rummy? Bridge?" I joked.

"Umm, no. Let's just say, the last time I visited, a bunch of them were playing poker… strip poker."

I laughed and nearly spit my beer out.

"Wow, that is hilarious. I mean, it's also quite disturbing, and might have caused me to throw up in my mouth a little bit too."

"Oh, trust me," she said, "I threw up in my mouth a lot of bit!"

We both started laughing. When our laughter subsided, she said, "Unfortunately, no one in our family wanted to take over the cottage. So we just sold it."

"I'm surprised you didn't want it?" I said.

"I would have loved to, but… financially, it just wasn't in the cards. Long story."

That's the Elise I knew, brushing off and avoiding anything too personal. I know I said I wasn't going to tackle the elephant in the room, but I did decide to give the elephant a little nudge.

"Do you know how many times I drove by your grandparents' cottage in hopes of seeing your car there?" I chuckled.

She didn't share in my chuckle. Instead, she quietly lowered her eyes to the floor of my deck.

"I don't know what I would have done if I saw it there. Probably nothing. Kind of embarrassing, I know." Again, I chuckled, and again, she didn't.

And there it was, the infamous and uncomfortable moment of silence. We had obviously run out of small talk, and anything further would surely start to involve that elephant. It really was nice to see her again, and even nicer to chat with her again, so I decided not to go down that road. You know, the road where I would do my old babbling routine and say something utterly stupid. Instead, I decided to make it short and sweet.

"Well, I'll let you get back to hanging out with Kelli. I just wanted to come over and say hi. It was really nice to see you again, Elise."

I held my gaze and smiled at her for a second then slowly turned and walked off. That's when it happened.

"I'm sorry, Josh." There was a break in her voice, and as I turned back around, she emotionally continued. "I'm so sorry for the way I ended things that summer… and for being such a bitch."

"Oh Elise, you weren't anywhere near being a bitch that summer."

"I was at Freddy's party."

I smirked and said, "Yea, I'll give you that one."

My attempt at humor only made her more emotional.

"I was so horrible to you that night. I really hope you know I didn't mean all those things I said to you."

"Really, it's okay, Elise. You were beyond drunk that night, and I kind of assumed you didn't mean most of what you said."

I said "most" because I know no matter how drunk someone is, and no matter what stupid things they say, there's always more than a hint of truth to some of it.

"No, you don't understand, I didn't mean *any* of it," she pleaded.

At that point, my smirk had faded, and my mind traveled back to the night of Freddy's party all those years ago—to Elise drinking with Chad—to Chad hitting on Elise—to Elise barely being able to stand up—to me trying to rescue Elise—to Elise blasting and embarrassing me(and herself) in front of everyone—to me punching Chad square in the face (That was the only good part of that night).

I shrugged at her declaration and said, "If none of it was true, then why didn't you ever say goodbye? Or ever talk to me again?"

By now, the elephant was in full view. The lighting on my porch wasn't the greatest, but from where I stood, it looked like there were tears forming in her eyes.

"Did you ever get the letter I wrote you? The one I left on your windshield?"

She swiped at a tear and nodded yes.

"I just couldn't face you again. I was way too embarrassed," she said.

"I get it, I do, but… I guess I just wish I really knew how you felt that summer. Personally, I thought we had something pretty cool and real going on. But after that party, I didn't know what was real. I just kept thinking, maybe what I *thought* we had was just in my head, ya know?"

She again swiped at her tears and softly said, "No, it wasn't it your head. Not at all. I guess it just freaked me out how badly you wanted to get to know me."

"It was my fifty-seven-question list, huh?" I smiled.

Through her tears, she laughed and said, "Well, yea, that was part of it."

"I'm sorry, Elise. It was just a case of the more I got to know you, the more I wanted to know about you, if that makes any sense? I know I was a bit overwhelming with my questions and with wanting us to hang out so much." I paused, shrugged then said, "I guess I was just trying to make up for all the years of not knowing you, so I tried to do it all at once. I'm sorry."

"Josh, you have nothing to be sorry about! No one has ever treated me as well as you did that summer, and no one has ever said things to me like you did."

"You referring to my babbling?"

"I loved your babbling! Nobody has ever compared me to

a greatest hits album!" she laughed through her tears.

"And crack. Don't forget I kinda sorta compared you to crack."

"Trust me," she giggled, "I could never forget that."

"They sounded much better in my head than when I actually said them aloud."

"They were some of the strangest, yet sweetest and most sincere compliments I've ever received. Ever. And I loved our non, date, dates or group get-togethers or whatever you called them."

I smiled, knowing that's exactly what I called them.

"And despite what I might have said, I loved our five-minute walk to my car at night. And our date—our actual date, date—it was hands down the best date I've ever had."

Everything she just blurted out was everything I had ever wanted her to say—and to feel. I still didn't understand. If she really felt that way then why sabotage it? And why never ever call or see me again? It was as if Elise read my mind, for she began to explain herself.

"Do you remember what I did to my boyfriend and my best friend in high school?" she asked.

I nodded.

"The rest of my senior year I was miserable. Alone and miserable. By the time I went to college, I was determined to make a fresh start. I was also determined not to get caught up in the party scene. I did go to parties, but I was extremely cognizant of my drinking. Surprisingly, I never let myself get out of control.

"That being said, it didn't prevent me from falling for stupid come-on lines from boys. I grew up in a tiny town and went to school with the same people from K thru twelve. Being at college, especially a college party, I was more than a bit overwhelmed… and more than a bit naïve. Embarrassingly, I fell for line after line and would wake up the following morning and hate myself. Don't get me wrong, I wasn't that innocent. There were definitely times I knew the guy only wanted a one-night stand, and I was… well, I was fine with it. But then there were the occasions that I fell for their stupid lines and I actually believed they cared about me… for more than sex."

She paused then cringed, and without making too much eye-contact, she said, "You think I'm a slut, don't you?"

"What? God no, Elise. Are you forgetting that I grew up in York Beach… and spent most of my twenties single… with Doug as my wingman and sidekick? There's no way I'd be the one to throw rocks."

She gave a slight smile and continued.

"The sad part was that their lines became so predictable. Crap like, '*You're not like most girls around here,*' or '*I know we just met, but I feel such a connection to you.*' Or the classic, '*I can't believe someone as cool and cute as you is still single.*' Those are just the most popular ones."

It was my turn to cringe, for I may or may not have used each and every one of those lines once upon a time. As Elise paused, I had a quick flashback of the time Scott and I used the same line at the same party. No, it wasn't on the same girl, but the two girls were best friends. In separate parts of the house, we hooked up with them, and I guess afterwards the girls got to talking… and started to compare notes. Apparently, it's not just guys who do that. Anyway, long story short, we were quickly approached by two angry girls.

"Do you guys rehearse this shit?" one of them said. "At least be creative enough to use different fuckin' lines!" she said before they both stormed out.

Ironically, it was not rehearsed or planned. The fact that we used the same lines at the same party and at the same time was just a huge coincidence. Pathetic, I know, but come on, admit it, it's kind of funny.

I snapped out of my flashback when Elise continued her story.

"I suppose the really sad part was that I still fell for them. Most of the time, the guys never called again, or if they did, it was just a late-night booty call. By the time my sophomore year came around, I guess I had developed an *I don't give a shit* attitude. I was done looking for Mr. Right. I decided to just go with the flow. I started partying more, like way more. It wasn't until midway through my junior year that I snapped out of it. Honestly, the whole party scene had become monotonous, not to mention, my grades were suffering."

Elise's story was interrupted when a couple of people came over to say goodbye to me. As soon as they left, I turned to Elise and said, "I'm sorry about that."

"It's okay. I'm sure you don't wanna spend your whole party listening to me babble."

"Seriously? As much as I babbled to you that summer, I think it's about time the tables were turned," I smiled. "So, you started to party less and concentrated more on your grades?"

She nodded and continued.

"By the time my senior year rolled around, my grades were back up where they needed to be, and my partying was pretty much non-existent. My housemates were partiers, but I was good at keeping to myself and avoiding that whole scene. I did stick around for their Christmas party. Our house was packed, and I barely had anything to drink, but I actually had a good time. It was at that party where I met Jacob. We immediately clicked. We talked and laughed the whole night. And no, we didn't hookup. Well, we did kiss a little, but that was it. He said he'd call me after Christmas break…"

"He didn't call, did he?" I asked.

"Oh, he called. Trust me, I didn't think he would either, especially seeing as I didn't give it up to him at the party. To my surprise, he actually took me out on a real date."

"One that didn't involve loud music or a keg?" I laughed.

"Exactly," she said. "He took me out to a nice dinner and then we went bowling. I wanted to take it slow, so we ended the night by just kissing. It was nice, really nice. From that point on, we started hanging out more and more, and for the first time in a long time, I was truly happy. I was a senior, my grades were high, and I honestly thought I had finally found my Mr. Right."

I knew the story was about to take a turn for the worse, so I said, "You really don't have to tell me all of this, you know?"

"Yea I do. I owe it to you to explain. I was so sure he was *the one* that I let my guard down and let him in. Completely let him in."

Although Elise didn't specify, I assumed she meant let him into heart as well as her pants.

"Soon after that, his calls came less often, and we barely hung out anymore. Until one day, he just stopped calling all together, and whenever I tried calling him, I would just get his answering machine."

I felt bad for Elise, but in my head, I knew it could have been much worse. It's not like she walked in on him having sex with another chick. Let's just say, it was a good thing I kept that thought in my head.

"One night, I got so fed up that I decided to go over to his place and get some answers."

Yup, good thing I kept my thoughts to myself.

"Long story short, he had been screwing around with one of my roommates for weeks."

It was at this point, a few tears began to roll down her cheek. Although I could totally relate to this, I figured now was not the time to compare notes on walking in on such a thing. Sympathetically, I reached out and touched her arm.

"I'm so sorry, Elise."

"It's okay. It was karma… for what I did in high school."

As her tears flowed more freely, I stood there touching her arm and trying to find the right words to say.

"My roommate was beside herself with guilt and embarrassment," said Elise.

"She should be," I said.

"That's the thing, *she* felt guilty, but I don't think *he* did. He didn't seem remorseful in the least. He did follow me out to my car. I just remember I kept asking him why. Why would he do this to me?"

I knew this wasn't going to be good.

"He told me he thought things were getting a little too 'stale' between us."

"He said that?"

"That's not even the worst part," she said. "So, I said to him, 'Things are stale, so that means you start dating my roommate?' To which he just laughed and said, 'Dating? We're not dating. This is my final year in college, I'm just looking for fun and exciting.' I just stood there like a lost little puppy."

Elise paused and wiped her tears on her sleeve.

"The worst part was I made the mistake of asking him,

'What, I'm not fun and exciting?' I swear to God, Josh, he looked at me with a straight face and said, 'You used to be, but things have just gotten boring lately. No offense, Elise, but I'm not looking for serious, I just want that new car smell.' After he said that, I just turned and drove home."

I moved my hand to her shoulder and said, "Oh, Elise, I'm so sorry."

With tears now pouring down her cheek, she looked up at me and said, "So that's why I built up those walls… and why I was so anti-relationship that summer."

Before I could say a word, she continued.

"As devastated as I was by it, it made me take a long, hard look at myself. That's when I realized it might just be me. Maybe I *am* boring. Maybe I'm only good for that newness phase."

"Elise, stop. You know that's not true."

She looked away and shrugged.

"Seriously, you at least know that's not how I felt about you, right? Please tell me you knew my feelings were sincere?"

Again, she shrugged and said, "I was so screwed up, I didn't know what was real. I thought you were genuine, but… but I also thought Jacob was genuine too. I guess I was just scared."

"Scared of me?"

"Scared that once we were past the newness/fifty-seven question phase, and once I completely let you into my heart, it would be just like the others. I was so afraid if I let you inside, you'd be disappointed with what you found."

No matter how hard she fought it, and no matter how quickly she swiped at them, tears poured out from her eyes—from her perfect brown eyes.

"So, I know it's nine years too late, but I just want to say

I'm sorry… and thank you. Thank you for being such a wonderful person that summer, and for seeing things in me that I couldn't see myself."

A couple of party-goers walked onto the deck and headed inside my house. Elise frantically tried to wipe her face and eyes, and when she was semi-composed, she looked out at the people gathered by the fire.

"And now that I've made a total fool of myself, I think I should probably go."

"Really?" I said. "Because I was thinking, we should go sit inside, grab a couple more beers, and then you let *me* babble to you. It's been nine years… I have a shit-ton of babbling to make up for. Besides, I have Kleenex inside. They're much more effective than your sleeve."

Through her tear-soaked eyes, she began to laugh.

"Soooo? Living room? Beers? Babbling? Kleenex? Sound like a plan or what?"

"It sounds perfect," she smiled.

With that, we made our way into my living room.

36

"FEAR" – Blue October

I motioned for Elise to have a seat in the corner chair by the window. I grabbed another chair, two beers, and yes, a box of Kleenex, and I joined her. I watched as she went through a half a box, wiping and blowing her nose. When she was completely composed, I handed her a beer and proceeded to clink our bottles together.

"Cheers," I said.

When she finished taking a well-deserved swig, I noticed her face. She seemed lighter, and why wouldn't she, she had just spent the last half hour pouring her heart (and tears) out to me. It was like a huge weight had been lifted from her. It must have felt very cathartic for her. Much like taking a whole bottle of lighter fluid to a box of memorabilia and lighting the fucker on fire. Yup, I knew exactly how she felt.

Elise wasn't the only one who felt lighter. Everything she just said to me was everything I ever wanted her to say. For nine years, I was left to wonder how she really felt about me that summer. Now that the elephant in the room had been spotted, talked about, and shoved away, we were left wondering what we should say to one another.

It was probably too soon to ask her about her dating life or about her current relationship status. And no, I wasn't thinking about asking her out or trying to pick up where we left off nine years earlier. Seriously, I wasn't.

Honestly, I was still in shock that Elise Carlile was sitting in front of me. I wasn't thinking about the summer of '95, or where our friendship would go from here, I was very content living and enjoying the here and now.

Elise was the first to break the silence. "I can't believe you own that coffeeshop. What's it called again?"

"The Eclectic Café and Coffeeshop."

She widely smiled. "I knew you'd be an owner one day, but I always thought it would be Murphy's."

I went on to explain to her about Mr. Murphy's offer—and how I turned it down—and how I recommended Todd.

"And you said Todd still owns it?" she asked.

"Yup."

Just then, Pete entered the house.

"How's it going out there?" I asked.

"There's just a handful of people left. Apparently, there's another big party down the road with a live band."

"Pffft, they've got nothing on Frank and Doug," I said.

"Ha, you missed it earlier. Frank was playing that Crash Test Dummy song…"

"The Superman one?" I asked.

"No. You know, the one that goes 'Mmmm Mmmmmm'… whatever it's called."

"I actually think it's called Mmmmmm Mmmm."

"Hmm, makes sense," laughed Pete. "Anyway, Doug was making up his own lyrics. Basically, he was just singing about a bunch of different beers, followed by Mmmmmm Mmmmmm. I have to admit, it was pretty funny. He even worked in a Zima and Stroh's reference."

Elise and I laughed, shaking our heads.

"I'm surprised he didn't work in a vagina reference," I joked.

"Oh, don't worry, he did," laughed Pete. "Anyway, I think I'm heading home though."

"You can crash here tonight, if you want?"

"Thanks, but I think Doug is going to Joanna's, so I'll have the place to myself."

I stood up and gave him a hug (man hug) goodbye.

"We should try to do a round of golf this week," I said.

"Definitely, let me know."

Pete said his goodbyes to Elise then headed out. No sooner did he leave, then Doug, Joanna, and Kelli entered.

"Successful party, or what?" boasted Doug.

"It was fun… and interesting," I said, looking over at Elise then back to Doug and Joanna. "Thanks for organizing it all."

"Of course, bro. And don't worry, I'll be by in the morning to help clean up. Tomorrow afternoon at the latest. Early evening at the very latest!" he smiled.

"Uh huh," I said. "Is the fire out?"

"Just about," answered Doug. "Don't worry, I'll take a piss on it and put it the rest of the way out."

"Umm, or you can use the hose. I prefer you to use the

hose. I order you to use the hose."

"Yea, yea, yea. Well, we're heading to Portsmouth for last call and then hitting Gilley's. You guys in?"

I took a chance and answered for both of us.

"Um, I think we're just gonna hang here."

I hesitantly looked over at Elise and was pleasantly surprised when she nodded in agreement.

"I'm heading out too," Kelli said.

"What?" exclaimed Doug. "But we're going to Gilley's."

"Some of us have to get up at five thirty to work."

"That's right," smiled Joanna. "Get some rest, and I'll be thinking of you while I'm still snuggling in bed until noon."

"Yea, yea, rub it in," laughed Kelli. She then approached Elise. "Thanks for coming tonight! I still can't believe I ran into you after all these years!"

"I know, right?" Elise said, giving her a hug. "Thanks for inviting me."

"Call me. We still have a lot to catch up on."

"I will," said Elise, giving her a hug (girl hug) goodbye.

After Kelli left, Doug turned to us and said, "You guys sure you don't wanna come?"

"Yea, we're sure. Hey, are you guys okay to drive?"

"He's not," Joanna said, nudging Doug, "but I only had a couple drinks tonight, strictly for this reason."

"Isn't she the bestest?" slurred Doug.

"Yea, the bestest," I echoed.

"It was nice meeting you, Elise," said Joanna.

"You too," replied Elise.

"Elise," began Doug, "it was very… interesting seeing you again."

Joanna glared at Doug, smacking his arm.

"What? Trust me, that's the politest way to put it," said Doug.

Elise smiled and said, "It was interesting seeing you again too, Doug."

"Hey, remember when we all went out drinking at the Golden Fortune Cookie?" he asked.

"I do," said Elise. "You were quite… animated that night."

"Pfft, I was quite drunk, you mean?"

"Yea, I was trying to be polite," she giggled.

"Good ol' Mr. Wong," I chimed in.

Elise laughed then said, "I've told so many people about the whole Confucius/Sting thing. Sooo funny. I drove by there the other day, it looks like it's a bar now."

"Well, yea," interrupted Doug. "That's my bar. Mr. Wong sold it to me."

"No," Elise said in disbelief.

"What, you didn't tell her about my bar?" Doug said to me.

"Sorry," I said, "I didn't get around to it yet. But yea, Elise, Here Hey Hoohahs is most certainly Doug's bar."

She laughed and said, "Here Hey Hoohahs? Where did you come up with that name?"

"I'll tell ya what, come by for a drink sometime, and I'll fill you in on it," said Doug.

"Deal," she said. "Do you have your own version of Mr. Wong's Shaolin Punch?"

"No, but I should!" Doug said excitedly.

"Oh, Josh," interrupted Joanna, "can you cover for me next Saturday night? Doug is taking me to see *Cats* at the Ogunquit Playhouse. Isn't that so sweet of him?"

"Yea, so sweet… and creative. How do you come up with such great date ideas?" I asked, smirking at Doug.

"Just a gift. I guess," he shrugged.

With that, Doug smiled, grabbed Joanna's hand and started towards the door. He stopped short and turned around and addressed Elise.

"By the way, with all the talking you two have done tonight, I hope you gave Josh a really good apology for ripping his heart out that summer."

Elise lowered her eyes in embarrassment. I raised my eyes and glared at Doug. Joanna raised her hand and smacked Doug.

"What? Trust me," said Doug, "He was not fun to live with for those next few months."

"Don't mind him," Joanna apologized.

"It's okay," Elise quietly said. "I suppose I deserved that. And yes, I apologized to him."

"Well good for you," he smiled. He then opened the front door and left with Joanna.

"He hasn't changed a bit, has he?" laughed Elise.

I just rolled my eyes and shook my head.

"They seem like a cute couple," she said.

"I hate to admit it, but yea, yea they do."

When I was sure the fire was put out (properly), I came back inside and turned off some of the lights in the house. No, I wasn't trying to make it all romantic-like. I was just being practical. It was late at night, everyone had gone, and we just didn't need so many lights on, especially with all the candles that were lit. Relax people! I didn't just light them. The candles had been burning all night! And just because I switched out my upbeat party mix and put in a more mellow mix, it still didn't mean I was trying to get all romantical-like!!

When the music and the lighting were at an appropriate

level, I grabbed two beers and we returned to our chairs by the window.

"Doug really owns a bar, huh?" she asked.

"Yes he does."

I went on to fill her in on everything about Hoohahs. I told her that I used to not only work there, but was Doug's partner for a few years.

"It was fun, but I think I always knew it was a stepping stone until I figured out what I really wanted to do."

"The coffeeshop?"

"I think so."

"It totally suits you," she said. "I should have known when I walked in that you were behind it. The records on the wall, the posters, the music… yup, just like the Josh I remember."

The way she said that, the way she said, *just like the Josh I remember…* it was nice. Really nice. I also went on to tell her how I met Joanna, and how she was one of the baristas at the coffeeshop I used to do all my writing in.

"Your writing?" she asked.

It was right then that I realized I had never told her about my writing. All of my screenplays happened post 1995-Elise. I ended up filling her in on everything. How I attempted my first screenplay at age 19. How I lit it on fire, and how I never wrote again for over ten years.

"I think that is so cool," she said. "Do you think any of them will be made into a movie?"

I shrugged. "The reality is probably not. That's why my newest idea is to turn them into novels. I figured it might be easier getting a book published rather than dealing with Hollywood and trying to find the huge financing."

"Sounds smart. What kind of stories do you write?"

"Umm, I have a couple of silly comedies, a couple of dramas, and a couple few that are loosely based on me and my friends growing up here at the beach. I've actually started turning a few of them into a trilogy and I'm calling it – The Soundtrack to my Life trilogy."

She widely smiled and said, "I love it. I'm sure Doug alone provides you with plenty of material."

I looked at her and smiled. "A lot of people have provided me with material over the years."

Her expression went blank as I continued smiling at her.

"You didn't write about me, did you?"

"Let's just say, book one of the trilogy takes place in the summer of 1995."

"Oh, God. I'm totally the bitch character, aren't I?"

"Relax. I actually think you'll enjoy it… sorta."

"Can I read it?"

"Um, well… it's not a real book yet, and it still needs some editing, but… yea, if you really want to."

I have to admit, the thought of Elise reading a story I had written about her was kind of… strange, and weird, and surreal, and a little bit scary. But I suppose it was also kind of cool as well.

"Can I edit my character," she asked.

"No."

"Can I suggest edits to my character?"

"No."

"Fine," she smirked. "I can't wait to read it. What's it called?"

"It's called *The Empty Beach*."

"Awww, I love it."

I didn't fill her in on book two – *Between Hello and Goodbye*.

It had already been an emotional night, so I didn't really want to get into the whole story about Anna. My hope was to keep the rest of our conversations that night more on the lighter side. With that in mind, I decided to avoid asking her about her relationships over the past nine years, and I certainly avoided talking about mine.

We spent a lot of time reminiscing about the summer of '95. From Freddy to Megan to Duct tape Phil, we covered them all.

"Oh my God," she burst out, "I hope you included Geoff in your book."

"Da ha ha ha, are you joking or serious?" I laughed.

"I have told soooo many people about him, especially his bathroom antics. Most people think I'm just pulling their leg or that I'm exaggerating. Is he still around?"

"I still see him once in a while riding his bike or walking his dog. I think the last time I saw him, he was pretending to strike a match at me."

The next couple of hours flew by and consisted of funny memories, cold beers, and great tunes. In other words, it was frickin' perfect. By 2 AM, our drinking pace had slowed considerably, and so had our reminiscing. Not wanting the night to end, I searched for something new to talk about. It was at that point, I decided to dip my toe in her *past-relationships* water.

"I can't believe you're sitting here in my house. I swear, I thought I'd never see you again. I just assumed you'd be married with kids and living up in a cute little Vermont town. You know, the whole white picket fence thing," I laughed.

She didn't share in my laughter. Her smile faded and her expression saddened a bit. *Oh shit*, I thought. Maybe she's married. I had already checked once, but just to be sure, I double/tripled checked her ring finger. Empty! Hmmmm, maybe she was one of those chicks who is married but doesn't wear her rings. Doug had warned me about those types. Now that her mood had changed, I couldn't *not* say something.

"You're not married, are you?"

Her lips curled back into a smile, and she gave me a little laugh then said, "No. But I was."

"You were? No way." I was both relieved and intrigued.

"Way," she said, continuing to smile. "Let's just say, this party tonight lasted longer than my marriage."

"Really?"

"Well, I'm exaggerating a little, but not much."

"I'm sorry."

"It's okay. It was my own fault. It was just this world-wind type of romance. It was fun and exciting, and it moved way too quickly. And despite everybody warning me to slow down, I got caught up in the excitement, and the next thing I knew, we were saying *I do*."

"Was he from your town?"

"No. I met him when I was visiting some friends over in Burlington one weekend. His band was playing at the bar we were at. We ended up mingling afterwards and just sorta hit it off. The crazy thing was, he really wasn't even my type."

As soon as she said Burlington, Vermont… and band, my mind was totally picturing some hippie dude with Birkenstocks. A dude with long hair and a scraggly beard. A dude who didn't believe in deodorant—or soap. For whatever reason, I was picturing the lead singer of The Spin Doctors, but with lots of tie dye.

"Not only was he not my type, but his band's music wasn't my type either. They were heavy into grunge music," she said.

My mind switched gears—and Birkenstocks and tie dye were replaced with ripped jeans and flannel. I still pictured him with long hair, but definitely with lots of flannel. Soap and deodorant were still optional. Basically, I was now picturing her married to Eddie Vedder from Pearl Jam.

Elise continued. "His music was loud and aggressive, but in person, he was so laid back. He had this coolness about him."

I didn't even know this dude, yet I was jealous of him. I wondered if anyone had ever said that about me; that I had a coolness about me. I'm thinking probably not.

"I was pleasantly surprised at how deep and thoughtful he was," she said. "Actually, he had been a philosophy major but dropped out to pursue music. Like I said, we just hit it off. He was very engaging, and when I talked, he seemed legitimately interested in what I had to say. And I loved how he always, always had a famous quote or song lyric for every occasion."

Images of Eddie Vedder and the Spin Doctor dude were quickly replaced by the image of Ethan Hawke's character in the movie *Reality Bites*. So, as my mind pictured a chain-smoking-philopsophizing-guitar-playing Ethan Hawke, Elise continued to tell her story.

"The next thing I knew, I was working Monday through Friday back at home, and then I'd stay with him and his roommates in Burlington on the weekends. My parents and most of my friends didn't really like him, which I suppose made me like him even more."

"Funny how that works," I laughed.

"In retrospect, I guess I was just going through the phase of trying to find myself, and Vince had a way of making me feel special. Long story short, within a year he asked me to marry him, and stupidly, I said yes. We didn't even make it to our first anniversary before I filed for a divorce."

"I'm sorry, Elise."

"You don't have to be sorry for my stupidity."

"Eh, we all make mistakes."

"Yea, but we don't all get married to them."

I had no response. The woman had a point.

"Anyway, after we got married, we got a place together, and by *we*, I mean, *I* got us a place! He didn't have a penny to his name. Do you realize, it took me that long to find out that most of his gigs just paid them in free beers?"

"He didn't have a job? Like a real job?"

Elise laughed then said, "I can't tell you how many *real* jobs he'd been fired from. The funny thing is, he always had a justification of why he got fired—and it was never his fault. Pathetically, the whole time we were dating, I bought into each and every one of his justifications. I knew he wasn't making much from the band, but he had a way of telling me that true art wasn't about money." Elise paused and laughed. "I actually remember admiring the hell out of him for that."

"Unfortunately, artistic integrity doesn't always pay the bills," I said.

"Agreed. Less than two months after we were married and living together, all those qualities that I used to love and admire about him, started to —"

"Annoy the hell out of you?" I smiled.

"Yes! He'd be out until two or three in the morning with his friends, and on most days would still be sleeping when I got home from work at five. And don't even get me started about his friggin philosophies or his constant spewing of famous quotes. I finally lost it. I was like, Jesus Christ, enough with the quotes. How hard is it to have an original thought?

And how hard is it to wake up before noon? Or hold a job for three consecutive days??"

This was the most animated and loud that she had been all night. I laughed, placing my hand on her shoulder in a calming manner.

"Whoa, settle down, killer. It's in the past. You've moved on, and you're a better person for it."

Elise blushed when she realized she was getting a little too worked up.

"Sorry."

"It's okay," I laughed.

She took a long swig of her beer then said, "What about you?"

"Me? Nope, I've never been married to a flannel wearing-philosophy drop out. Nope, never."

"Ha, ha, ha. Very funny. Seriously, have you ever been married? Or engaged?"

I guess I should have known, if I was going to dip my toe in her relationship history that she would follow suit and dip her toe in mine.

"Umm, never married. Engaged once… kinda. Well, not really. Though, I did propose and I gave her a ring, which she accepted… kinda. I mean, she never actually said yes… and eventually gave the ring back and left town. Anyway, whatever, it's a long story. I won't bore you."

"Oh, no, no, no," she said, sitting up straighter. "After everything I just told you, you totally owe me a story."

I polished off the rest of my beer, sighed, then said, "Fine, but I'm gonna need another drink. You?"

She finished off her Corona, handed me the empty, and said, "Yes, please."

After a quick bathroom break, I returned with two cold beers and my final box of Chicken in a Biskits. Okay, full disclosure: when I went to the bathroom, I may or may not have talked to myself in the mirror, and it might have sounded something like:

Holy shit, dude! Can you believe Elise Carlile is sitting in your living room? Drinking beers with you? At late o'clock at night? And she seems like she's enjoying it too, don't ya think? Ya, me too. Just don't ruin it by saying something stupid. Good talk, good talk.

Yea, that's right, I sometimes talk to myself in the mirror—and talk to my Cusack poster. Don't judge!

Anyway, after I returned to the living room, I proceeded to tell Elise the saga of Jane Wheeler, and even though I told her the abridged version, it still took the better part of an hour.

When I finally finished, all she could say was, "Wow."

"Yea, wow," I echoed.

"So, Jane just got married last week?"

"Yup. A week ago today."

"Right here at the beach?"

"Right here *on* the beach. The same beach we used to walk on together," I said.

"And you went to the wedding?"

"Front and center. Well, actually more like, left and to the rear, but you know what I mean," I said, offering her some Chicken in a Biskits.

"I've never heard of these. Are they any good?" she said, digging her hand in the box.

"Are you kidding me? You've never had one before? Who are you?"

Elise rolled her eyes at me then shoved a few in her mouth. I watched in anticipation for her reaction.

"Mmmm. These are good. They taste like—"

"Like Grandma's chicken soup shoved into a delicious cracker?"

She pondered then smiled and nodded in agreement. There's nothing like watching someone pop their Chicken in a Biskit cherry for the first time. When our cracker-craze subsided, I continued my story.

"Oh, I didn't tell you the other part."

"Uh oh," she smiled.

"So, two weeks ago, I was kind of seeing someone. Well, I thought I was seeing someone. Apparently, she didn't get the memo, or if she did get the memo, she certainly wasn't following proper dating protocol. Anyway, I heard she wasn't feeling well, so I went over to surprise her with some feel-good remedies. Let's just say, I was the one who ended up surprised—and not feeling well. I walked in on her getting banged by her hip hop roommate while 50 Cent played, loudly. Oh, and I spilled hot soup on my leg, and it kinda really hurt."

"Wow, I'm sorry, Josh."

"It's okay. I put some burn cream on it. My leg is fine now," I smirked.

She returned my smirk, and again rolled her eyes at me.

"So let me get this straight," she started, "two weeks ago your sort of girlfriend was—"

"Having wild hip hop sex with Eminem Jr. and was raising her legs in the air and waving them like she just didn't care."

"Yea, that," she giggled. "And then, a week later, your long-time romantic interest got married right here in York Beach?"

I slowly nodded.

"And then, another week later, the girl who treated you like shit nine years ago, shows up at a party at your house."

I smiled and nodded.

"Wow," she laughed. "You've had quite the shitty month, huh?"

I joined her in laughing then thought for a second and said, "Well, if sitting here all night talking to you is considered part of a shitty month, then I'll take that any day."

"Awww, still a sweet-talker," I see.

Yup. I still had it! I might have been thirty-four, but I could still dish out a sweet compliment. I looked over and gave my Cusack poster a wink (Again, don't judge!).

"Just being honest. Extremely drunk, but honest nonetheless," I said to her.

She shook her head then stood up and announced, "Pee break." She then headed down the hall towards the bathroom. I could tell by her voice and her not-so-straight walking, that she too had crossed the buzzed/drunk line. While she was on her pee break, I might have had a quick chat with Mr. Cusack, but I can't really reveal what was said, guy code and shit.

When she returned, she had a huge smile on her face.

"I know this is random, but for the last nine years, every time I hear 'I Melt with You' on the radio, I totally think of you. Remember? From that first day we met on the beach?"

"Ah yes. You mean the day you tripped and fell over your chair and spilled your drink and landed on the tube of lotion, shooting a glob of it perfectly onto Frenchy's nutsack?"

She covered her embarrassed face and said, "Yea, that day."

"Or the day you got a dose of my first official babbling session?" I said.

"Aww, I loved your babbling sessions. They were endearing."

"Endearing? You really are drunk," I laughed.

"Extremely drunk, but honest nonetheless," she winked.

"Touche," I said. "Speaking of songs, do you know what song reminds me of you?"

"What?" she asked suspiciously.

"Queen's 'Somebody to Love.' Remember when you and Freddy did that at karaoke?"

She again covered her red face and said, "Oh yea. You mean the time I did a face plant on the stage?"

"Yea, that time," I laughed. "Just kidding. You were amazing. I still can't believe how good you were. Do you still do any singing?"

"Nah, strictly relegated to the shower now."

"Too bad. You were really good."

"Why, thank you."

As we sat there drinking our beers and eating our C&B's, The Smiths "There Is A Light That Never Goes Out" started to play on the stereo. It was one of the songs I had put on Elise's mixtape all those years ago. About halfway through the song, my curiosity finally took hold, and I had to ask her.

"Okay, I have to know something," I said in a somewhat serious tone. "And you have to be completely honest."

"Uh oh," she hesitantly replied.

"That mixtape I made you… the one I put on your windshield with your letter… did you ever actually listen to it? Like, the whole thing?"

I looked directly at her, trying to get a good read on her expression. As soon as I posed my mixtape question, her eyes looked away, and there was a hesitation in her response. Her hesitation caused a voice to pop into my head. It was Doug's voice, and it was saying, *Ha, ha, Josh! I told you, chicks rarely ever listen to the mixtapes you give them. Not only are they a kiss of death, but they're a huge waste of time*!

I hate Doug's voice in my head and hated even more when he was right. When Doug's snide voice faded out, I listened as Elise offered her response.

"Umm, to be honest, I didn't listen to it at first. I was still so mad at myself for how I treated you, and then, when I read your letter, I felt even worse. I just couldn't bring myself to listen to it."

At any second, I expected Doug's evil *I told you so* laughter to reappear in my head, but before it did, Elise continued her thoughts.

"It took me three months before I finally listened to it."

"Wait! So you *did* listen to it?"

"I did," she smiled. "And even though I hadn't heard of most of the songs before, I grew to love them. Well, most of them anyway."

"You grew to love them?" I repeated her words.

"Don't let this go to your head, but it ended up being my most favorite mixtape ever."

"Shut up!"

"It's true, and those two Cure songs were my faves."

"Ahh, 'Pictures of You' and 'A Letter to Elise.' "

"Yup. I loved them! And not just because one is my namesake, but because they are two of the most beautifully sad songs I've ever heard."

"Why yes, yes they are," I excitedly agreed.

"And don't let this go to your head either, but you totally got me into The Cure. So much so, that I went and saw them on their Bloodflowers tour."

"I saw that tour!" I said with a little too much enthusiasm. Elise finished her beer and laughed at my excitement.

"Do you still have it? The mixtape?" I asked.

"Sadly, no. It met its demise on my way home from work one day."

"Ahh, your tape player ate it?"

"Sure did. Completely mangled beyond repair. I did end up downloading all of those songs and putting them on my iPod though."

Before I said another word to Elise, I paused and addressed Doug's voice in my head.

Ha! Take that, you fucker! Not only did she LOVE my mixtape, but now they're on her iPod!

Doug's voice in my head had nothing left to say. Bam!

My excitement led me into the kitchen for another round of beers. As I cracked them open, I was sure there was a perma-smile on my face, and why wouldn't there be? One of my many, many mixtapes had actually resonated with someone—for nine years! I mean, I would like to think there were others out there who also appreciated and loved their mixes, but I also knew there was a lot of truth in what Doug's voice had said. I'm sure most of my mixes went unlistened to, or worse, unappreciated.

I sat back in my chair and handed Elise her beer.

"A toast," I announced.

"To?"

"To my amazing mixtape, of course!"

She smiled and humored me with a clink of my beer. She took a short, worn-out sip then set her ice-cold Corona on the window sill.

"Well, no offense to your amazing mixtape, but I think I'm done."

Although my sip was longer than hers, my sentiment was the same. There was no way I was finishing that beer.

"Yea, I think I'm done too," I said, placing my bottle next to hers. After that, we sat and listened to the rest of "Never Tear Us Apart" by INXS. Then it hit me. "Wait, how did you get here tonight? Wasn't Kelli your ride?"

"No, I have my car here. I followed her over. That being said, there's no way I can drive."

"Ya think?" I joked.

"Do you mind if I crash on your couch?"

"Of course. But you don't need to sleep on the couch. You can sleep in my bed. Not with me in it!" I clarified. "I just did laundry today, so it's all fresh sheets and shit. Or better yet, the bed in the guest room is made up too."

"Thanks, but a pillow, a blanket, and the couch are all I'll need," she smiled.

"You sure?"

"I am positive."

"Okay, suit yourself."

I headed into the other room and returned with a pillow and a blanket.

"Thanks," she said as I handed them to her.

I shut off the remaining lights and blew out the candles, although most had already burned themselves out. As I made my way over to shut the stereo off, Elise stopped me.

"You can leave that on, if you don't mind? I like falling asleep to music."

"Yea, of course. Me too, by the way. I either need music or the TV on to fall asleep."

Elise nodded as she spread out the blanket on my couch. As I stood there, I tried desperately through my drunken haze to come up with the perfect goodnight speech. I wanted to sum up just how much I enjoyed the last six hours or so.

Unfortunately, my alcohol consumption was clouding my creative thoughts, and I couldn't seem to form the right or meaningful words.

"I'll see you in the morning. Tonight was pretty weirdly cool, huh?"

"To say the least," she laughed.

"Well, goodnight, Elise."

"Night, Josh."

With that, I stumbled to my bedroom and crawled into bed. As I stared up at my ceiling, I mumbled, "Weirdly cool? You're a fuckin' idiot, Josh."

Normally, I would have tossed and turned for hours, thinking and over-thinking about the night's events, but I didn't. It wasn't because I was a more mature or refined version of myself, it was simply due to the fact I was too drunk to focus or to keep my eyes open. I was certain, however, that I passed out with a ginormous smile on my face. And why wouldn't I, Elise effing Carlile was sleeping on my couch.

And for the record, NO, I wasn't thinking ahead, and I wasn't even thinking about trying to pick up where we left off nine years ago. I swear, I wasn't! I was just extremely happy to see her again and to finally get some answers and closure from that summer.

Elise was right, it had been a shitty month for me, but as I lay there in my bed that night, I fell asleep with an overwhelming feeling of contentment. That, combined with my alcohol consumption, caused me to have one of my best night's sleep ever. I slept like a friggin' baby. It was the kind of sleep that usually followed a night of great sex—or followed a great masturbation session. I think you get the picture.

37

"THE RING ON THE SILL" – Cowboy Junkies

It was nearly noon when my eyes finally reopened. Despite my hangover-headache, I still felt well-rested. So, before I took what might have been the longest piss of my life, I sat up in bed and pondered. How should I handle the *wake up*? Should I start cooking her breakfast? Or was that reserved for more intimate sleepovers? Should I offer to go out to breakfast? Brunch?

I would have sat in bed over-thinking this more, except, like I said, I had to take a major piss. As I exited the bathroom and headed down the hall towards the living room, I decided to just be cool and play it by ear. Unfortunately, the decision was made for me, for when I entered the living room, the couch was empty. The blanket was neatly folded and placed on the pillow. I'm not going to lie, my heart sank into a pool of disappointment.

In no particular order, here are the thoughts that went through my mind:

1. Just like that, she was gone—again. Déjà fuckin' vu! Was it going to be another nine years before I saw her again?

2. She had a lot to drink last night, and maybe when she woke up, she regretted everything. She regretted us hanging out, talking, laughing, crying—everything! She probably couldn't leave here fast enough.

2a. Pffft, she probably made up that whole story about loving my mixtape too.

3. Hmmm, I also had a ton to drink last night, so maybe the whole Elise thing was just a drunken figment of my imagination. Maybe she was never even here.

4. If it *was* real, then maybe, just maybe, because she too had a ton to drink, Elise left early simply because she wasn't feeling well. I lost track of exactly how many Coronas she had, but that many Coronas were sure to give anyone the morning beer-shits. Yea, that was it! Maybe she didn't feel comfortable destroying my toilet, so she decided to rush home. Been there, done that.

I knew that #3 and #4 were a stretch, but I was kind of pining my hopes on #4.

The other thought that was in my head was that I desperately needed some water and Advil. That was the only thought I knew was real. I made my way into the kitchen and grabbed a glass of water and the bottle of Advil. I re-entered my living room and plopped myself in the same chair from the night before. I popped three Advil then chugged the water. It wasn't until I placed the glass on the window sill that I saw it. "It" being a crisply folded note leaning up against a mostly full

Corona bottle—Elise's Corona bottle.

The good news: I could scratch #3 off this list. Last night was not a figment of my imagination.

The bad news: Elise left a note, and chances are, it wasn't a good note. More than likely, the note would probably reflect on #2 and #2a.

I suppose it could have just been a random piece of paper, or maybe it wasn't even for me. Those theories were quickly shot down when I saw *Josh* was beautifully handwritten on the front of it.

You know what, I thought to myself, *I'm too old for this shit*! I wasn't going to sit there staring at a stupid piece of paper and let my mind race. Fuck it! I grabbed the note and opened it up.

Just for good measure, I popped another Advil. As I unfolded the note, I thought, *Why do chicks insist on disappearing and leaving me with Dear John letters… on the fuckin' window sill!*

I took a deep breath and began reading.

Josh,

I took off early this morning but just wanted to thank you so much for last night. I hope I didn't embarrass myself too much with being all emotional and stuff. I really need you to know how sorry I am for the way I ended things all those years ago. I'd been carrying around that guilt for years, so thank you for letting me unload on you, and most of all, thank you for accepting my apology.

I totally understand if you don't want to, but now that I'm living here, I would love to go out sometime on a non-date, date… or otherwise. Hopefully I'll talk to you soon!

Elise

With the letter still in my hand, I leaned back in the chair and let out a happy and relieved exhale. Holy shit! That might just be the best note I've ever received. Just to be sure, I opened the note and reread the *non, date, date… or otherwise* line. I wasn't crazy, was I? She was totally hinting at going on a real date—with me!

Before I could reread it again, I was interrupted by the ringing of my phone. I walked over to the table by the couch and answered it.

"Hello?"

"Sooo, did ya get lucky last night? She still there?"

"No and no, Doug," I said.

"Aw, that sucks. I thought for sure you'd get some apology sex."

"Apology sex?"

"Apology sex, sympathy sex, either way, she owed you some sort of sex."

"Well, there was no sex of any kind," I said.

"Oh well, maybe next time."

I was tempted to tell him about her note. In particular, the *or otherwise* phrase, but I thought better of it and decided to save the conversation for another time.

"Hey, are there still plenty of beers left?" Doug asked.

"Yea, why?"

"I figured I could come over later for a little Tiger Woods Playstation action."

"And to also help me clean, right?"

"Yea, that's what I meant," he laughed.

"Uh huh. Well, come over whenever. I'll be here."

"K, sounds good. Later."

With the phone in one hand, and her note in the other, I

started to walk back to my chair. I had only gone two paces when the phone rang again.

Without hesitation, I answered and chuckled, "Yes, Doug, I told you, we still have plenty of beer."

"Don't tell me you guys are gonna drink again?" said a female's voice. "I'm still recovering over here," she giggled.

And by *she*, I mean Elise.

"Elise?"

"Hey, how are you?" she said. "I didn't wake you, did I?"

'No, not at all. I got up a little bit ago. And just to clarify, *Doug* plans on drinking again, not me. I'm still recovering here too. Wait, how did you get my number?"

"Oh… I went by your coffeeshop earlier and asked Kelli for it. I hope that's okay?"

"Yea, of course it's okay. Just a little surprised to hear from you, that's all. You know, seeing as you bolted so early today."

"Sorry about that," she replied. "I always have a hard time sleeping anywhere new, not to mention, I had way too much to drink. I woke up early and couldn't go back to sleep. I didn't want to wake you, so I just decided to go home to my own bed. I didn't want you to think I left early because I had a bad time. That's why I left you a note."

"Yea, I just read it. Thanks."

"Pretty silly and cheesy, I know, but I just wanted you to know I had a great time last night."

"Not cheesy at all. I had a great time too—and I'd love to go out sometime—if the offer still stands, that is?"

"Actually, that's why I called you. I just remembered my new boss offered me Red Sox tickets whenever I wanted. So, I was kinda wondering if you might wanna go to tonight's game? They're not playing anyone good, and they're probably not that great of seats, and I know it's last minute, but —"

"I would love to go!"

Whether this was a non-date, date or a real date, it didn't matter. I was just asked out by Elise Carlile to go to a Red Sox game! It was the perfect cap-off to the last twenty-four hours.

After I hung up with Elise, I carefully returned the note against the beer bottle, and I leaned back in my chair. I can only imagine that I was smiling like a mofo. As I sat there smiling, I began to fixate on the window sill.

I remembered sitting there a year earlier and feeling I had hit my lowest point. With Jane's goodbye note in my hand, and the ring on the sill staring back at me, I honestly felt like I was destined to be alone and miserable. Dramatic, I know, but that's how I really felt. It was as if Jane's note and her ring on the sill became a symbol of my pathetic life.

But now, almost exactly a year later, I sat in the same chair and didn't feel so pathetic or depressed. I honestly felt like a new chapter was about to begin. A happier chapter.

It wasn't until I picked up Elise's note and her beer bottle that it hit me. As I lifted her bottle, I noticed it had left a water ring on the sill. Yup, ironically, my new chapter would also be symbolized by a note… and a ring on the sill.

I know, I know, cheesy and stupidly laughable. As a matter of fact, as I stared at the note and the water ring, I actually started laughing out loud. My first thought was Doug's comment from last week. He was dead right—God was most certainly one funny fucker!

38

"THE WORLD IS…" – Matthew Ryan

If I haven't already, I want to thank everyone for reading (& hopefully enjoying) this silly little trilogy I created. Although it's a mixture of fact and fiction (mostly fiction), there are definitely enough pieces of me in it to make it very personal. So, the fact that you read not one, but all three books, means the world to me.

When I originally came up with this Soundtrack to My Life idea, I honestly thought my only audience would be my friends and family and maybe some locals who grew up in York Beach. Needless to say, I was pleasantly blown away that these books have resonated with so many strangers of different age groups from all over the country. I am forever grateful for everyone's kind words and support.

I know, I know, you guys are probably saying, *Wait! So how does the story end? Did Doug and Joanna end up together? Did Pete and Michelle work things out? Is Elise "the one"?*

Have you guys ever heard a certain song, and its lyrics create such imagery and meaning that it was as if the artist wrote it about the exact situation you were in? And have you ever read an interview with that artist, and when they explain what that song was *actually* about, you realize it was nowhere close to how you interpreted it? I mean, you still love the song, and it still means something to you, but you kind of wish you never read that interview.

I'm sure I worded that wrong and none of what I just said probably makes any sense to you, but I guess what I'm trying to say is sometimes not knowing is better. With that in mind, I think I'll let you interpret how you want the ending to be.

I will say this: Elise and I had an amazing time at the Sox game! Not only did they win that night, but a month later they ended their 86-year curse and won the World Series! With my friends and Elise by my side, we all sat at Hoohahs and witnessed this miraculous event together.

Well, technically I wasn't at Hoohahs for the final out. Before the ninth inning started, I drove over to my grandparents' house to watch the end with my grandfather. He was the one who got me into the Red Sox and baseball in general. He took me to my first Sox game, he was my Little League coach, and he taught me how to properly yell and swear and throw things at the TV when they lost. On that particular night, there wasn't any yelling or swearing. There were just satisfied smiles and looks of long-overdue relief.

In the past, I've been known to be a bit of a humbug during the holiday season, but that following Christmas with Elise was nothing short of magical. And speaking of grandfathers, one of the presents I bought Elise was a remastered DVD version of *It's a Wonderful Life.* I remembered her telling me how she used to watch it every year with her grandfather. So, from cutting our own tree, to decorating it, to watching *It's a Wonderful Life* together, that Christmas was one of my favorites.

One of my favorite singer/songwriters is this dude named Matthew Ryan, and one of my favorite songs of his is called "The World Is…" In particular, I love the lyric:

"The world is held together
With lies and promises
And broken hearts
And brand-new days
For you to start—All over again."

I'm not sure exactly what Mr. Ryan was thinking when he wrote this song, nor do I really care to know, all I know is what that lyric means to *me.* I'm certainly not an old man, but I have been around the block a few times, and I have most-definitely experienced lies, and promises, and broken hearts. As a matter of fact, from heartbreaks to mixtapes, and everything in between, I think I've seen it all. I've been beaten down, defeated, and have felt hopelessly depressed, but through it all, my one saving grace, was the hope of tomorrow being a brand-new day… a brand-new day for me to start all over again.

I guess I'll end this trilogy with one final thought: If there's one thing I've learned along this journey, it's that life doesn't always turn out the way you plan it. As a matter of fact, life will probably NEVER turn out the way you plan it, but I promise you this, it'll ALWAYS turn out the way it's supposed to.

~ The End ~

About The Author

Jody grew up in the Kittery/York area of southern Maine. He originally started out as a screenwriter. As of now, he has written nine feature-length screenplays ranging from dramas, to dramedies, to comedies. Not only did Jody grow up in Maine, but he makes it a point to utilize and represent his state as much as possible. From Maine's scenic rocky coast, to its remotely pristine backwoods, to its eclectic characters; all serve as backdrops and pay homage to his beloved state. His ultimate goal is not to just sell his scripts, but to have them filmed right here in the great state of Maine.

Unfortunately, searching for the proper financing has been a long, tiring, and at times, disheartening process. Feeling helpless in the whole 'funding' process, Jody decided to reverse the typical Hollywood blueprint. That blueprint being: It's almost ALWAYS a novel that gets turned into a screenplay and not a screenplay which gets turned into a novel. Jody's thought process was simple: It's much easier to self-publish a book rather than self-finance a movie, and who knows, maybe, just maybe, this will be a screenplay that gets turned into a book only to eventually get turned back into a movie! But even if this wild idea never comes to fruition, at least by turning it into a novel, the *stories* themselves will be able to be enjoyed by the public. Whether it's two or two million people who buy his books, Jody is just happy that they are no longer collecting dust in a desk drawer.

Other books by Jody Clark

"The Empty Beach"
The Soundtrack to My Life Trilogy-Book One

"Between Hello and Goodbye"
The Soundtrack to My Life Trilogy-Book Two

"The Wild Irish Rose"

"Livin' on a Prayer – The Untold Tommy & Gina Story"

Available at
www.vacationlandbooks.com

I do most of my posting & promoting via my Facebook profile so feel free to friend me!!!

Jody Clark(vacationlandbooks)